P

1

PAST GLORIES

Newsletter

Receive T M Goble's Occasional Newsletter
containing
Information about future publications
(there are many to come across different genres)
Deriving plots and characters
Choosing Locations
Researching books (both fiction and non fiction)
Recipes (cookery books - coming soon)
Full details at the end of the book

01

The last piece of Black Forest gateau grabbed my concentration. A dark cherry, peeking from the moist chocolate filling, made my mouth water. The slice lay among the scattered crumbs on the blue weave patterned plate.

With a sigh of determination, I straightened my back and clenched my jaw to resist the temptation of the spoon. This is ridiculous, I'm a grown woman, of course, I'll resist!

My head ached, my stomach churned, and saliva filled my mouth with longing, as I imagined the rich, gorgeous taste. Focusing on the cherry, I blinked away the tears while my hand edged closer to its destination.

Huddling at the kitchen table, the howling November wind battered the old farmhouse windows and doors which rattled through the empty house. The draught of the icy wind whipped across the stone-flagged floor and nipped at my toes.

Half of the designer kitchen had been fitted to perfection. The bright red drawers and cupboard fronts flooded the kitchen with a reflected bloody crimson light. Halogen down lights glinted on the stainless-steel trims which edged the mottled grey marble worktops.

The remaining unfinished walls, floor and windows

had made the eccentric Victorian farmer proud, but time had pitted, dirtied and dulled them to a dirty brown. The juxtaposition of the old and new, created a stark contrast and illustrated an apt reflection of my life.

Blinking, I tried to stem the tears leaking from my eyes, but they dribbled across my cheeks and dripped from the end of my chin. Breathing in tight angry gasps, I yearned that one day the chaos would vanish.

Shivering in the cold farmhouse, I longed for the central heating of the London apartment which had been home. Tightening my fleece, I hoped for deliverance from this icy nightmare.

The memories of the heady days of my early twenties produced a small smile which tweaked at my lips through the tears. For fifteen glorious years I'd whirled around London with success that had been the envy of my friends. I'd become the top fashion designer in London and the world's best at accessories.

The ecstatic life of London had improved beyond my wildest dreams, when I fell in love with the dashing and handsome Justin. Arriving from Harvard he had the pick of the plum well-paid jobs in the City of London. How different my planned life had turned out. World class accomplishments littered my past. My present is shivering and crying alone in this deserted farmhouse.

The day at Royal Ascot races when I fell in love is imprinted on my memory. Wearing a large multicoloured hat, one of my own designs, I had concentrated my attention on a photographer who had focused his camera in my direction. Would a picture of me and my designer hat be on the front pages of a daily newspaper? Flashing a broad smile and striking an elegant pose, my eyes sparkled as an irrepressible giggle escaped my lips. Posing for multiple shots, I collided with Justin, who emerged from the swirling crowds around me.

In a flurry of apologies our eyes met. A whirlwind romance, and then a glittering marriage. Long-term success followed. Serious money lined the route to the top as we join the famed list of celebrity couples. Everyone wanted our friendship, so invitations poured in. I'd only made one mistake along the way in my successful career. Hopefully, it has been forgotten, as Caroline would have moved on to bigger and better successes.

02

Tears ran down my cheeks and I whimpered from the cold touch as my fingers caressed the spoon. What should I do? Little money and immense hassle summed up the future, but its clarity had vanished, and a veil of misty grey tulle had replaced it. The enforced isolation away from the teeming life of the glistening city had drained my ebullient confidence.

Chocolate cake provided solace and distraction as my life spiralled downwards. Substantial supplies would be needed as my existence had hit rock bottom. Tugging at the waistband of my skirt, I ignored the tightness, flicked the curls from my face, and gripped the spoon. The temptation of the gooey slice had become overpowering. The spoon hovered in anticipation.

Battering gusts and swirling drizzle hit the ageing farmhouse. The panes rattled and I quivered. The old farm, Cloughside, had been neglected. Only a mile from the isolated village of Mossmoor, but a lifetime from the glitz of London.

The horrendous short journey to the village increased my sense of isolation. The half-mile of rutted and muddy farm track reached a small potholed winding lane, which dipped through a ravine with a stream crossing the road. It then veered up and over the hill to reach the village. No pavements or streetlights graced my journey, when driven by necessity to venture across the hostile landscape for provisions.

With a cold shudder, the image of the wild scenery of the windswept moors, dominated by straggling hills, filled my mind. Not a skyscraper in sight, only dark craggy rocks on the distant horizon. Few outsiders ventured to Mossmoor.

In its glory days, packhorse trails merged in the village centre, giving a bustling life to the many pubs. The plethora of them had dwindled to one, which struggled to gain an income. Built of local limestone, The Jaggers, now weathered after centuries of battering from the elements, appeared forlorn and forgotten. Even its sign, depicting the name and a picture of a packhorse laden down with heavy panniers, had faded. The historic market centre for the vast expanses of moorland areas, with their isolated farms and small hamlets, had one general store. Modern-day residents, mostly supermarket shoppers, had to endure a twelve-mile journey to Braxton.

03

Why had my life hit a downward spiral? Should I accept the blame? Had I changed? No. I'd been delighted with family life in London, with friends and a social life to be envied. The change in Justin's character had created the descent into the nightmare.

But why had my husband changed? The bright lights and social whirl no longer satisfied him. If only he'd stayed the same as the day we'd married.

A promotion to the Head of the Environment Division at Twitchard Management Consultants should have been another step up his ascending career ladder, but the new role created changes in his personality and outlook.

With a strange eagerness he studied 'eco' labels, swapped his car to an electric hybrid and became determined to save the planet. Quoting statistics to anybody who would listen, about pollution, the ozone layer and alternative energy resources, he became obsessive. Light-hearted dinner party conversation eluded him, and invitations dwindled to non-existent.

The new approach never appealed to me, but our two teenage children embraced his ideas. Three against one, assigned me no chance of winning, and they discounted my views as naïve and outdated. For me, the hammer blow landed when Justin's company announced staff could work from home.

The idea of moving from London to a small holding obsessed him. As the 'eco' bug increased, he developed delusions of rural harmony and self-sufficiency. Perhaps he viewed the future through rose-tinted glasses where the sun always shone. Storms, howling gales and mud had no place in his dream of living in the countryside. The children embraced his every suggestion. Justin became determined to run a full-size organic farm.

Why did he think he could move from the city to become a farmer, with no experience or background in agriculture? Although I objected long and hard, he bought this farm in the northern counties of England. It became an impossibility to drop into London to meet friends. Surrounded by crumbling roads and a hostile environment, the distance and isolation, presented a frightening contrast to my former life. Why hadn't he chosen a pretty, sheltered valley in the southern counties?

Outside the rain splattered window, the grey marbled sky loomed with menace. With a long sigh I rubbed a hand across my tear-stained face, straightened my shoulders and resolved that tomorrow I would be positive.

With relish, I focused my attention back to that last slice of gateau. I licked my lips in anticipation. With a large intake of breath and a small smile of eagerness, I raised a spoonful of cake towards my awaiting lips.

04

Before I had a chance to taste the exquisite gateau, a dreadful sound filled the air, drowning out the howling gale raging outside. Banging and braying emanated from the farmyard.

The farmhouse door shuddered and rattled from the kicking but remained closed. How long would it withstand the onslaught? The beast outside showed no signs of relenting, and the noise continued unabated. With an authoritative edge to my voice, 'Go away, Angela!' The kicking stopped. A sigh of relief escaped as I returned my attention to the cake.

My mother-in-law, who had no sense of humour, had not discovered the donkey had been named after her. Throughout the years, since my marriage to Justin, I had never been sure of our fragile relationship. Justin's successes were her only interest as he sprang from one promotion to the next. Despite my best endeavours, she only tolerated me, and didn't acknowledge my success in the fashion world. But then fashion didn't interest her.

Old before her time she embraced a dowdy and dated appearance, in pale twin sets, fake pearls and a sensible tweed skirt. My flamboyant, floaty and frivolous dress style was eyed with a moue of distaste. The scruffy stained farm clothes I wore today were a stark reminder that my life had changed. No frivolity or flamboyance existed in the grey bleak world which I now inhabited.

She lived in North London, but Justin had assured her, that he would visit and stay with her when he was in town on business. But somehow, she didn't seem bothered about seeing me.

Before I took a mouthful of the scrumptious cake, the banging and scuffling noise started again. 'No, Angela! How many times do I have to say no!' My high-pitched yelling and screaming heightened the noise outside. Would the door resist the battering from the huge grey beast? How did a donkey know I would give in and throw her inappropriate food?

A reward would stop her attack. A donkey in the kitchen would be the last straw, and the imagined scenario filled me with horror. I dropped the spoon back onto the plate with a clatter and admitted defeat. With my lips pressed in a firm line, I approached the large square oak door which needed both hands to open, as the wood had swelled in the damp conditions.

As soon as the gap appeared the donkey's head sprung in. Angela had the upper hand as I hadn't engaged brain and thought through my actions. 'Get out, Angela!' I screamed, as I pushed the large grey head. As she retreated, I sensed victory, but I hadn't won yet. Then another mistake leapt to the fore as my woollen socks slid on the flagstone floor. Dealing with Angela without wellies became impossible.

Picturing myself sloshing through the farmyard mud in woollen socks sent a shiver through me. I needed a different approach to subdue the donkey. Battling to push Angela's head back into the yard while putting on my wellies became an uneven contest. A one-handed push didn't succeed with such a strong animal. As I wobbled around on one leg attempting to pull on a Wellington boot, the wind and rain howled through the open door.

If I didn't take command, she would be in the kitchen, as with each wobble she edged through the doorway. Angela wanted cake, so in desperation I reached back to the table, grabbed a handful of chocolate goo and rubbed it across her mouth. She curled her top lip and exposed her teeth as though laughing at me. The large animal terrified the life out of me. Fear clogged my throat and my hands shook.

Holding my breath, I smeared more cake onto the curled lips then threw the rest of the handful into the yard. The donkey had won again and backed up to eat today's treat.

With chocolate daubed down the front of my scruffy drab brown fleece jacket, I leaned against the doorframe in one welly boot and a muddy sock. The rain and wind lashed across my face and my wet hair sent cold dribbles down my neck. I shivered. Tears once again filled my eyes. Their presence dominated my life and were ready to cascade across my face at any opportunity.

Angela enjoyed her cake and strutted around the yard searching for more, licking up crumbs as she moved. The farmyard enclosed on three sides by the house and barns had become a mess. Mud intermixed with straw covered the rough cobbles. The cows sought shelter here and the resulting smell became overpowering, but I had no idea how to remove the stench. I would never enjoy rural aromas! The pervading odour permeated my clothes, made my hair smell and attached to me when shopping in the village.

05

A tall man in his late forties, wearing smart trousers, a check shirt and tweed jacket, strode into the farm-yard, and a frisson of alarm made me grip the doorframe. Who is he? Why had he come to the farm?

'What is the reason for this noise? Why is the donkey braying? And what's it eating?'

Handsome men received the best side of me, but not today. 'Who the hell do you think you're shouting at?' I snarled with my hands on my hips.

Approaching the donkey, he pulled her head up, 'That's chocolate cake!' Raising his arm, he pointed his finger at me. 'What a stupid woman!' He grabbed the donkey's collar and tugged it away from the last crumbs of the cake. 'This yard is a disgrace. It's dangerous and hazardous for the animals. Get it cleaned up!' He held Angela's collar, so the animal couldn't move her head, making the remains of the cake out of reach.

'Leave my Angela alone!' Forgetting I only had one welly on, I stepped towards the man. 'Don't come to my farm and issue orders! I'll give her what I like.' I picked up a piece of chocolate cake from the cobbles, placed it in the palm of my hand, then reached towards the donkey.

'You will not!' Knocking the cake from my hand he stamped it into the mud as he glared with narrowed eyes and clenched jaw. His face turned red. Alone with this irate man on an isolated farm caused a shiver of apprehension to slide down my spine. Although my mouth opened, no words emerged.

Fear clogged my throat and I whimpered, covering my face with my hands to block out the sight of the furious man. Not a sensible move as my hands had been covered in chocolate cake. Did I now look as though I'd been indulging in tribal face painting?

Tears as usual drizzled their way across my cheeks. The furious man held Angela's harness and he controlled the willful donkey with self-assurance.

Even in my distressed state I appreciated his handsome features. Angular cheekbones, steely eyes and tousled nut-brown hair complemented his smart appearance. What must he think of me? Why had I been so rude? Am I turning into a crazy depressed woman?

It's Justin's fault for forcing me to live in a farmhouse in the middle of nowhere. Tension drained from my shoulders and my breathing returned to normal as my anger, frustration and humiliation seeped away.

As the man's temper subsided, his face relaxed. He whispered as he stroked the donkey, 'Come on old girl, let's get you back into the field.' Angela snorted at me but plodded alongside him, and he picked up a handful of hay to encourage her progress. How did he make dealing with a rebellious donkey appear so easy? The calmed animal left the yard munching hay.

Closing the battered door to keep out the strong cold wind, I removed my single welly and wet muddy socks. What should I say to the stranger? Who is he? Why's he on the farm? It's as though he knows the layout, so he must have visited before, but I don't remember him. As he marched across the yard, I reopened the door. The frown and anger had gone.

'Please come in,' I clutched the door for support, 'I've been rude to you, I'm sorry.'

His first words on entering the kitchen surprised me, 'It's not warm in here and you've nothing on your feet. These flagstones must be freezing. Isn't the Aga working?'

I attempted not to sound pathetic but didn't succeed. With a groan, my shoulders slumped, and I focused my attention on my bare muddy feet. 'My husband lit it last week, but it's gone out. I don't know how it works and he's not here to relight it.'

The instant flash of amazement left his face. A smile tugged at his lips and removing his jacket, he rolled up his sleeves, then set to work on the Aga. Within a few minutes he climbed back to his feet brushing the dust from his trousers, 'It will be hot soon and I'll show you how it works before I leave.'

Why did he intend staying? What did he want? Why had he come here? All these questions and more hurtled through my mind but I remained silent. I'd done enough damage to my reputation for one day, so I busied myself cleaning the chocolate covered plate. Although I stood with my back to him, his gaze bored into me while I washed the dishes in cold water. Pondering the situation, I chewed on my lower lip. When I had exhausted my delaying tactics, I joined him at the kitchen table.

06

'To business,' with narrow eyes he watched my face for a reaction. 'Don't feed chocolate cake to any animal.' His eyes focused on the chocolate stained fleece. 'It's not good for humans either, but they are supposed to make rational choices.'

How dare he criticise! I raised my head and straightened my back but wouldn't make a second spectacle of myself, so I pressed my lips together to restrain the words of indignation that threatened to emerge.

First and foremost, I needed to know why he had ventured to this remote place? The embarrassment of my behaviour and appearance hadn't gone. If my posh friends in London could see me, they would be appalled, and I squirmed. With an effort I concentrated and hoped my voice sounded calm and reasonable when the words emerged, 'Who are you?'

A frown of disbelief creased his forehead, his eyes opened wide and his mouth dropped open. Before he spoke, he recovered his composure. 'I'm David Hunstanton, the owner of the local Veterinary Practice, and I've an appointment to be here this afternoon.' He had a hint of pomposity and disbelief in his voice.

To avoid his enquiring and quizzical gaze, I turned my head away and closed my eyes. Why had I been such an idiot? What must he think of me?

He drummed his fingers on the kitchen table, 'Justin arranged the appointment during a round of golf in Braxton a fortnight ago. He asked me to check the animals as they are new to his farm.'

As a way of distracting myself, I moved away from the table and took plates from the draining board and put them in the cupboard. How to handle this situation?

'We only moved here a few months ago.' Even to my own ears my voice sounded flat and had an edge of weariness. 'Justin is away on business.'

'Are the animals in?' he frowned, and his jaw clenched.

'I don't know.' I rubbed a hand across my face acknowledging that I must appear pathetic and weak. Large animals terrified me, and I had no intention of approaching them. My confidence had gone.

Puffing out my cheeks I let out a long slow breath and pulled at my fleece to make it smarter, but improvements were a forlorn hope. With alarming intensity, he watched my every move which caused a self-conscious flush to creep across my cheeks. My scruffy, dirty appearance didn't help my confidence. I had become a mess. Wet hair continued to send trickles of water down my back and I shivered.

'You come from London, don't you? His tone had accusation and challenge. 'Do you know how to care for farm animals?'

With a glower of resentment, I attempted to hide my incompetence, but a whimper slipped from my lips, and I wriggled on the chair and cringed with shame, 'Justin, Clyde and Paris have cared for them.'

'Clyde and Paris are your children?' I nodded.

'Are they here?'

'No.' I sniffed and pulled a grubby handkerchief from my sleeve and wiped my nose. 'Clyde is at Uni and Paris has chosen a boarding school for her sixth form.' Tears streamed down my cheeks, and I struggled to resist the temptation to put my head in my hands and sob. Embarrassment consumed me and a harrowing headache pounded my forehead.

'May I guess the length of Justin's business trip is unpredictable?' He didn't expect an answer but pushed back his chair and headed towards the door. 'Give me a few minutes.'

As I wandered across to the grubby kitchen window, he strode past the barns, under the arch in the farm buildings and then disappeared towards the nearby fields and animal sheds.

Silence filled the house, except for a puttering sound from the shiny red Aga, which emanated a welcome heat. The howling wind had subsided and the windows no longer shook and rattled. Sliding the rocking chair close to the Aga, I slumped down onto the soft cushion and warmed my hands, relishing the heat on my cold, numb fingers.

My predicament on a farm intensified because cattle frightened me and as I'd never liked birds, the chickens also created a problem. Having no idea how to care for sheep I'd left them to fend for themselves in a field.

As for the farmyard animals, the donkey, the peacock and geese, I'd thrown food at them. Over the past week I'd done my best and attempted to copy the routines I'd observed the rest of the family perform. In hindsight my attempts had been pathetic and hadn't worked.

Rubbing the damp hair at the back of my neck, I groaned in exasperation and resolved positive action. I couldn't continue sitting around and crying my life away.

The waft of warm air from the Aga floated across me. Taking off the old fleece, I smoothed my hand over my top and skirt, then ran my fingers through my hair. Picking up a colourful scarf discarded over a nearby chair, I draped it on my shoulders to smarten myself.

By the time he'd returned, I'd splashed my face with cold water, removed the smears of chocolate cake from my cheeks and resolved to ask for help.

David Hunstanton marched into the kitchen, grabbed a kitchen chair and settled himself down next to the Aga. For several long seconds he regarded me with an expression of pained tolerance. 'No damage is done, but you should've asked for help.' His insistent voice cut through the pulsing in my head, 'The animals need attention.'

'I...' I stuttered, but I had nothing to say in my defence. The situation had become hopeless.

'I'll be blunt,' he raised his chin and shot me a penetrating look. 'Can you afford to pay for help?'

Too exhausted and frustrated to elaborate, I whispered, 'Yes.'

After a few minutes on the house phone in the hall, he returned and informed me, that the eldest of the Drinkwater sons from a neighbouring farm would arrive within the hour.

07

Liam Drinkwater left the yard on his quad bike in the evening darkness as the long shadows of the lime trees settled on Cloughside Farm. Two energetic sheep-dogs perched on the back as he drove, with nonchalant expertise, along the rutted track to the village.

A tall and wiry man in his early thirties, with short hair, he had an all-weather tanned face. Wearing dark colored work clothes, a thick windproof jacket and huge muddy boots, he had taken control and instructed me to stay indoors.

A man of few words, he had an air of assurance as he moved through the farm dealing with the neglected animals. My willingness to ask questions never surfaced and I'd left him to the mess.

Twice he'd come into the kitchen to ask about the farm, but I couldn't answer his questions. After mumbling a few words, he'd left with a frown furrowing his forehead. The short terse interactions left me with the conviction that he had been unimpressed with my knowledge.

With no assistance from me he attended to the needs of the animals. A great weight had been lifted from my shoulders. As the evening approached, I relaxed. The heat of the Aga wrapped around me and generated positive thoughts.

With renewed energy in a warm kitchen I cleaned up the mess left by a week's neglect. What to do next? Being alone had never occurred before. Decisions needed to be made.

As the house quietened, apart from the strange animal noises from the barns on the far side of the farmyard, I walked into the hall at the centre of the old farmhouse. Wide stairs with elaborate bannisters and intricately carved spindles rose to the middle landing before turning and climbing to the first floor.

Justin had promised to decorate the hall when we'd moved in, but the brown raised anaglypta wallpaper, dark wooden stairs and hallstand remained. The terracotta carpet, patterned with swirls in shades of mustard and beige with the occasional splash of red, had a musty smell, although I'd vacuumed it many times.

The old cream phone resided on a wonky telephone table next to the grandfather clock which chimed nine. The intricate carvings on the top of the clock acted as a magnet for dust and spiders' webs. Justin had bought the clock at an auction for several thousand pounds, but it needed winding when I remembered, and gave a variable accuracy of the time.

The huge brass pendulum swung rhythmically backwards and forwards. The loud ticking filled the hall announcing the relentless passage of time. Uncertainty and loneliness gripped me, as the regular beat poured itself into my mind, dragging me towards the uncertain future like a pulsating time bomb.

No mobile phone reception reached the farm. Messages and invitations had filled my phone in London. In those days I never appreciated the swathes of countryside where mobile phones failed to operate. Living in Moss-moor had become a regression to the dark ages. The empty social calendar, and lack of chatter and interaction with my friends, forced lonely evenings.

08

Standing in the middle of the hall, my heart pounded, and my mouth dried. Why do it again? Although my body trembled and my eyes overflowed with tears, I couldn't resist the masochism. Forcing myself, I reached my trembling finger towards the answer phone. Once again, I pressed the play button. I'd lost count of the number of times I'd listened to the solitary message.

The words hadn't changed. When would I find the courage to erase the distressing world-shattering communication? Only the one message remained on the machine. Justin's tinny resonant tone on the cheap Taiwanese recorder made his voice sound idiotic.

'Hi Jess,' his quiet voice hesitated, and I sank onto my knees and leaned in closer to the machine. 'I don't dare to speak to you, and I can't write it down.' Tension twisted my stomach as I waited for the next part.

After a long silence, he blurted out, 'I've met someone else in Germany, so I'm not coming back. The farm and animals are yours.' His voice quavered, 'I'll contact the solicitor to put everything in your name.' After another lengthy pause, he whispered, 'Sorry.' Then a click. Silence. Emptiness.

Tears spilled across my cheeks every time I listened to it. I pulled out a crumpled tissue and wept with compulsive sobs that shook my body. The message didn't change. Of course, it didn't. No matter how many times I played it, the message remained resolute. Why did I torture myself by repeated listening? He'd left me.

A new female filled his life. Had he chosen a young and beautiful woman? How had they met? When had the relationship started? The questions had tumbled through my mind for the past week, but no answers appeared.

Images formed in my head of the two of them laughing, holding hands, making love. An aching void of rejection and loneliness settled on me and I had no one for comfort. The inevitable question kept resurfacing although I tried to ignore it. Had I driven him into the arms of another woman?

I'd started with disbelief and had attempted to ring him, but his mobile number had been unobtainable. Before he'd left for Germany, he'd been on edge throughout the weekend. All his daylight hours had been spent with the animals and in the evenings, he'd shut himself in his office and wouldn't come out.

Early Monday morning, last week, he had flown to Germany. He'd been backwards and forwards to Berlin and Munich for the previous six weeks, after his boss assigned him to a problem with the German side of the business.

My disbelief dwindled as he didn't return my messages. In the first days I'd been confused but blamed myself, so I'd kept an even tone when I'd spoken to Paris and Clyde on the phone.

They enjoyed their new lives, Paris in her boarding school and Clyde in his first year at Uni. Justin hadn't informed them of his departure, so how and when would I break the news?

Becoming frustrated with Justin's silence, my self-doubts increased. Each day my confidence had sunk another notch. Emptiness, disbelief and loneliness consumed me, making coherent thought impossible. This afternoon's scene with the vet had been an embarrassment but displayed how far I had slid. My vibrant and positive personality had vanished.

Since Justin had left the message I'd been in a befuddling and humiliating trance. I'd let many days drift past, with no idea of what action to take. Alone in this isolated farm filled me with horror, and to add to the escalating problems, I didn't drive. Weakness flooded over me, but unlike the past few days, I had a determination to resist. I'd cried enough. The tears made my head ache, my eyes red and produced no positive benefit.

09

With a need to plan my next move, I struggled from the floor and settled on the chair near the phone. Sitting up straight, I clenched my jaw to stifle a sob, and took a notepad and pencil from the drawer.

Paris and Clyde must take priority. Separate meetings would be best. Justin's departure would produce different reactions. Paris will be distraught and won't stop talking, a sign of nervousness. Clyde will retreat into his shell. During a private meeting I can coax him into talking. At the top of the list, Contact Justin and then added in large letters, Don't accept failure.

My mind cleared. Michael! Justin's boss. I had his direct number after meeting him at a corporate event. After making notes, I dialled. Michael answered in a curt business manner.

'Hello, it's Jessica Southwick.'

'Hello, Jessica, how are you?' But the words faded away and he stopped talking.

The pad contained the words I'd organised before ringing. Taking a deep breath, I concentrated on keeping my voice even and calm, 'Justin's number is unobtainable. Has he acquired a new company phone? Can you give me his number as I need to contact him?' My voice had remained steady and controlled. I'd reached the end of the sentences with no telltale signs of distress.

'Oh, my God!' The quiet words echoed down the line.

'What is it?'

'Justin hasn't told you, has he?'

'What hasn't he told me?' I stammered.

'Justin flew into Munich last Monday, travelled to our office, handed in his resignation and walked out. The company has written to him, but there's been no reply.'

My eyes rested on the pile of unopened letters addressed to him which I'd stacked beside the phone. Realising that Michael had continued to talk, I concentrated, 'Will you ask him to ring me?'

'Justin's left me. And I'm on my own.' With unnecessary force I slammed down the phone, threw my notebook and pencil down the hall, put my head in my hands and sobbed.

10

The headlights of Clyde's old Ford Fiesta pierced the gloom as it bounced along the ruts of the farm track. The tortuous Friday journey from London had no doubt been gruelling and slow.

A heavy grey sky covered the moors, sucking colour from the landscape, and a bitter wind blew from the northwest as a portent of forthcoming sleet and snow.

Three weeks ago, I'd had separate meetings with my two children in London. With carefully chosen words I'd told them the news of their dad's desertion for another woman.

As I'd predicted Clyde had clammed up refusing to discuss the issue and the implications. Paris hadn't met my expectations because she'd taken the news calmly, by asking what I'd done to drive him away. The accusation had hurt, and still stung.

Can I convince Paris that Justin's departure has not been my fault? For some reason I can't believe Justin would never return. His infatuation might fade. Why did Paris think his departure had been my fault?

I nipped back into the cosy kitchen to wait. Despite the windows and doors rattling in the wind, the Aga spread warmth throughout the house. The sweet smell of baking hung in the air as I'd made scones. In years past, they had been the children's favourite when they returned home after a day at school. Rolling my head from side to side I attempted to alleviate the tension in my neck.

Paris had always been a daddy's girl and from a young age, she'd idolised him. They had formed a close bond. Taking that into consideration she would blame me for the split.

How would we readjust to Justin's absence? In our regular calls, they'd not mentioned their father. The excitement of their new lives had been the sole focus of their conversations. Would the separation from Justin have a long-term effect on them?

At seventeen and nineteen they should be able to cope, but concern niggled about their ability to deal with the change in their lives. My emptiness would not be resolved, I would have to accept my isolation for the foreseeable future.

Justin had sent factual emails, but he ignored the questions I posted in return. What a coward! Did he think that he could ignore his previous life?

The farm had been transformed by Liam. The heavy rain hadn't daunted him. The farmyard cobbles had been cleaned, so mud no longer dragged into the house. The terrible stench had disappeared. Even to my inexperienced eyes and ears the improvements had made the animals content. Also, he had cleared the yard of those I found difficult.

Angela, the donkey, lived on a pasture away from the farmhouse along with the geese. Though the peacock remained in the farmyard, strutting around, looking magnificent with its iridescent tail, I stayed out of its way. It's pointed beak and strange piercing noises filled me with concern.

Liam popped into the house on a regular basis to update me on progress, but he did not smile. A pity for a handsome man. When talking to me he appeared tense and ill at ease. As soon as he'd given me the requisite information he left. I'd offered him a cup of tea on every occasion, but he'd never accepted. Perhaps he didn't like me because of my background as a townie.

Liam's low wages I could afford, although the installation of new lighting in the barns had been expensive. On a confident day I'd travelled into Braxton, the nearest town, by bus. A second-hand bicycle, dark olive green complete with a wicker basket on the front, provided a shaky ride for local journeys.

I'd had tumbles when the wheels had stuck in the deep farm ruts, but I had persevered. Although quicker than walking I had to push it on the steep inclines. The trips to the village store had been embarrassing. Justin's desertion had become village knowledge. In small close-knit communities nothing stayed hidden for long and they found out everyone's mishaps one way or the other. There were no secrets in Mossmoor.

I checked my appearance in the large oak framed mirror in the boot room next to the kitchen. The swirling flared skirt in shades of pink and purple, teemed with a flattering textured lace blouse, boosted my confidence. I straightened my clothes then listened for the approaching noise of the engine. The scarf draped around my shoulders, came from a collection of my own creations, and I ran my fingers over the soft cashmere enjoying its luxurious texture.

The strong winds eradicated sounds, but they returned during lulls in the gusty battering. I took a few deep breaths to calm my quivering insides. Pausing to plaster a smile across my face, I grabbed my long cashmere cardigan and draped it across my shoulders, then ventured outside to meet the old car as it pulled onto the farmyard cobbles.

11

Paris leapt out and threw her arms around my neck. Clyde scrambled from the car, kissed me on the cheek and squeezed my shoulders.

Clyde, leaner than his father whose business lunches had added to his waistline, had become tall and good looking. Paris had the hallmark of being a younger version of me. Although a little overweight, her pretty round face and wonderful ice blue eyes were more striking than mine had ever been.

We assembled in the warmth of the kitchen and gravitated towards the Aga. Paris gabbling about the slow journey from London, swept up a buttered scone and in between mouthfuls, 'You're smart this evening, Ma. Your hair looks good. Is that a new outfit? It's stylish.'

Clyde munched on his scone with obvious enjoyment. 'The country life is suiting you, mum.' My pleasure at the compliments rankled because they remained under the illusion, I enjoyed country life. How could they come to that conclusion when I'd fought so hard to stop the move and remain in London? I yearned to return to the bustling metropolis. Thinking about the city cheered me but I missed the noise, energy and bustle of the people.

When they had relaxed and settled in for the weekend, I would reveal my news. Selling the farm and moving back to London had become of prime importance in my plans. Paris continued to ramble about the journey, when the door opened and David Hunstanton, the vet, entered.

The initial scene between us with the donkey had been forgotten, and I'd found him helpful over the past weeks. A charming man, his face beamed as he entered the kitchen.

Paris switched her gaze between our faces with a puzzled frown, 'Mum, what's happening here?' But I took no notice of her sharp tone and introduced David. Paris scowled, managed a curt hello but fell silent. What's the matter with her? She has career aspirations to be a vet, and I'd anticipated she would enjoy talking to David about his career. Clyde nodded and fiddled with his mobile phone.

Paris flopped into the rocking chair next to the Aga, turned her back and studied her scarlet finger nails. Her blonde hair flopped forward but didn't conceal the frown on her face. I chatted with David and ignored the sullen silence from Paris, while Clyde stared out the window. Their rude and unfriendly behaviour confused me.

David informed me the heifer, he'd been called to examine, had improved. He declined an invitation for supper. Having passed on his information, he left.

Paris leapt to her feet, with fists clenched by her sides and tears in her eyes. 'What's the matter darling?' I stepped towards her. Anger filled her eyes.

'Keep away from me, how dare you?' Her voice ran up the scale and cracked, 'It's only been a few weeks.'

'What are you talking about?'

Tears ran down her cheeks and she drew her arms across her chest, then huffed in annoyance. 'It's your behavior that forced dad to leave as your flirting is so blatant.' With burning reproachful eyes, she glowered at me. 'The new hairstyle and clothes. Huh! It's so obvious. I thought you'd dressed for us but you made the effort so you could flirt with David! How can you make eyes at him?'

12

Words failed me. The accusations brought a lump to my throat. If Paris had been older, she would have accused me of having an affair. David had been calm and helpful over the past difficult weeks. A good-looking man, he deserved to be treated in a friendly, welcoming manner.

In Paris's mind, the decision had been made, I'd deserted her father and had begun an affair with the local vet. Didn't she understand Justin had left me for another woman? A flash of annoyance ripped through me at the injustice. Neither Paris nor Clyde had asked me how I coped with his abandonment. Tears caught in my throat and I took a deep breath to steady myself, as I hadn't even thought about another man.

I opened my mouth to defend myself, but it would lead to an argument and that wouldn't help. A bloody mess, made worse by my children's attitude, caused a wave of indignation to sweep through me. Justin's abrupt departure had smashed my life to smithereens and left me adrift, not knowing which way to turn.

Every day became a challenge. The long empty nights with images of Justin and his new woman flickered through my living nightmare.

Amidst a new flow of tears, Paris rounded on me, 'Clyde and I hoped your separation would be temporary, we assumed you would wait for him! It'll take time for dad to tire of his fascination with his new woman.'

As though an arbiter in the dispute and able to guide our decisions, Paris and I turned to Clyde but didn't expect him to speak. 'It's so obvious, mum.' Without another word, he picked up his bag and Paris did the same.

The kitchen door opened again. This time Liam stood in the doorway and contemplated Clyde, and then Paris. The large waterproof jacket dripped water on the kitchen floor tiles. His hair, wild and windswept, enhanced his rugged handsome features even without a smile. He had no change to his usual deadpan expression.

'Jessica, all's done for today, I'm off to town tomorrow. Young Jackie will see to the animals. We will be here on Sunday to start the tupping. It's late. Should've been done earlier.'

I'd already met Jackie, Liam's younger sister. I caught Paris's eye, and with a jerk of rebellion I gave Liam my best smile.

To my utter amazement, Paris fluttered her eyelashes, and skipped across the room, 'We haven't been introduced. Come in, it's draughty.' Liam hesitated with a frown of confusion but stepped inside and closed the door.

'I'm Paris and this is Clyde.' She gave a wide smile accompanied by the tossing of her long blonde hair. 'It's late, why not stay for supper?'

A clouded, puzzled look appeared on his unsmiling face, 'No thanks, miss. The dogs are settled on the back of the quad and I'm having supper at The Jaggers.'

Liam left, and Paris stood in the doorway peering into the darkness. The quad bike started up and pulled away, then closing the door she wandered back towards the warmth of the Aga, 'Mmm! He's dishy.'

Then she must have remembered our previous conversation and her smile disappeared. In one flowing movement, she picked up her bag and flounced from the kitchen.

13

Two hours later I called the children to supper. There had been no friendly chatting which I had anticipated, because they'd been ensconced upstairs. I had hoped the visit would ease the loneliness of recent weeks, but they had chosen to ignore me.

Footsteps along the soft carpet of the landing indicated they had responded. For the special occasion, I'd set up the dining room. I adjusted my scarf as I waited for them to descend. My nerves quivered with anxiety at the poor beginning to the weekend. The atmosphere had been chilly and awkward as they blamed me for Justin's departure.

Entering the dining room, I smoothed the glaring white linen cloth which covered the dark oak table. Then I rearranged the matching embroidered serviettes, folding them with neat precision and putting them beside each place setting.

The heavy shining cutlery, bought by Justin to complement the traditional room, glinted in the warm light from the oak standard lamps. The tarragon and garlic aroma of a beef and vegetable casserole filled the room. Perching on the carver chair at the head of the table, Justin's usual place, I wrung my hands hoping for a happy evening and vowed to avoid controversy.

The meal progressed but became filled by long and awkward silences. For a short while Paris jabbered away about her school friends. Clyde stayed preoccupied with his thoughts.

Throughout the meal, Paris had been studying me with intense scrutiny and a direct challenge in her blue eyes. Although I wanted to know her thoughts, I daren't ask, fearing a tirade about my behaviour and Justin's departure.

The meal ended without argument although the atmosphere had an undercurrent of strained tolerance from Clyde and Paris. Choosing my words with care while my face assumed a serious expression, 'It's difficult, but we must have a serious talk about the current situation, not least money.'

Paris screwed up her face and twisted her body away, a sure sign she would not participate. 'If you and dad were reunited, we wouldn't need this heavy stuff. Please, can you make it up with him!'

'It's not that easy.' My tone implied I wouldn't make the first move.

'You want him back, don't you?' I nibbled my lip. The direct question surprised me. My mind twisted in turmoil as I searched for an answer.

If he asked to return, could I forgive him? My fractured marriage and broken heart would not mend overnight. The image of Justin and his floosy leapt unbidden into my mind. My body trembled as I struggled to push the thoughts away.

Stacking the plates in a slow and methodical manner I composed an answer to satisfy Paris. 'Darling, you have to accept reality. Talking to him is essential, but the differences may be too great for reconciliation.'

'It's only been a few weeks,' she banged the flat of her hand on the dining table making the stacked dishes and cutlery rattle, 'your relationship with dad can't have changed in that short period. He's a middle-aged man, so it must be a midlife crisis.' Paris, undaunted by my lack of response, and with no understanding or sympathy for my feelings continued to air her views. 'He's infatuated because she's young and famous.'

Paris's words stopped me in my tracks as their significance hit me like a rock in the stomach, 'If you know that, you've spoken to him. Have you?' I studied her face with a worried frown.

Clyde's deep voice interjected, 'Oh Paris! We agreed during the journey home we wouldn't mention his calls as we didn't want to upset mum.'

'Sorry, Clyde,' mumbled Paris.

Although keen to find out more, I resisted the temptation to quiz them. They had spoken to Justin, but he refused to return my calls and messages. How many calls had taken place? What had been discussed? Had Justin intimated the collapse of our marriage had been my fault?

Loneliness and disappointment surged through me. Did no one consider the torment that had consumed me over the last few weeks? The pain of rejection and the fears for the future, had filled my devastated mind.

I had no energy or inclination left to humour my children. With an effort I composed myself, 'Okay, we're tired, so it's not the time to have a difficult conversation. Let's leave it until tomorrow. I will clear the table in the morning.

As we left the dining room, I flicked off the lights and stood in the hall as an awkward silence descended, 'I've a headache, so I'm going to bed.' After kissing them goodnight I plodded up the stairs.

The mixture of anger and loneliness increased with every step. As I closed my bedroom door, I stammered, 'It's still three against one.' Flinging myself onto the bed,

I sobbed.

14

When my children were young, and I needed to talk with them, we sat in the kitchen, so I laid the traditional oak kitchen table for Sunday lunch. Why did I fuss so much? The children needed to accept life as it existed, not how they desired it to be. I moved towards the window. The sun's rays covered the barn roof tiles giving them a rosy glow. My mind drifted, it would be a difficult few hours.

The weekend hadn't progressed as planned. Friday evening's confrontation and accusations set the tone for Saturday. Neither wanted to chat about the problems, so the family meeting hadn't happened.

Early Saturday morning Paris had received an invitation from a friend and Clyde offered to drive her there. After he returned, he took me to Braxton, but wouldn't talk about his father. Paris stayed the evening with her friend while Clyde chatted to Jackie, who had arrived to feed the animals and then gave her a lift home.

I'd been anticipating their visit throughout the week, as an opportunity to have someone in the house to talk to about my feelings for the current predicament. Their disinterest in me and inability to understand my fragile and worrying dilemma filled me with sadness. Had I raised them to be so self-centered?

Sunday lunch would be the final opportunity to discuss the future. The smell of the roast beef filled the kitchen as I opened the Aga oven. The meat, burnt on the outside, oozed blood from the middle. The potatoes hard like stones or fell apart when touched. For many years I had produced perfect Yorkshire puddings, but today's offering had burnt edges and had never risen. I turned up my nose at the colourless and limp vegetables.

If I'd concentrated on cooking rather than thinking about my situation, I could have presented a succulent meal. Paris and Clyde hadn't been near me during the morning. Why come home and then avoid me?

It had to be Justin's fault. What had they discussed on the phone? I stepped into the hall and called them to lunch, but the house remained silent. They must be outside, but where?

I pulled on my wellies, put on my new olive-green fleece which matched my bike, then rubbed a weary hand over my face and set off to find them. The overnight rain had made the cobbles slippery. Walking carefully over the uneven ground, I avoided the peacock but admired his plumage, a brilliant shade of blue tinged with green as it glowed in the dim light. The cattle grazed in a nearby field and their raucous sound filled the air.

I pulled the fleece tight as I traipsed across the farmyard and found Paris and Clyde in the animal sheds talking to Jackie and Liam. The tall double doors of the barn had been pushed open wide. The floor had scattered straw among the water buckets and feed troughs. Floating dust and chaff swirled in the sunlit air.

Liam scraped a shovel along the floor, and the screech of metal against the flagstones filled the shed, setting my nerves on edge. Chickens squawked and clucked as they scratched the straw for food. The stench from the overnight confinement of the cattle hit me as I stood in the doorway.

Paris, loud and girlie, perched on a straw bale with crossed legs. She looked American in her washed out fashionably ripped jeans, denim jacket and a pale pink baseball cap with Paris inscribed across the front. Flirting and giggling she chatted to Liam.

Touching her lips and playing with her hair, she fluttered her eyelashes, which made Liam smile but didn't please me. She must have asked Clyde to tag along as he sat on a bale of straw chatting to Jackie. I shuffled my feet and hovered in the doorway, too scared to approach the chickens which clucked as they pecked the floor searching for food. With cold feet and rising irritation, I waited for them to finish their conversations.

15

Liam and Jackie declined to join us for lunch, which came as a relief, as I wanted the three of us to have a meaningful conversation about the future.

Discarding my fleece and wellies, I settled at the kitchen table and lifted the lids from the dishes. The colour of the meat ranged from black to bright red. The vegetables appeared unappetizing and had deteriorated since I'd drained them. I'd been pleased when they were young as they'd had a healthy and unfussy approach to eating. 'Would you like your meat well done or rare, Paris?'

'Ugh! Meat! No way!' Her face winced in disgust. 'Haven't you realised, I don't eat meat! Only Yorkshire pudding, potatoes and vegetables for me, please.' Before I managed to reply, Paris sized up the Yorkshire, raised her eyebrows, 'I'll do without the pudding.'

Frowning in irritation, my smile vanished, 'When did you become vegetarian?'

'What's wrong with that? I didn't eat the meat in the casserole on Friday, but you didn't notice!'

Clamping my lips together so that no words could escape, I concentrated on carving the meat. I had no control anymore. No one asked my opinion or appeared to care about my views. 'Sorry, Mum. I didn't mean to snap. You don't have a problem with me being a vegetarian, do you?'

'No, darling. If I'd known I would've prepared a different meal.' Paris surveyed the food in the serving dishes.

'I didn't want to create extra work for you, a few vegetables and those broken potatoes will be fine.'

Clyde had taken no meat. 'Would you like beef, Clyde?' I gave a false laugh. 'You haven't become vegetarian, have you?'

'Did it come from animal-friendly managed farms?'

'I've no idea.' An exasperated sigh escaped from my lips, 'I bought it at the supermarket.'

'Okay, I'll have a little today, but I would appreciate you checking the labels before you buy.'

The arrogant tone and attitude irritated me. I had hoped for support from my two children, but they wanted to make a tricky situation more difficult. I'd attempted to bring them up to be caring and thoughtful, but judging by their behaviour this weekend, I'd been a miserable failure. With a meaningful glare and no smile, 'You're welcome to do the shopping.' No comment came following my sarcastic remark, they lowered their heads and avoided eye contact.

Silence held firm during the meal. The bellowing of the cattle, as they were moved back into the barn, filled the kitchen. Paris pushed the vegetables around her plate eating only a few. Clyde helped himself to food but never turned his attention to me.

At the end of the meal, the food on the table appeared untouched. I'd spent the morning preparing the meal but neither of them wanted it, they hadn't appreciated the effort, and didn't want to be at the table with me.

The timing couldn't be worse, but I decided we would talk. They needed to face facts so I pulled back my shoulders, 'You'll be leaving soon so we must talk about serious matters. No excuses and no complaints, let's sit in the front room, I'll clear the table later.'

16

Neither would challenge me, so with long faces, they sat next to each other on the brand-new rustic settee. The blue patterned upholstery needed years of wear to dull the brightness so it would fit with the dark wood cupboards in the room. The suite of furniture had been another of Justin's impulsive buys and I hadn't been consulted.

The muffled sound of the animals filtered through from the farmyard and the grandfather clock ticked, marking the countdown to their departure back to London.

'None of us wish to have this meeting.' My voice was bleak and low-pitched, 'But it must be done.' Neither reacted, so I carried on, 'The first issue is money.'

'Oh, mum, this is awful!' Paris folded her arms across her chest and heaved a dramatic sigh, 'Do what you think is best.'

Clyde added, 'I agree with Paris, it's better to leave it to you.'

'Life is not that simple.' The discomfort on their faces increased, it reminded me of reprimanding them when young. They would sit there and bear it but wouldn't respond. At some point, Paris would cry.

Clyde's shoulders drooped, 'It's the first time we've

been together without dad.' Paris put a tissue to her eyes.

'You've upset your sister.'

'It's not me! Dad leaving home has caused this weekend's problems.' They held me to blame. A silence extended.

'What do you want to say Clyde?' I had no optimism he would solve the difficulties.

'The first weekend without dad is over, so our next visit will be easier, and we'll be able to cope with a serious discussion.'

'But these matters are urgent!'

'They can wait until next weekend!' Paris sniffed and mopped at her eyes; her voice sounded petulant like a child wheedling.

'Are you coming next weekend?' They nodded in unison. A strange decision after the disaster of the weekend I'd endured. With a conscious effort I ensured my voice sounded bright and positive, 'That's lovely, but don't you want to stay in London with your new friends?'

Clyde muttered, 'I've found some shared interests with Jackie. We're seeing a film together next Saturday. She's super. Quite different from other girls I know. Hopefully, it will be more than once.' A smile hovered on his lips, but the carpet held his attention.

My mind whirled and my mouth opened with surprise. No support for me, only his own interest. Disappointment swept through me at his uncaring and self-centred attitude.

The sooner I sold the farm and returned to London the happier I would be. But for now, I had to make the best of living in this bleak and hostile environment filled with animals, mud and loneliness.

Jackie, with her work clothes and short cropped hair wanted to be the equal of her four brothers. It surprised me that Clyde had taken an interest in her and I didn't know how to respond.

Paris had a smug expression, 'Next Saturday Liam is taking me to the village barn dance.' Her face held a defiant expression.

'What! He is not! Liam is far too old for you. And that's final!' I stood up, quivering with indignation while a flush spread across my cheeks.

Paris clenched her hands into fists and squealed, 'I'm seventeen and he's only about thirty. Dad is four years older than you, so difference in age is not important.'

Controlling myself became impossible. Pressures had built up during the weekend and Paris sat in the firing line. 'You are a silly girl,' I put the flat of my hands on the table and leaned forward, 'it's not about age, but maturity. Liam is a sensible and mature man. You're a schoolgirl and a silly, immature one! You will do as I say. I will not consider the matter. The decision is made!' I slammed my fist down on the table.

Her agitated high pitch voice squealed, 'It's a pity dad's not here, he would have been sympathetic.'

'You're not going!'

'You've changed so much since he left,' her blue eyes blazed with wild indignation, 'you used to be friendly and understanding. Now you're harder, edgier and unapproachable.'

Her comments rendered me speechless. So that's what she thinks of me. A chill crept through my body. Loneliness engulfed me as even my children had turned against me, and I had nobody to give me comfort or advice.

Paris, burst into tears, leapt up from her chair and ran from the room, slamming the door behind her. As usual she acted like a drama queen, blowing the situation out of proportion to achieve her own ends. The hysterical outburst, typical of her self-centred behaviour, showed no respect for my views.

Tension overwhelmed me as tears ran down my cheeks. My throat scratched and my vision blurred. After a few minutes of tense silence, I shuffled towards the door, 'I'd better check on Paris.'

I had no enthusiasm for the forthcoming confrontation. Paris wanted her own way and I intended to dig in my heels.

With surprising speed, Clyde jumped to his feet, 'It's better if I go.' I slumped in the chair and placed my head in my hands. The weekend had turned into a disaster.

The grandfather clock ticked marking the passage of time with rhythmic certainty. Emptiness and loneliness stretched before me. No one had yet asked how I had coped since Justin's departure. The hurt, rejection and sadness that swirled through me had no avenue for escape. It festered and overwhelmed me day by day. No one cared.

The visit had been an unmitigated disaster. Swiping away the tears I forced myself into action. Stomping into the kitchen I crashed the dirty roasting pans into the sink. A few minutes later Clyde announced they were leaving.

'Is she okay?' I'd upset her but remained adamant that Paris wouldn't go to the dance with Liam. Should I sack him? If I did, who would replace him? I wouldn't know where to start. I couldn't ask David because he had recommended him in the first place. Liam had the expertise to run the farm, which I lacked.

My mind cleared, I'll patch up the quarrel with Paris with no decision one way or another. Perhaps a chat with Liam might persuade him to drop the idea. Yes, that would be the best solution.

Paris walked into the kitchen, 'Bye mum, take care of yourself, let's talk next week.' The tantrum and accusations appeared forgotten, and although we hugged briefly, she had no warmth and no smile.

'Yes, let's chat next weekend. Have a safe journey.'

Clyde kissed me on the cheek but didn't speak. Neither gave a backward glance as they walked to the car chatting and laughing. Tears formed in my eyes, but I blinked them away, I'd shed too many.

17

Liam strode into the kitchen as I opened the black plastic bag for the leftovers on the plates. He gave several glances at the beef joint which remained on the table. 'Have you had your lunch?'

'Jackie and I had a cheese roll a couple of hours ago.'

'Young people become hungry working so hard in the cold weather, I am grateful for your help, so let me make you and Jackie a beef sandwich.'

'Thanks, the meat looks tasty.' For the first time, he stayed but showed no signs of relaxing and moved between his feet, shaking his head when I pointed to a chair.

As I put the final touches to the huge sandwiches, I drew in a deep breath, 'We need to talk, Liam.' I needed my voice to sound friendly. 'Are you taking Paris to the village barn dance next Saturday? If so, I have concerns...'

Liam blushed, lowered his head and shoved his hands into his jacket pockets. 'I don't want to take her. This morning in the barn she kept pestering me and wouldn't let me work. I didn't want to upset anyone, so I agreed.' He talked faster than before. 'If you say she cannot attend, then that's fine, I won't be mardy.' He ran his hands through his already disheveled hair and sadness clouded his features. 'I will be with a large group, so joining us would be the easiest way. She will hate it.'

'Do you think so?'

'She comes from London, with sophisticated clubs and the views of a townie, if you'll excuse the expression.' I couldn't take offence as the label townie applied to me. 'It will not be a young people's dance; the whole village will be there. Paris will not like the music or the skittle competition, where I will be throughout the evening, as I'm the village champion.'

'It would be good for her to get it out of her system.'

'That's my hope. It will stop her pestering me and allow me to carry on with my work. If you let her come, one of my girl cousins will keep an eye on her, as Jackie's not going this year.'

It would avoid an argument with Paris and make next weekend's conversations easier. I gave him the sandwiches with two hot mugs of tea. Liam mumbled his thanks and departed to find Jackie. He's a good man!

The conversation had been easier than anticipated. Paris won't have Liam's undivided attention. Tough! I threw the cold deflated Yorkshire pudding into the black bag with disgust, and wrapped the rest of the beef in foil, in case Liam wanted another sandwich.

18

The noise and smell hit me. The chickens squealed for food as they danced around my legs. I suppressed a shiver. The flapping and squawking unnerved me.

'Hi, Mrs Southwick. I'm packing eggs for tomorrow. If you are searching for Liam, he's in the top pastures with the dogs, they are rounding up stray sheep.'

'Did you want another sandwich?'

'No, thanks.' Jackie pushed her hair away from her face.' I studied the young woman with interest as Clyde liked her, and they would be going to see a film together next weekend.

Thickset, short cropped hair and strong arms didn't make her a striking female, and I struggled to understand why Clyde would find her attractive. The worry about Liam and Paris nagged. While I had been assured by his words, I still held a doubt that Paris would be pushed aside so easily.

'Clyde mentioned that you and he are going to the pictures in Braxton next week.'

Jackie stopped packing the eggs and faced me. 'I'm not dating him. You've got the wrong impression.' Her jaw clenched with no smile. 'We have a shared interest in the cinema, so it makes sense to go together. That's all. It's not a date.'

Without further comment, I made my weary way back to the kitchen and sat for ages at the kitchen table brooding. I worried about Clyde, as he had always been a sensitive boy when young and took any form of rebuttal badly.

For some reason, he liked Jackie, but from the conversation, she had no reciprocal feelings. That might make him morose.

This weekend I'd wanted to tell Paris and Clyde that I intended selling the farm, but the opportunity hadn't presented itself. Somehow their visit had been out of my control. It would be another week before I could start the selling process.

My thoughts returned to the earlier part of the weekend. Paris and Clyde considered the separation my fault. Why did they think that? Justin had left me to live with a German floozy. What had their father told them? Why did they believe him and not me? Sadness and bewilderment settled over me like a dark grey blanket.

An obvious reason crept to the forefront of my mind. When Justin switched his affinity to the environment, I'd urged caution. Thought before action, I'd repeated, but no one listened. It became three against one in the family. I'd given in, but we had a flaming row about buying this isolated farm. Perhaps Paris and Clyde thought I tried to undermine Justin instead of supporting his new venture. Maybe that's why they had taken his side.

What on earth had Paris been thinking when she'd accused me of making eyes at David Hunstanton? Perhaps she's been reading too many romantic novels. What do I think of David? Handsome, confident, pompous, but kind. I jumped as the door opened and the wind blew in. David stood in the doorway wearing his overalls with a woolly hat pulled down on his head.

19

Despite the shock of him appearing when he had been in my thoughts, I attempted to act as normal. David slipped off his wellington boots and complained about the cold, so he accepted the offer of a coffee with a nip of brandy, then sat close to the Aga. Rubbing a hand across his forehead, he screwed up his eyes as though warding off an impending headache.

Switching off the harsh overhead fluorescent lights, the worktop downlighting gave the kitchen a softer glow and enhanced the shadows.

'Liam and Jackie have left.' He rubbed his forehead again, 'I've given the heifer an injection and it can return to the herd tomorrow.' I nodded and would pass the information on to Liam in the morning.

David clenched the mug in his hands and leaned against the Aga deep in thought. 'It's my last call today, another vet is taking over for the night shift.' Stretching his long legs out in front of him, he warmed his toes against the oven. 'It's been a hard day.'

'Thanks for coming, I appreciate it. Have you far to go, your eyes look red and tired?'

'Only about five miles as I live on the Braxton to

Meek road in an Elizabethan farmhouse. I keep meaning to sell it as there's only me.'

I didn't want to sound nosy, but my curiosity had become aroused about this handsome man. 'Only you?'

'I'm a widower, my wife died in a diving accident five years ago, our only son is a medical man in Australia.'

'I'm sorry about your wife.' It sounded weak and cliched, but more appropriate words failed me.

David's quiet voice broke the silence, 'Jessica? Would you come with me to the village barn dance next week?'

My stomach lurched and despite the heat in the kitchen, a shiver swept through me. He'd asked me out, but to the same dance as Paris. But he had asked me out! A date. With a man.

Hesitating, my head cleared, and I sized up the situation, 'I don't think it's my scene as I never enjoyed them as corporate events in London.' An image of the last event I'd attended sprang to my mind. Too much alcohol and careering around the dance floor like a maniac. David grinned, threw back his head and laughed. 'What's so funny?'

'Comparing a London corporate event with a Mossmoor barn dance is beyond funny, it's hilarious.' David continued to chuckle.

'I don't understand.' A small smile lurked as his amusement was infectious.

'The locals don't have a village hall, although they have been trying to build one for years. It's called a barn dance because it takes place in a barn.'

A real barn! That would not be cosy. 'Isn't it cold at this time of year?'

'There's a bonfire, lanterns and many heaters, it's a village event.'

'I don't think it's my scene.'

'There's a bar, some traditional dancing for the older

ones, and the side barn has children's entertainment.'

'What about country dancing?'

'Little, except when the Young Farmers want to whip everyone into a frenzy.' Shaking my head, it didn't sound a perfect evening. A barn would be draughty and dusty. 'Let me finish as you haven't lived in the village for a full year. Everyone who goes, regardless of age, is expected to take a partner. There's no implication attending with me, but I must go.'

'Why?'

'A tradition that goes back into the mists of time. The village farmers give me a token gift of their appreciation each year. Often it's a bottle of whiskey or brandy.' He gave a small smile. 'Keeps me in spirits for the rest of the year, they did it with my grandfather, father and now me.'

'That's kind of them.'

'Not at all,' he chuckled, 'I must stand there while the farmers come up from the audience to tell stories of the mishaps I've had. They are recounted in detail and often with embellishments, before they'll give me the gift.'

'Such as?'

'This year's prime story will be Albert Drinkwater, that's Liam's uncle, who will describe how fast I can run when an irate cow chases me down a narrow lane.' I laughed. An enjoyable and welcome sensation I hadn't experienced in recent weeks. 'Please say you'll come, we only need to arrive together, that's what counts in local folklore. After that, you don't have to talk to me.'

With a flash, I realised the positive aspects of attending, I would be able to keep an eye on Paris and be seen to support the village. 'I'll come, but no country dancing.' David laughed. His face lit up. I liked that smile.

20

After the supermarkets of London, Mossmoor's General Store reminded me of shops from the sepia prints of bygone days. Vegetable sacks lay loose in battered wooden compartments along one wall. The shop, crammed with shelves, allowed little light from the outside, and the low watt bulbs made reading the labels difficult. Earthy smells from the potatoes filled the shop, while an ancient electric till sat on the wooden counter with a permanently open drawer.

Cate, the wife of the landlord of The Jaggers pub, had finished paying for a few items as I wandered in clutching my shopping bag. The camel winter coat covered black trousers and knee-length boots. Her black hair had recently been styled. Without doubt her elegance resonated with the hot spots of London, not a bleak village in the middle of the moors.

Michael worked hard building a successful business by making the pub attractive to the richer market, while Cate spent all day in the garden bar. During daylight hours she drank coffee, but in the evening, she swapped to gin and tonic. In her mid-forties and a little overweight, she loved the glamorous life and did little to support her husband, Michael, even if they were busy. Village gossip centred on how they afforded luxurious holidays and extensive wardrobes.

I nodded hello to Maureen, the owner of the shop, who appeared dowdy next to Cate. The drab grey overall hung on her slight bony body. Her sixty-fifth birthday approached, but she'd declined any interest in a celebration. When she attended a village event, she wore clothes common in her mother's time.

On my first visit to the store after we'd moved in, Maureen had been welcoming and friendly, she didn't judge people in the village or any newcomers who arrived. Maureen and her husband, Stan, had been stalwarts of the village for years.

They had suffered the declining fortune of rural stores, and their prospects for an imminent retirement had deteriorated. They told anyone prepared to listen, they'd hoped to convert a barn and their nearby land into a much bigger shop with a car park. The lack of capital, and difficulties with planning meant that their hoped-for retirement nest-egg wouldn't happen.

Maureen took the money for my purchases and smiled, 'David Hunstanton is a charming man. We're pleased you accompanied him to the barn dance despite the difficulties you're having.'

Meeting people from the village had afforded me the opportunity to chat, and I appreciated how they made me feel a part of the local community. The encouragement to become involved in village life hadn't changed my mind about returning to London, but it had slowed the urgency. The feeling of isolation had evaporated. Much to my surprise, I'd received invitations to visit others in the village and there were many offers to help on the farm. I'd been overwhelmed with the reception I'd received.

David had been a perfect escort at the barn dance

as he'd introduced me to many local people. Although he had been kind, and thoughtful throughout the evening, he hadn't asked me out again which had been my only regret. No doubt I would have refused because I didn't want to get involved.

Cate having packed her purchases stood to one side while Maureen served me, 'Your knowledge of fashion is amazing, Jessica. We won the ladies quiz night at The Jaggers easily. I've already invited Jess around to have a serious talk about clothes.' As she announced this her eyes swept over Maureen's dismal appearance.

I'd only attended the quiz as several of the women at the barn dance had pressed me. The questions had been easy to answer. No one from the village knew my fashion background, as when I'd arrived, I had been referred to as Justin's wife. It had annoyed me, but I'd never set the record straight.

'Stan and I don't go out as my ninety-year-old mother lives with us and needs constant attention.'

Cate, who always liked to be the source of gossip, raised her eyebrows, 'There's a rumour in the village, Maureen, you will close the shop next year and not sell it on.'

For the first time, the gentle smile disappeared from Maureen's face, she avoided eye contact and her bottom lip quivered. 'It's no rumour, Cate. Business has been declining for years so we've not been able to build the extension. Stan reaches retirement age soon so it's not worth staying open. We will close and stay where we are.'

'That's sad.'

'We've seen it coming for years.' Maureen's voice sounded flat as she focused on rearranging the shelves on the far side of the shop.

21

Struggling against the wind, I drew my new wax jacket tight and put my groceries in the front basket of my bicycle. Calm, sunny and cold weather this morning encouraged me to wear a thick flowing skirt. The blustery wind and rain that now swept through the village meant it had been a bad choice for the cycle home.

The thought of the mud and water filled me with gloom. In London drizzle, I would have hailed a black cab and sailed home listening to the chatter of the driver. Those days had gone. I braced myself as it wouldn't be a good ride home in the gathering gloom of twilight.

Cate called out, 'Don't be long getting home. The rain is turning to snow on the tops.' She pointed to the moorland hills that rose to the west of the village, 'It'll be laying soon.'

For reasons I didn't understand the lights on my bike had stopped working. It didn't concern me as there would be no traffic, unless I encountered a tractor. The past week had improved my mood considerably as I'd become more sociable in the village. I sang and strolled up the hill.

The barn dance had been far better than I'd expected. The weekend with Paris and Clyde had passed without friction. They were disappointed I wanted to sell the farm but hadn't protested too much.

Preoccupied with their forthcoming dates they had made little comment about my plans. When had they changed from friendly and approachable children to the self centred and uncaring young adults? Clyde hadn't spoken about his evening with Jackie and Paris spent the evening at the barn dance sulking, because Liam never left the skittle competition.

The official papers had arrived confirming the farm ownership had been transferred to me. Now I could sell but hadn't put it on the market as one final matter needed resolution. Another week had passed, and Justin still hadn't spoken to me. I would never have considered it in the past, but he had become a spineless coward. What had happened to the dashing, handsome and confident man I had married?

Last night I'd come up with an excellent strategy to force him to ring. I'd emailed him stating that unless he rang, I would use a private detective to discover his whereabouts and then travel to Germany to confront him. My confidence had returned, and I anticipated moving to London to find a job with a new found enthusiasm.

Although I hadn't designed fashions for several years, I still had talent. When the children were born, I gave up my career to be a full-time mother and devote myself to family life. I lost touch with most of my fashion associates, although my social life still blossomed with Justin's connections and other mothers also coping with young toddlers. There would be only one leftover problem from my past in the world of fashion, but I could handle it.

22

The darkening sky silhouetted the moorland hills, but I would be home before twilight faded. A limestone wall flanked the lane and deep potholes scarred the bumpy road surface. Still pushing the bike, I plodded up the hill with head bent against the wind howling across the open moor.

The only concern would be the ford on the lane, which had been high on the way into Mossmoor. With last night's weather, the stream would deepen during the day as the water drained from the hills. When I reached the top of the hill, puffing a little from the exertion, I mounted my bike.

For the next quarter of a mile, the lane dipped downhill towards the ford, so I set off. Pedalling furiously, I gripped the handlebars in preparation for the splash as the bike swished through the water. With grim determination my speed increased as my legs pumped the pedals.

The cold air and snowflakes brushed against my cheeks, but the anorak, gloves and billowing skirt, with thick tights, kept out the cold. I increased speed.

The water in the stream glistened as it crossed the road. At about six inches deep I would lift my feet from the pedals and let momentum take me through the water. The stout mudguards would keep me dry. I'd crossed the brook many times in this manner when the water had been deep. My method had been honed to perfection.

As I approached the water, I caught a fleeting glance of a car with no lights on the far side of the ford. With no time to stare, I concentrated on steering through the swirling stream. Screwing up my eyes, I focused on the water manoeuvre.

Success! I didn't get wet and with furious pedalling emerged from the ford, intending to use my impetus to gain traction on the upslope.

A man kneeling on the road emerged from the blackness, his sudden appearance prohibited me from shouting a warning. Hurtling towards him, his eyes widened, and he raised his palms to me. Although he made a late fruitless attempt to jump out of my path, my body and bike caught him a glancing blow.

With a look of surprise, he bounced into the side of his car and banged his head. Staying on the bike for a few yards, I lost balance on reaching the bank at the side of the road. The steep incline of the roadside gave me a gentle fall into the thick moss and grass. The man hadn't fared well, and he staggered backwards. 'Mind out!' I pointed towards the water, but my warning came too late.

Disorientated from the impact, he tripped on a rock and fell into the stream head first.

'Oh, my God!' I stumbled back down the lane. The shadows of the trees reduced the light, but he sprawled unmoving in the stream. As his legs remained on the road, I grabbed and hauled with all my strength. With a second hard pull, I dragged him clear of the water.

Panic engulfed me. Had I killed him? Relief spread through me as he groaned. One final tug moved him away from the gushing stream. 'Don't hit me again, please, I beg of you, don't hit me.'

Stepping towards him, I crouched down to check if he had been injured, but the darkness became pitch black near the water. As I grabbed his shoulders, his voice became clearer. 'Take my wallet, my cards. The keys are in the car. Don't hit me again. Please!'

The poor man sounded confused. Perhaps he had hurt his head. 'I haven't mugged you.' I shook his shoulders, 'I hit you with my bike.'

'I don't care what you hit me with, please don't do it again.' He wriggled free from my grasp and on all fours scrambled away. In the darkness he lost his orientation and scuttled in the direction of the stream. I grabbed him by the arm and pulled with all my might to stop him. 'Police, police! I'm being mugged!'

The ridiculousness of the man's plea gave me a sense of realism. If he was calling for the police in the middle of an isolated moor in a snowstorm, he must be delirious. 'Don't go back into the stream!' I shouted at the top of my voice. 'It's dark and you weren't visible! What are you doing in the middle of the moors with your car in this weather?'

The man stopped struggling and sat up. I crouched down next to him, peering at his face. Why wear a light suit in this weather? His clothes were soaked through. 'Let me help you?' I offered my hand.

He garbled, 'I didn't realise that a river flowed across the road.' The moon appeared briefly between the stormy clouds, highlighting his sports car with the bonnet raised. 'It stalled, so I tried to restart it.' He shivered. 'The bike had no lights! I shall tell the police.'

The accident had been my fault so I couldn't let him fend for himself. Dressed for a normal day at the office he would suffer hypothermia unless I acted. 'It's a long walk to my farm, will your car go, otherwise you'll freeze to death.'

'I'm so cold,' he moaned.

The pitiful voice annoyed me, and I had little sympathy for him. Pathetic, sprung to mind.

23

'Try the car,' I instructed. He dropped the bonnet and to my surprise followed my orders and jumped in the car. The engine spluttered into life. Leaving my bike on the bank, I grabbed my shopping and leapt into the passenger seat shouting, 'Drive! Let's get moving!' The engine whined as he let the clutch out, but the car juddered forward up the hill. 'Turn right along that track!'

The man shivered and moaned. When we reach the farmhouse, I will check for any major injuries and he can warm up. The underneath of the car banged, and the ruts threw it sideways. With white knuckles, he gripped the steering wheel and shivered, 'It's ruining my car.'

'You won't be alive to enjoy it unless you reach the warmth! Keep driving!' His hands shook as he hunched over the steering wheel peering through the windscreen. When he hesitated again, after hitting a large rut, 'Nearly there.' At least I hoped it sounded that way as we still had a quarter of a mile before reaching the farmyard.

On the last rut near the farmhouse, the engine roared. 'The exhaust has fallen off!' he shouted.

'Drive between those buildings and into the farmyard.' The enclosed yard became a calm haven compared to the rough weather screeching over the moors. The welcome glare of the automatic security lights calmed me, and highlighted the wisps of hay, which danced in the air as the wind swirled and roared. Liam had left, as no lights shone in the outbuildings. Pity, I could have done with his assistance. 'Come on, this way!'

With determination I pushed him along in front of me as he wobbled across the cobbles, confused and disorientated. The warmth of the kitchen hit us.

He gasped as the hot air reached his lungs, then shivered. With one last shove, I pointed towards the rocking chair next to the Aga, 'Sit there and don't move.' In the full light of the kitchen, I assessed the cold, wet and bedraggled man huddled in the seat.

In his late twenties, he wore a light green summer suit, sodden with water and streaked with mud. His black shoes, the lightweight slip-on style, had both been torn. The brown sludge from the stream mixed into the blonde highlights in his hair. What a mess!

Only his suit and car gave me confidence that he wouldn't be a down-and-out or a burglar. Rushing upstairs I grabbed a pair of Justin's old jeans, a rugby shirt and a thick woollen dressing gown. As I returned to the kitchen he flinched, his wide startled eyes appeared like a rabbit's caught in the headlights. His sallow complexion had paled as his body drained of energy.

'This way, follow me!' Pulling at his arm to ensure he understood, I led the way through the door into the boot room. The cold and clinical emulsioned walls coupled with the tiled floor, emanated a sharp chill after the kitchen. It smelt of disinfectant and the fluorescent lights cast a harsh glow. Justin had boxed off a side room as a shower unit for occasions when he was dirty from farm work. 'A shower will warm you, then dress in these clothes.'

24

Mossmoor had been cut off by the snow, the breakdown service had informed us they were unable to rescue him and his car. I'd never been cut off before. When I lived in London, it would have been a worry but the people in the village took the bad weather in their stride. They made sure the animals were safe and didn't travel far until conditions improved. In an emergency a tractor could reach any destination.

Although I didn't like the idea, the stranger had to stay in the spare room. Tomorrow I would make alternative arrangements if the bad weather continued. Liam might be able to provide him with temporary accommodation. The snow had been forecast to change to rain overnight, but can the weatherman be relied on?

With a sad expression he hunched in the chair next to the Aga, wearing the odd assortment of clothes I'd provided. I'd heated minestrone soup and served it with warm crusty bread which he'd eaten balancing the bowl on a tray in front of the Aga. A long evening beckoned. Sitting in my kitchen with a total stranger while a snowstorm raged outside was a new experience.

For my own peace of mind, I would endeavour

to elicit information about his background. All I had gleaned about him had been his name; Miles. Well Miles had been miles away from civilization this evening. The pun brought a small smile to my lips. Why had he been on the road to nowhere in such hostile weather conditions, in unsuitable clothing, and an inappropriate car for such rough country tracks?

Pulling a spare chair across the kitchen I joined him next to the Aga. I handed him a mug of hot tea and with my best grin, 'Miles, what job do you have?' A spark of interest appeared on his face, 'I work for Renewable Energies Limited.'

Inwardly groaning, I'd had enough of the greens and renewables to last me a lifetime. Justin's adoption of the green agenda had been the catalyst for the end of my marriage and my life of luxury in London. 'On the technical side?'

'No, I'm a salesman selling renewable solutions.'

Keeping my hostile thoughts to myself I persevered with the conversation. 'Have you come far as you weren't dressed for the moors?'

'Birmingham.' It would be a long evening, as he gave short and abrupt answers.

Perhaps he didn't enjoy idle chatter with a woman who he thought had mugged him, but I wouldn't give up. 'Where were you travelling to when you crashed?'

'On a hopeless cause, I suspect. My sales have been terrible this month. I'm clutching at any chance, otherwise they will sack me.' His shoulders sagged which accentuated his hunched posture. He lowered his head to study his hands which clutched his mug of tea.

'Christmas won't be long?' I attempted to add a cheerful note, but it didn't bring the desired effect.

'They're ruthless! If you don't meet the figures, you're out, and I haven't managed a single order this month.' With a wince he moved closer to the Aga. A pang of sorrow for his dilemma passed through me. Perhaps he'd unseen injuries that had been inflicted by me.

'Let me get you another cushion.'

'Thanks, you've been kind. You saved my life. It's terrible out there.' The colour had returned to his cheeks. A good-looking man, younger than me, with mesmerising mink brown eyes. As he relaxed, a cheeky sparkle emerged and an attractive smile lit up his face. Having finished his tea, he settled with another cushion and a shot of whiskey.

25

Miles swirled the amber liquid in his glass, 'A rumour spread in the office that a director of a big company's environment division had brought a farm near here.' As I'd relaxed with my whiskey, my mind had been drifting, but the words brought me to full focus. 'A long shot,' he licked his lips after a sip of whiskey, 'but I decided to try. At least he would be sympathetic to renewable energy, but it took a few hours at the office to find the name of the farm. So, I set off late, but I didn't expect it to be so remote.'

Although I didn't want to pursue this conversation, I needed to determine whether I'd come to the correct conclusion. Had he been searching for Justin? 'Have you details of the farm?' Keeping my voice casual, I sat up straight in the chair and hoped for an inane reply. 'Yes, but I became lost on the moors. The man's name is Justin Southwick, and the farm is called Cloughside.'

My heart sank as he named the farm. It would be impossible to send him on his way tomorrow without telling him. When he reached the bottom of the track in daylight, he would notice the sign, Cloughside Farm, The Home of the Southwick family. I had no alternative, 'My name is Jessica Southwick. Justin is my husband.'

'Excellent!' His eyes brightened and his face lit into a devastating smile. Finishing his whiskey in one large gulp, he put the glass down and rubbed his hands together. The snippet of news made him excited. 'The paperwork is in the car.'

'Hang on,' I put out my hand and patted him on the arm, to stall his movement while racking my brains for an excuse, 'it's not time for business.'

'I've recovered, but do I need to speak to your husband rather than you.'

The remark annoyed me. Sexist pig! I swallowed my pride, 'Yes, perhaps you'd better talk to him.'

Miles stared out of the window, 'He won't be coming back in this weather, will he?'

On my own in a vulnerable situation I had no intention of enlightening him as to the details, 'Oh, yes,' I prevaricated, 'it's only light snow for here. He has a Range Rover and knows the road.' Did my lie sound convincing?

'Yes, I'm more used to the town,' he yawned and glanced at his watch. 'Perhaps it would be better to catch him in the morning. I'm exhausted.'

With a huge internal sigh of relief, I showed him the spare room with its odd mixture of old and new furniture. Keeping my safety in mind I'd chosen the room furthest from mine. I would rise early and complete jobs outside near Liam, then I would have little contact with Miles.

The snow could have cleared by morning allowing the breakdown truck access, then I could pack Miles back to Birmingham.

As I locked up for the night, a letter from today's post lay on the front door mat. Recognising the bank's envelope I ripped it open. My hand trembled as I digested the information that they wanted to talk to me about the accounts.

26

Pulling back the curtains in my room at seven o'clock, a misty drizzle swirled through the farmyard. Snow had turned to rain. In the hollows, and the field-edges along the walls, the snow lingered, but the moors and fields were clear.

A blustery light shower blew across the farmhouse, but weak sunshine lit the distant hills. The breakdown service can reach the farm. Miles can return to Birmingham. Wearing my thick pink and green dressing gown and my matching slipper boots, I nipped to the kitchen to set the Aga and central heating full on. Despite being temperamental, I'd become adept at managing the heating, governed by the bright red beast which dominated the kitchen.

A knock and rattling at the door made me jump. Assuming Liam at this early hour, I twisted the key and put the kettle on to make the first cup of tea of the morning. 'Good morning, Jessica,' the deep voice resonated around the empty kitchen. It wasn't Liam, so I spun around.

'David, why are you here so early? Is there something wrong with the animals?' He shook his head. His pale face and glazed eyes gave him a gaunt look. He slumped onto the chair with a huge sigh. 'What's the matter? What has happened?'

'On a nearby farm, the animals became trapped by the rising brook and the snow after a fence failed. Several had been injured so we've been rescuing them throughout the night.' Without asking I put a hot cup of tea in front of him. 'They only have a small farm and limited facilities, so they were grateful for my support. I can't be sure about snow on the tops. As I'm too tired to spend an hour battling through the lanes to get home, I thought...'

'Of course, David, you're welcome. There's a shower through there. Some of Justin's overalls and trainers are hanging up. Get yourself clean and warm. I'll make breakfast.' Relief spread across his face.

'Thanks, I won't be long, I'm starving.'

A warmth spread through me that he'd come to me for help. But my mind soon jolted back to the letter from the bank. During the long and restless night, I'd fretted about the bank's letter. Although I hadn't checked recently, there should be money in the account.

Agitation had been with me ever since I blinked my eyes open this morning. I hadn't combed my hair, and no one ever caught sight of me without minimal make-up.

It had been my intention to change from my dressing gown while the breakfast cooked, but David appeared before I'd organised the kitchen. 'That's better! The cooking smells good.'

Running my fingers through my hair would not improve the shame of my appearance. I shuddered when I caught sight of myself in the mirror, hair all over the place and a pale face stared back at me. The image filled me with shame. I'd let myself go.

What had happened to the glossy curls and subtle makeup? The smile had also disappeared. A large silent groan escaped my lips and I closed my eyes. First, I would serve breakfast, then I needed to make significant improvements to my appearance.

As I placed a large breakfast plate in front of David, a sleepy Miles, wearing Justin's dressing gown and thick socks, entered the kitchen. Not the best timing in the world. Would David jump to the wrong conclusion? Did it matter? Nobody could possibly fancy the person I'd glimpsed in the mirror.

'Morning, Jessica,' Miles stood in the doorway, stopped and focused. David with a fork halfway to his mouth stopped eating. He closed his mouth and appraised the new arrival. Miles judged the scene before him and expected to understand the pattern of events.

In three large strides he reached the table, and held out his hand, 'Good morning, Justin, I'm Miles from Renewable Energies, perhaps we might have a chat after breakfast.' Because David had been taken by surprise, he didn't react. My mind raced at the meeting under these circumstances. Miles added, 'That breakfast smells good.' A clear hint which I would ignore. As soon as he'd appeared, I'd intended telling him to ring the breakdown service. But the morning hadn't gone according to plan.

About to order Miles to make the phone call, a car roared into the yard. As the noise didn't match the quad-bike, I assumed Jackie had come in a Land Rover.

'Miles, no. This isn't Justin.' The door to the yard opened.

27

I stopped, frozen to the spot and my smile slipped, 'Justin!'

Miles hadn't picked up the tone of the room. Confusion spread across his face, but ever the salesman, he approached Justin to shake hands, 'Good morning, Justin, I'm Miles from Renewable Energies.' Miles had met his potential client.

My body shook forcing me to grab the back of a kitchen chair for support. After the confusion with Miles, the entrance of Justin bewildered David even further.

Why had life become so complicated? One moment alone in an isolated farmhouse, then three men have appeared. I counted five breaths to appraise the situation, but my eyes never left Justin's face.

He must have reacted to the ultimatum and travelled from Germany, only to find two men in the kitchen with his wife wearing her dressing gown. Justin's eyes flashed between the two men and me. What is he thinking? Do I care?

No doubt he'll recognise David, but will wonder why he's here before dawn, wearing his clothes and having breakfast. As for the other man, I'm not bothered what he thinks, but he's also wearing Justin's clothes. The irony of the situation hit me, but I didn't find it amusing.

I had other things on my mind, so I focused on the deceitful, cowardly man who stood in the doorway. His pale face and hollow eyes stood out and his dishevelled appearance came as a shock.

The old farm mud-streaked anorak and his crumpled trousers looked as though he'd slept in them. Taking in a huge breath he rested his hands on his hips and snarled, 'What are these men doing here?'

His words angered me, 'How dare you! You lying, deceitful man!' I screamed as heat burned my cheeks. 'What have you done to the bank accounts? You have the audacity to arrive without warning and then make judgements about me!' The hostility of my over loud voice shocked me. Justin stared wide eyed and open mouthed. David's voice cut through the sudden quietness, 'I'd better be going.'

My face became hot and I clenched my hands into fists. 'David, for goodness' sake sit down and finish your breakfast.' My attention switched to Miles, 'Get dressed, ring the breakdown service, then leave.'

Directing my most emphatic message at my husband, I emulated his pose. Putting my hands on my hips, I bellowed. 'You pathetic man! Stop making a fool of yourself. Go into the front room.' Scowling as anger bubbled and roared through me, I pointed towards the kitchen door. 'You can then explain what you've done to the bank accounts. Then I shall kick you off my farm!'

To make my point, I emphasised the word 'my' in case he had forgotten that he no longer had any right to be here. The three men became statues. 'Do as I say, now!'

None of them relished disagreeing with me and followed instructions. David sat down and picked up his knife and fork.

Miles left the confrontational atmosphere of the kitchen. Justin with his hands shoved into his anorak pockets and a red face, crossed the kitchen and followed Miles into the hall.

I stalked behind them scowling in cold fury, while my hands itched to shake Justin until his teeth rattled and he answered my questions. A tendency towards violence had never been a part of my character, as I usually took the role of peacekeeper. Not today.

With Justin behind him, Miles hesitated. With a flash of annoyance, I pointed to the stairs, 'Miles, do as you are told!' Without another word he scampered up the stairs like a naughty child.

Stopping at the threshold to the room I attempted to relax, but it didn't work, and my stomach knotted, and nausea filled my throat.

Over the long weeks since Justin's departure I'd rehearsed what I would say, but I'd expected to talk to him on the phone, not face to face. He'd come here!

Several matters needed resolving between us and I would not let him leave until they had been agreed. Forcing my shoulders down, I straightened my spine then marched into the room. Justin faced the empty fireplace.

28

Giving him a few minutes silence to organise my thoughts, I perched on the arm of the settee.

'Jessica, I've...'

In a quiet, firm but icy voice, 'Justin, I will not talk to your back, turn and speak to my face. After all you are supposed to be a grown man and should be able to deal with difficult situations.' Pausing I waited for a reaction. 'Stop being a wimp!' I snarled through gritted teeth while gripping the sofa for support. I'd been certain we would never meet again. With my heart thudding, my breathing became more rapid. Shuffling his body around he lifted his eyes.

Scouring his face, I tried to read his mind, which lurked behind an embarrassed facial expression. The lacklustre eyes focused on me, causing a shiver to track through my body. Did I have any reaction to meeting him? Would he ask to come back? The sadness and lack of sparkle gave him a crestfallen appearance, which contrasted to the confident and arrogant man I had married. Did I still love him?

A rush of adrenaline clouded my thoughts and impaired my judgement. Justin had hurt and humiliated me.

Could I ever forgive him?

'I've met someone else in Germany.'

'You explained that weeks ago.' I frowned and my eyes narrowed with unmitigated fury, 'Why have you refused to communicate?'

Pale and gaunt, he had aged since that fateful Monday morning when he'd left for Germany, never intending to return. Sorrow filled me, but not enough to push aside the acute hurt of the past weeks and months.

'It's time for our final settlement before we separate.' With hesitancy in his voice, the confidence, which he had in abundance, had evaporated.

'The bank accounts!' The pitch of my voice rose and cracked with hysteria. He stammered but closed his mouth. 'Tell me!' My fists balled and every muscle in my body tensed.

'Jess, Jess, let's part as friends, we are too mature for unnecessary anger.'

'Tell me, I want the truth, the whole truth.' Attempting to regain control of my loud and harsh voice, I drew in a large lungful of air. What had he done to the bank accounts?

'I added together the money in the bank, the shares and the amount we paid for the farm, and divided it into two, and I've taken half.'

'You've done what!' I sprang up and took a step towards him with my fists clenched. 'You've left me with this ramshackle farm! And taken the cash, while I have to care for the kids.' I didn't draw breath, 'And tell the kids the truth and stop trying to blame me because you've gone off with a German tart!' Before he moved, I shouted and flung out my arm. 'Get out! I never want to see you again! Ever! And I'm suing you for every penny!' My voice ascended to a shrill scream.

His slow walk to the door irritated me and I wanted

to pick up the flower vase to throw, but I resisted. 'The courts will return the money!' I ground out in a strangled tone to his retreating back.

'They cannot as I've given most of it away, it's gone to a good cause.' The door closed with a resounding click. I swung my arm in frustration and stamped my foot. The movements tipped over the occasional table and the flower vase crashed to the floor.

29

I emerged from the hot and humid smells of the tube station and pulled my coat to keep out the cold. It would be a difficult morning and the outcome would be uncertain. The massive cupola of St Paul's Cathedral towered above me as I crossed Paternoster Square.

The wide stone slabbed piazza, edged by numerous coffee shops with outside tables and chairs, created a Mediterranean impression, but the icy breeze of London on a winter's day soon pushed the illusion away. A few hardy souls craving their cigarettes sat wrapped in anoraks and overcoats.

The sweet memories of past years brought a smile despite today's tension. I'd launched a new collection and we'd hit this square in mid-afternoon after rave reviews from the critics. Happy memories.

The heady times of years ago had disappeared, today would be a complete contrast. I'd come to London to see an old friend, John Mantle, who held a key position in the hiring and firing of personnel in the fashion business. A well-paid job had become a high necessity for survival.

The pain and despair of one of the worst Christmases ever, wouldn't go away. After the fiasco of Justin's visit,

I'd had no contact from the three men. David Hunstanton had never visited, and another vet tended to the animals when Liam required expert help. The breakdown service had taken away Miles and his car. He hadn't returned to sell me a Renewable Energy Solution. And in the same pattern, as before his surprise visit, Justin would not communicate with me.

It had been the first festive period without their father. The children's local romances had collapsed much to my relief, so Paris and Clyde only stayed a day before returning to their friends near London. I had a big argument with them coming up to the New Year, as Justin had invited them to Germany for a visit. When they asked me for the travel fare, I refused expecting their father to pay.

After several days of arguments, they elected to go by coach, but concerned for their safety, I caved in and gave them the money for the flights. But the ill-feeling that the arguments had created didn't lift, and apart from a few short phone calls, I'd had little communication from them.

The village residents had been the bright spot of a dismal holiday period. In The Jaggers pub, Cate plied me with drinks so I would talk about the fashion world, as she loved to hear the details and became enthralled by my designed accessories.

I'd accepted a few invitations for coffee but spent my time at the farm working on the finances. The farm only raised enough income to pay for Liam and Jackie. My most depressing news had been from the estate agent. The selling price of farms had fallen with little activity in the market. It might take a long time to sell the property, so I needed a job because Justin had cleared our bank accounts.

In my heyday, as a top designer, head-hunters pursued me, but time had passed, and I'd lost all contact with my old colleagues in the fashion industry. The knot in my stomach tightened as I reached the door to the elaborate office block near the Stock Exchange. This morning before leaving the farm, I'd dressed smartly as today would make or break me. The mulberry wool and cashmere coat wasn't new, but looked stylish with a loose tie belt and rose gold buttons. The matching handbag and shoes which I'd designed completed the outfit to perfection.

While my confidence had sunk, smart clothes and well styled hair, helped me hang to a false assurance, and I hoped it would fool the people I planned to meet. In the glory days I'd refused many offers and opportunities. On today's visit, if necessary, I would beg for a job.

30

The security guard announced me by my designer name, Jesse James, as he showed me into John Mantle's office. The full-length windows, stainless steel and glass furniture, gave the room a corporate style.

'Hello, Jesse darling, so wonderful to see you again,' John Mantle halfheartedly held my shoulders and brushed each cheek. A small, skinny man, about the same age as me, wearing coloured trousers teamed with a short-sleeved shirt without a tie. He dangled with jewellery and a few subtle tattoos adorned his bare arms. 'It would be lovely to meet for some bubbly and talk about old times.' With an exaggerated glance at the Rolex on his wrist, 'Can't do it now as I'm pushed this morning.'

I hadn't expected to be welcomed with open arms but giving in had never been my style. During the train journey to London this morning I'd prepared what to say to John, a society climber. In order to give the impression that I still had friends in the fashion industry, I countered his lack of interest with a quick lie, 'I haven't much time today, as I've so many people to meet.' I forced a smile onto my unwilling lips.

'Now that I've finished my career break, I'm back in

business.' John Mantel screwed up his face and his sneer held a note of mockery. Pretending not to notice I strutted across to the window, attempting to give the illusion of confidence, although my heart raced with uncertainty. I needed his help. To re-emphasise my point that I was back in business, I waved an arm around indicating the room. 'I thought your office would be grander, you haven't been taking a career break to have a family, have you?'

In the silence that followed my sarcastic outburst he lifted his head and glowered at me. 'While I'm in town I intend visiting the new kids on the fashion block. I flicked my hand through my curls and fixed my eyes on his face. 'It's important to meet the people, with real influence, who pull the strings of the industry.' With a false air of superiority, I gave another exaggerated glance around the office.

'Darling, I would love to help you, but your death knell has been rung.' John puffed out his chest and sneered with icy contempt, making it obvious that he had juicy gossip concerning me, which he was anxious to reveal.

'What are you talking about?' I tried to sound haughty as I strolled around his small office with my head held high. A small flicker crossed his lips as he searched through a pile of papers and magazines. Then with an exaggerated flourish of triumph, he extracted one of the glossies. Placing it down on his desk with a theatrical flourish, he opened the double page spread and pointed, 'You must have missed this, darling! Out of touch, are we?'

Sinking down into the nearby chair my eyes were fixed on the most prominent photo on the page. Covered in mud, I pushed my bike up Mossmoor Hill following a puncture. The angle of the picture didn't do me any favours, I appeared overweight, while my hair, completely dishevelled, blew in the wind.

31

Caroline Darken, the author of the damning article, I did not wish to encounter ever again. Our history stretched back to my early days in the industry. My poor behavior towards her made me squirm, so I wanted to forget her.

Caroline had bad mouthed me, and many others who supported me, then gave up her design career to become a fashion journalist. After she took that role, I left the industry to become a full-time mother. I didn't need to read the article to know it would be vitriolic.

Squaring my shoulders, 'Caroline can't design and can't write. She has no influence.'

'Darling, like it or not, she holds sway over the industry. Those she favours receive good contracts.' Rubbing my hands together I narrowed my eyes. John had been taken in by the article which meant others would share his views. I didn't need this sort of publicity as I tried to re-establish myself.

John continued, in a caustic manner, 'You are a mess in the photo! Whatever made you move to the remotest place on earth?' My heart sank because John had been my best bet of a helping hand in the industry, but I wouldn't crumble, I wouldn't.

In the past, he would have done his level best to keep me on his side as I had been head-hunted by several agencies. Those were the days!

I steeled myself, stood, and raked my fingers through my hair, 'I'd hoped for so much more from you John than being taken in by Caroline. Can't you see I've been out in the wilds getting an authentic view for my next collection.'

'Wallowing in mud and pushing a broken bike,' he sneered, scrutinising the photo.

Huh! He's right. What to say next? Clutching at straws, I tapped the embarrassing photo with my finger, 'A leading fashion magazine in recent months predicted a rustic theme in next year's fashions.' I allowed a moment's pause for him to digest this information. 'Let's face it, rustic is no good on the drawing boards of fashion houses in fancy offices in London, you have to experience the great outdoors first.

It registered with John, who missed little in trends, 'I might well contact Caroline and ask her for the original. It will make a good picture as the signature photo for my Rustic Realism Collection. Eat your heart out, Barbour!' With a flourish, I walked towards the door. 'Got to fly, catch up sometime for drinkies!'

I managed to leave the office block before I broke into tears. The sun had gone, and a light drizzle swept through the air, but I wouldn't remove my sunglasses. Coffee would help to calm me. Although I'd tried my old confidence with John, it hadn't worked, and I'd blurted out anything to readdress the humiliation of the article. As I'd left his office, I'd snatched up the magazine and as an act of masochism, I would read it.

The cost of a cup of coffee and a piece of chocolate cake were overpriced but I needed comfort food. A solitary convenient armchair in the window enabled me to face out to the square. The rich aroma of the coffee mingled with the damp smell of heavy coats.

The chocolate cake, although delicious, didn't help the nastiness of the article with Caroline at her most spiteful. Gone were the heady days when money flowed, now the financial road ahead would be difficult. The bank accounts had been emptied, leaving me on my own. The future would be bleak. I kept my sunglasses on, lifted the magazine in front of my face, and sobbed.

32

'Jessica? Jessica?' a quiet man's voice penetrated the misery. Trapped in the low chair in the coffee shop window, I had no hope of avoiding the person. I didn't recognise the voice, but my heart sank as I removed the magazine and turned around.

'Hello, Miles, it's good to see you again,' I lied putting an edge of false cheerfulness in my voice. I hoped he would not attempt to sell me a renewable energy solution.

'I've been trying to contact you...' but his voice faded away as he studied my face.

'Bad cold,' I attempted to create a nasal sound.

Raising his eyebrows, he gave a quizzical smile which suggested he hadn't been fooled. As I struggled to push myself from the low chair, he offered his hand in support. I intended to make an excuse and leave, but stood transfixed at the difference in Miles, from the pathetic one I remembered.

The highlights had gone leaving a trimmed short hairstyle. The immaculate dark blue Armani suit complemented the pristine white shirt, dark tie and black leather shoes. Taking a deep breath, I opened my mouth to speak.

Before I had a chance to utter a single word he interrupted, 'Jess, you saved my life.'

Captivated by his doleful brown eyes, I chuckled,

'Hardly. I knocked you down.' An image of the pathetic figure sitting in the kitchen, bore no comparison to the confident handsome man standing before me, still clutching onto my hand. How had he managed such a transformation?

'Mere details,' Miles gave a wave of his hand, 'you helped me, so I intend reciprocating.'

'It's only a cold.' Although my eyes were still heavy with tears, I sniffed, to add a touch of realism to my blatant lie.

'A cold, of course.' He gave a grin of epic proportions which illuminated his handsome features, indicating that he'd seen through my bluff. With a hand on my elbow we left the coffee shop. As we stood in the gloomy drizzle, he removed my sunglasses, folded them and returned them with a boyish grin. 'For the cold, I propose a light lunch with a bottle of wine?'

I should have declined the offer, but my stomach rumbled, and the alternative would be wandering through London to find old friends.

33

Throughout the excellent lunch in an exclusive bistro, Miles had been witty and charming. The bottle of Chianti complemented an excellent chicken Caesar salad, which had been rounded off with a light and tasty lemon mousse. Several glasses of wine had helped to lift my low mood, although the prospects for a job had dived following my meeting with John Mantle. The red tablecloth and matching napkins, along with the elegant wine glasses and the sunshine through the window, suggested a leisurely lunch in Italian climes taking me back to holidays in Rome and Florence.

'Your company has lifted my spirits.'

Miles leaned forward and rested his elbows on the table, 'Now tell me what's the problem?'

'There isn't one,' I lied, but Miles raised his eyebrows.

'Is the sale of the farm progressing?'

The question brought me hurtling back to reality, 'Little chance of that according to the estate agent.'

Leaning back in his chair his eyes fixed onto my face. 'I guessed that would be a problem, so we need a serious chat.'

'What are you talking about Miles? You know nothing about the farm.'

Folding his napkin before replying, 'I thought you had a buyer.'

'What happened the morning you were at the farm?' With new steel in my voice, I leaned forward and put my elbows on the table.

'Nothing,' he shrugged, 'I talked to whoever was nearby while I waited for the breakdown.'

'You're not convincing me, Miles. Who did you speak to? I want to know, you're up to something.'

'Jessica, Jessica! Relax. Believe me, I'm glad to be away from that wild country, it's a nightmare, so I'm much happier in London with my new job. When I rang this morning, Liam told me the name of the agency you intended visiting.'

I would not let his interest in the farm pass until I understood the reason. 'Why were you talking to Liam?' My voice rose and a flush of colour warmed my cheeks. 'When?' Tell me!'

'Darling, darling, calm down! I rang you but Liam answered. The phone rings in the farmyard, I heard it myself.'

Curiosity and apprehension bubbled up and a fluttery sensation filled my stomach, 'Why did you ring?'

Miles leaned back with a wonderful smile and a glint in his eye, 'The whole world has changed for me. I've a super new job and I'm back in London, so no more working for a crappy company.' Reaching forward he covered my hand which rested on the table. 'I rang with an offer of thanks and an invitation to meet up when you were next in London. Liam informed me where you intended visiting. When I checked at the agency, they indicated you had left so I guessed you would go for a coffee.' His tone changed, 'I'm a feeling person, and I suspect you've garnered the wrong impression.' Removing his hand, he regarded me with a quizzical expression.

His vibrancy today contrasted to when I'd hit him with my bike. I believed him, so I changed the conversation to lighten the mood, 'Where's this new job? Are you still a salesman?'

'Of course, what else could I do,' he gave an effeminate wave of his hand. Is he gay? No. The doleful eyes and the intense focus confirmed a ladies' man, without doubt. 'I'm Sales Director, in a new 'Eco' division for a multinational. Liam said you were in London searching for a new job.'

Miles had twisted the topic of the conversation away from him. I nodded, as he paid the bill with a flourish and gave an outlandish tip. He caught my arm as we left, and chuckled, 'I don't know how to tell you this, but you won't find a job as a sheep farmer in London!'

34

Images of herding sheep through London in between the traffic made me giggle. What chaos that would cause! Standing on the pavement amidst the hustle and bustle of city life again, gave me a strange feeling. Miles caught my arm and we wandered through the hurrying crowds. The job-hunting mission to London had been a miserable failure, and my mood which had lifted over lunch, spiralled downwards.

'Before having my family,' I explained in a sorrowful voice, 'I worked as a fashion designer and I want to return to that world, but I might be too old and out of touch. A former colleague dismissed my efforts to return to work in a cruel manner this morning. That's why I've been upset.'

'Absolute rubbish. You're not too old, our generation should stick together, we've both youth and experience.' A strange statement as he's in his late twenties and I'm fast approaching forty. 'I'm older than I appear, I passed the big three zero some time ago and you are only mid-thirties.'

With that, he clutched my hand, closed his eyes and stopped walking. 'I know nothing about the fashion industry.'

'There's no reason why you should, but thanks for a lovely lunch and excellent company.'

He repeated, 'I know nothing about the fashion industry, but my auntie does.'

A smile hovered on my lips. Why does a man in his thirties refer to someone as auntie?

'Let's go to her office. I'll introduce you.' I half expected him to take me to a nursing home, but with his new ebullience, he grabbed my hand and set off at a quick pace. Struggling to keep up, I didn't have time to question him. Miles didn't believe in using pelican crossings, and he dodged the traffic pulling me along after him, so I had to concentrate on not being killed as the City of London traffic swept around the pair of us. A bus passed a few feet in front of me billowing out diesel fumes and I grimaced.

We skirted BT Headquarters and headed for the Barbican, where we crossed a few more roads, then Miles stopped outside the FCI building. The glass and concrete structure loomed above, while flags adorned with the company emblems and international links fluttered in the breeze. It presented a prestigious façade. 'Have you heard of FCI?'

'Of course, they own a multitude of fashion houses, clothing firms and shops. They used to be called Fashion and Clothing International but shortened it to FCI. Does your aunt work here?' Miles ignored my question and still holding my hand strode towards the main door.

'A job or a commission?'

'Either.' I stopped, pulling him back as uncertainty gripped me.

'Miles, who is your aunt? Does she have the power to give jobs or commissions for new fashion designs?'

'Oh, yes,' he gave a dismissive flap of his hand, 'her

name is Camilla Freshfield.'

I grabbed his hand and stood in front of him. My eyes and mouth opened wide. 'The Camilla Freshfield.' I spluttered as my breath caught in my throat and my stomach somersaulted. 'Is she the Chief Executive of FCI?'

'Yes, she's the boss, so she's plenty of influence to find you a job.'

'No, Miles, no!' I pulled away from his hand and began to retrace my steps.

'Why not?' he grabbed me by the shoulders then stood in front of me to stop my retreat. 'She knows the fashion world, I'm sure.'

I shook my head in disbelief, 'She's far too senior to deal with me. A long way out of my league,' and I added in a somewhat disbelieving voice, 'Are you sure your aunt is Camilla Freshfield?'

'Oh, yes, but we need to be lucky and hope that she's in?'

'Why?'

'Auntie thinks of me as a lazy little shit, so when reception ring her she'll want me to contact her this evening or at the weekend.'

'A nice try, Miles,' I gave his arm a reassuring squeeze, 'but it will not work.'

'Be positive, Jessica. I'm a salesman. I don't give in at the first set back.' We stood in the middle of a wide piazza at the front of the FCI building. The patterned flagstones with central fountains exuded big business. 'There! That's the help we need.'

'It's a woman leaving the building.'

'Yes, it's auntie's PA, Bernice, come on!' He grabbed my hand and strode towards the entrance. He studied the front desk with its row of receptionists and hovered until a selected one became free.

The large reception area buzzed with people moving

around the soothing waterfall situated in the middle of the atrium.

'Hi, Susan,' he read the name badge on her smart blue uniform then handed over his business card. 'Camilla mentioned to pop in this afternoon, can you ring Bernice who will okay it.'

The receptionist hesitated, 'Bernice has left the office.'

'Oh, that's so annoying as I've made a special trip.' With a slight raising of his voice, 'Can you contact Camilla?'

The receptionist squirmed under pressure, glancing at his business card again, either she had to ring Camilla or have an annoyed director in reception. She opted for the easy route out, 'I will give you passes, tell Camilla's team who you are. Have you been here before?'

'Yes, we take the left-hand lift.'

As the lift door closed. 'Have you been here before?'

'No, of course not. Auntie would never let me in, I've met Bernice at a family occasion.' I stood and considered my reflection in the mirrors which surrounded us. I was satisfied with my appearance as I'd picked my clothes with care this morning.

'Why the left lift?'

'This lift is the only one that goes to the top floors. The numbers are above the lift doors. The executives work on the top floors.'

I admired his composure and acumen. 'Why did you wait for that receptionist?'

'Always pick the youngest and most inexperienced. They never want to draw attention to themselves. She didn't want to ring the Chief Executive.' In a daze I stood next to him while the lift whooshed upwards. What awaited me when the doors swished open? I wanted to run away and hide.

35

Miles and I arrived on the top floor. The plush dark blue carpets were like walking on a sponge. Despite Miles' methods, I would never be allowed to meet Camilla. I rubbed my chin and flicked minor fluff from my coat. Bright sunlight spilled in from the large windows with views across the Thames.

The office bustled with activity; keyboards clicked, a printer whirred, and paper rustled. Several people sat at expansive desks with leather tops and walnut frames. Miles whispered, 'This must be her personal team.' In a brisk and positive manner to a nearby person with a smile glued to his face, 'Where's Bernice?' The door of an office had opened.

Camilla, in her early fifties, with short black hair and dressed in a blue business suit with black high-heeled shoes stood in the doorway to her office. The open neck white blouse revealed no jewellery, but her wrist had a slim gold watch. No one in the industry messed with her.

Camilla gave an intense frown as she recognised Miles, who remained unaware of her presence. This would never work! Camilla's voice came across the office clear and crisp, 'Miles, what on earth are you doing here?' As she crossed the office her expression darkened. No doubt she would be cross that someone uninvited had passed security and entered her private office. 'How did you get past reception?' But holding up her hand, 'Don't answer. Charm!'

I smiled, but it drew no response from Camilla.

'Do you know you are the most annoying little shit!' The people in the office waited for Miles' response.

'Hello, Auntie, we wanted to pay you a visit,' he kissed her on the cheek.

'For goodness sake stop that Auntie crap, I've told you before, use my name.'

'Yes, Auntie,' which brought smirks from those at nearby desks.

Camilla turned to them, 'This is the laziest and most bone-idle nephew it is possible to have. You'd better come in. You can only have two minutes,' she closed the door of her office behind us and positioned herself at her desk.

She didn't wait for us to be seated, 'How's your mother?'

Miles's face split into a broad grin, 'Fine but annoyed as you haven't visited.'

'Yes,' she flapped her hand, 'I'll come at the week-end. Will you tell her?' Miles nodded. 'I hear you have a new job.'

Miles passed her his business card, and she raised her eyebrows in evident surprise. Her eyes flicked towards me, 'And you are?'

I took a deep breath, 'Jesse James, Fashion Designer.'

Camilla poured herself a glass of water from the water cooler but didn't offer one to us. 'You have a minute to convince me of why you are here, and whether I should listen to you. Jesse over to you.'

I took a deep breath as I had nothing to lose, I focused and talked rapidly.

36

The subdued lighting of the restaurant, with the attentive but anonymous waiters, and classical background music, created the perfect atmosphere for an elaborate champagne dinner.

Since leaving FCI headquarters I'd been walking on air. When grilled by Camilla I'd risen to the challenge. My thoughts were lucid, and I had explained a summary of my ideas, made up on the spot, about the Rustic Collection.

After a short time with Camilla, we were passed to a sympathetic manager, Felix, who no doubt wanted to please the Chief Executive. To my absolute delight Felix decided my ideas were worth a detailed inspection. If I produced a few sample sketches, then a commission would be confirmed with a significant advance.

Miles had been charming company throughout the dinner, as we'd celebrated the day's success. A completely different man to the snivelling wreck I'd hit with my bike. Confident, amusing and most handsome, we enjoyed dinner as though we'd known each other for years. He told me stories and made me laugh while we shared the highs and lows of our lives.

Miles had a glint in his eye and a smile that made my knees shake. I hadn't anticipated, after the poor start to the day, the glorious end. The bedraggled photograph of me in Caroline's article showed me when I'd hit rock bottom. One of the most amazing days of my life had been made possible by Miles.

As we left the restaurant, he guided me to a quiet spot away from the busy thoroughfare. We stopped by railings that bounded a Georgian square. The roar of the London traffic receded when I met the gaze of those wonderful brown eyes as they wandered across my face.

'A great day, Jessica,' he paused, and his expression grew serious, 'You are lovely.' With his head tilted to one side, he leaned in. As our lips met, he pulled me closer and wrapped his arms around me.

The long and slow kiss radiated warmth through my body while I relaxed in his arms. When we paused, our eyes met, and I tried to calm my racing heart. He moved his hand and caressed my cheek with his thumb, then our lips met once more. The kiss obliterated everything. With exquisite timing, he stopped the kiss, stepped back and smiled at me.

His next action surprised me, as he lifted his arm to hail a passing taxi, 'The cab will take you back to your hotel and I'll get the tube home.'

I'd expected him to invite me back to his flat. Even as I left the restaurant, I had been undecided on my final decision. He kissed me on the lips and then ushered me into the taxi. Slumped back, I relived the sensation of being enveloped in his arms and the tenderness of his soft lips. What a day!

Although tired, a fresh energy filled me. I'd been convinced we were destined for his flat and would spend the night together after the tenderness of his kiss. Will there be invitations in the future? A warm glow spread through me. A handsome and desirable man.

37

A new drawing desk and sketch equipment had been delivered to the farm. Yesterday, as I travelled back from London, the ideas for the Rustic Realism Collection formed in my mind. The commission could solve my financial problems. As excited now as when I started out in the fashion world, my hearty voice rang out a rendition of Yellow Submarine, as I rode my bicycle.

Energy filled me as I pedalled along the rutted track. Crossing the stream my thoughts returned to Miles and I laughed at the memory of him in the water. Who'd have thought the pathetic man I'd met that night would transform into someone so handsome and charming.

His positive attitude changed my experience in London from disaster to euphoria. The full sun in a blue sky helped my mood as I parked behind the village shop.

Pulling my jacket tight against the brisk easterly wind, I wrinkled my nose as the stench of the manure from a muck spreader in a nearby field blew across the village. I scurried into the shop and closed the door.

Maureen, on her own, wiped the wooden counter. 'It's so disappointing.'

'What is?' I adopted a serious tone even though elated.

'You've put the farm up for sale which means you'll be leaving the village. It's a pity as you've settled in.'

'Needs must!' I responded with a wry smile. 'The farm only pays for Liam and Jackie so leaves nothing for me. I can't do without them as I don't know how to run a farm.'

'Farms are like my shop. They used to be prosperous but are declining.'

As I searched the freezer a small frown creased my forehead, 'Are you waiting for a delivery?'

'No. We only want a little stock left when we close.'

'Isn't that next year?'

'The shop isn't making money. We've a little set aside which we can live on until we draw our pension. It will happen sooner rather than later.'

'That's sad. How long have you worked here?'

'Fifty years, it'll be a wrench to close the shop.'

Despite feeling sorry for Maureen, the village had endured a steady decline for several years which would continue in the future. While getting the new commission had been brilliant, I hadn't fallen for London as in the past. People were rude!

The noise and bustle which I'd missed so much had become irritating after the quiet solitude of the moors. Everybody rushed about with bad manners and no one spoke or stopped to exchange a few words. Chatting with people I met in the village had become part of my life. The short spell of living in Mossmoor had proved to me it had advantages over London. Can I live on the farm and commute to London when necessary? Get a grip of yourself!

Fashion designers don't live in an isolated northern farmhouse. Success for the future lay in the big city. I'm not a farmer, animals terrify me. London is the place for me!

38

Leaving the shop with my groceries, I turned the corner and walked into David, his white complexion emphasised a thin and drawn face. The healthy glow had disappeared, I gasped, and my mouth fell open, 'David? Whatever has happened?'

Taking a handkerchief from his pocket he mopped his sweating brow. 'Haven't you heard?' I shook my head. 'I've been in hospital.' The once vibrant eyes had lost their sparkle, his hair fell limp, and his hands shook. 'The illness started in the evening after you gave me breakfast. I travelled home expecting to sleep off a hard night, but I woke in a sweat.'

'That happened long before Christmas.'

'By the next day, I'd been taken to the hospital and the day after the doctors moved me to intensive care.' He leaned back on the seat and a small grimace crossed his face. 'The hospital took a long time to stabilise me and subdue the virus.'

'Poor man. Sit on this bench, you need to rest. What happened then?'

'After staying in hospital over the holiday period,

I've been living with my sister in Manchester and have just returned to Mossmoor. Juliet has had the strain of caring for her family and me, so I can't impose on her any longer.'

'Why didn't you ring, I would have helped.'

'You were tied up with your own problems.'

A pang of guilt swept through me as I'd assumed David had snubbed me after that morning's breakfast, and I hadn't given him another thought. Struggling he leaned heavily on his stick. 'You are shaky, David.'

'It's an improvement on the past month but I am weak so I will rest and keep out of my sister's hair.'

'Do you have no one else?'

'No, I can't impose on friends or colleagues, they have families. I need to get my strength back.' A smile creased his drawn features, 'I'm picking up a few groceries and heading home.' The beads of sweat formed on his forehead even though a cold day.

'Stay on the bench, I'll shop for you.' David dropped onto the bench with a groan. While shopping, thoughts about David swirled through my head. The last time we had met, I'd hoped for the offer of a date. Since then he'd been unwell.

Placing his shopping on the seat I sat down, 'David. You're not fit enough to look after yourself,' I gave a small tentative smile. 'Come and stay with me for a few days.'

'It's kind of you, Jessica, but I can cope.' I'd guessed the refusal. 'Come on, we'll put my bike in the back of the Range Rover, then visit your house on the way back to the farm. You can pick up what you need, it's not a problem to have you to stay.'

'What about Justin?'

'It's complicated. Let's settle you in to the warmth of the farm and I'll explain what has happened.'

'Thanks, Jessica. But it will cause problems.'

'Nonsense!'

Within the hour, the Range Rover crawled along the track towards the farm. I had organised my thoughts, I would work on the designs while David rested. The lonely life on the farm would be lifted by David's company and would make a pleasant change. 'Take the books and computer into the kitchen, I'll put the cases in your room.'

39

Clyde's battered old Fiesta bounced along the track and drove into the yard. 'Paris and I received the text that you had returned from London, so we came for a surprise visit.' Paris's eyes moved to the cases in my hands as David came from the kitchen.

'What's happening, Mum? Who do those cases belong to?'

'There is a simple explanation.'

'Whose cases, mum?' snapped Paris, as the colour rose in her cheeks.

My spirits fell, but I pushed my shoulders back and resolved to tackle the problem head-on. 'The cases belong to David.' This would be tricky. 'I've invited him to stay for a few days because...'

'That's gross! I hate him!' shrieked Paris. 'How can you have him here behind Dad's back?' She burst into tears and fled to the back of the barns.

Clyde would be no help as his expression had changed to a glower. 'Mum, what have you done?' An explanation would fall on stony ground, so I didn't speak. Clyde wrung his hands together and scowled, 'I'll comfort Paris.'

'I sensed there would be problems, so I'd better go.' David stood next to me with an ashen face and leaned on his car for support. In the short drive from his house, he'd perked up. After my trip to London and the commission for my collection my confidence had returned. There might be setbacks, but I intended taking them in my stride.

With a determined smile, I once again picked up his cases, 'David, you're staying here! I've never tolerated Paris's temper tantrums and when she calms down, she'll receive a piece of my mind. How dare she try to tell me who I should invite into my house!'

'What about Justin?'

'The wretched man walked out the last time you were here, and I've not seen or spoken to him since. Despite Paris's rosy-eyed view of the whole proceedings, he's gone to live with his German tart and is not coming back.' My legs weakened as I'd never uttered the words out loud before, I repeated them, 'He's not coming back.'

After settling David in a chair next to the Aga, I marched across the yard, empty apart from Peter the peacock which perched on a stone wall at the far end.

Determination gripped me and I pushed up the sleeves of my jumper as though preparing for a fight. Such bad behavior from my children, I would not accept. Clyde sauntered around the corner of the barn. 'Clyde, it's delightful to see you and Paris. I'm pleased you gave up the time to travel and visit me.'

I waited for him to stop in front of me. 'Your behaviour smacks of immaturity. You need a tolerant and grown up attitude to make a success of your life. Decide after the facts are known. Jumping to conclusions is not acceptable, your rude and childish behavior is ridiculous.'

Clyde's eyes widened as it had been many years since I'd reprimanded him in such a forceful fashion. 'For your information, David has been seriously ill. He's recovering and will be a guest in this house for a few days. Now,'

I pressed my mouth into a thin hard line, 'Where's your sister?'

Without a word Clyde lifted a weak arm and pointed. I stomped back across the yard leaving Clyde to think through the dressing down I had given him.

As Paris entered the kitchen, I moved across, smiled and kissed her on the cheek, 'It's lovely to see you, darling, it's made my day.' I placed a cup of steaming tea next to David while Clyde hovered in the doorway. 'Clyde take these cases to the top landing please.' I caught Paris's hand, led her into the front room and closed the door behind us.

40

After five minutes and another serious reprimand I left a sniffy Paris and joined David in the kitchen. I'd been harsh with her, but she should consider the feelings of others and not jump to conclusions.

As her mother, I disliked being so annoyed with her, but such rude behaviour could not be tolerated. A little later she shuffled into the kitchen, with slumped shoulders and red-rimmed eyes. With an expressionless face, she approached David. 'Mr Hunstanton, I want to apologise for my outburst. You are a guest in our house and are entitled to be treated with politeness and civility. You have been ill and so it's rude of me to make you feel uncomfortable.'

Listening to the mature way that she'd dealt with the apology, brought a satisfied smile to my lips. Clyde walked through the door as Paris spoke. 'Sir, please accept my apologies.'

'Thank you both,' David rubbed his chin, 'I can assure you I'm only staying a few days. Then I'll be able to return home.'

A silence followed, but David then spoke to Paris, 'I believe you want to be a vet. Is that true?'

Paris's eyes brightened. 'Yes, sir, I hope to get into the Royal Vets College as we visited there last week.'

'That's my old college, sit down and tell me about it. What's it like now?' As Paris chatted away, I relaxed.

41

The flashing light showed two messages on the answering machine in the hall. 'Hi Jess.' Justin's tinny voice filled the air. Holding my breath, I waited for the message to continue. 'I'm impressed with how the kids have matured.' My eyes opened wide. Perhaps he'd experienced a different side to the one they had shown earlier. 'I'm ringing to say I might need your assistance soon. You won't have a high opinion of me, but we had many good years. Bye.'

Screwing up my eyes, I clenched my jaw from the shock of his voice. A frisson of annoyance crept through me. Why should I help after his behaviour? What did he mean by leaving such a message? My heart pounded and my hands trembled. Needing more information about him, I would tackle Paris and Clyde about the time they'd spent in Germany. So far, they've mentioned little about the visit. They might have more information about Justin's life in Germany. What is he up to?

The second message came from Miles, 'Hi, Jesse, please ring. Ta.'

Pleased that he'd contacted me, I picked up the phone and dialled his mobile. After an enthusiastic greeting, he moved to the reason for the call, 'Jessica can you come down to London for a few days? It's essential to have a chat and there are people I would like you to meet.'

'I'd love to come, but I've got three people staying here. They are only here for a few days and then I'll travel down.'

'Great, a couple of days is fine.'

'Can you tell me over the phone?'

'No, no,' he laughed, 'the information will keep.'

'Will it take long as I don't want to stay in London for an extended period as I've the collection to design!'

'I've a large flat with several rooms. There's one with a view over the river, it would make a perfect studio. You're welcome to stay unless you prefer a hotel.'

Attempting to untangle the ambiguity of his words, they could be a helpful offer, or perhaps he had an ulterior motive. Miles's handsome face appeared in my mind and although I liked him a great deal, would I start an affair with him? Indecision reigned, but I closed the call on a cheery note.

The three men present at the disastrous breakfast scenario had returned to my life. Thoughts of Justin were accompanied by a tightening of my stomach muscles. The damned man had abandoned me and treated me without consideration ever since. After the hurt, I'll never have him back, he can't expect it! Why the strange call? Did he expect me to offer support? His new German floozy must fill that role in the future.

Until today, I'd been under the apprehension that David had chosen to ignore me after that dreadful morning. But what would he have done if he had been fully fit? Would he have asked me out? Our fury and embarrassment about Angela and the chocolate cake had been long forgotten.

What should I do about Miles? Although younger

122

than me, but only by a few years, his kisses had left me breathless. Next time would it just be kisses or would it go further? I enjoyed his company and found him attractive, but indecision continued to flow through me. As a myriad of thoughts jumbled in my head, the phone ringing made me flinch.

42

'Mrs Southwick?' a woman's voice with an upper-class accent and a formal approach.

'Yes, how may I help?'

'This is Mrs Hastings, the Headteacher at Paris's school.'

'Do you wish to speak to Paris?'

'No, Mrs Southwick, I need to speak with you.'

My shoulders tightened, my brow furrowed, and I gripped the telephone as though an offensive weapon. 'Is there a problem?' The call didn't appear good news.

'I've chosen not to exclude Paris from school as I wished to talk with you first.'

I sank down onto a nearby chair as my legs gave way, 'What's she done?'

'It's a serious matter therefore I need the background before I decide on my action.' I sensed the conversation would be controlled by Mrs Hastings.

'Please tell me. I will supply background information if you wish.'

'Very well.' The tetchiness in Mrs Hastings' voice became evident. 'A teacher reprimanded Paris for arriving late to class. Your daughter lost her temper with the member of staff, then swore at her, which is unacceptable in this school. I tried in vain to contact you, but with no success so I phoned her older brother and we agreed she should return home until I'd spoken with you.'

'Oh dear! I'll speak to her, as she arrived a short time ago.'

'Has anything changed in her circumstances over the Christmas period. In her first term, she behaved as a model pupil. The staff monitored her due to your separation, but she worked hard on her lessons.'

'During the holiday period she visited her father in Germany.'

'There is no reason to suppose that would cause the change.'

'Is this an isolated incident?'

'No,' came the emphatic reply. 'Since she's been back this term she has fallen behind with her work and has been reprimanded for minor matters.' Had the breakup from Justin caused a delayed reaction? 'Because of the serious nature of yesterday's incident, I interviewed Paris and she did not impress me. While girls never play me up, her face showed insolence and defiance. Had she been contrite, I would have issued a reprimand, but her rebellious expression forced me to contact you. With her current attitude she is jeopardising her place in the school.'

Given the difficulties with Justin, I didn't want Paris adding to my problems, 'I will speak to her.'

'Perhaps, you will let me know the outcome?'

'Yes, I will ring you,' I replied in an automatic and distracted manner.

'Good afternoon, Mrs Southwick.'

Despite the nature of the call, I would give Paris a chance to tell her side of the story, but it would have to be convincing. What had my daughter been up to? Had Justin contributed to her rebellious streak?

43

The call from the school unsettled me, but I concentrated on organising the bedrooms.

'Mum, do you want a hand?'

'Yes, please.' Paris drifted into her own room. The fragrance from the fabric softener filled the air as I shook the sheets across the bed. The room, bright from the sunlight streaming through the windows, had the imprint of Paris's character in the decoration. Posters of pop groups and film stars filled the pink room.

'Mum, I need to speak with you.'

'What about?' I forced my shoulders to relax, perched on the edge of the bed and she joined me.

'I want to go to Germany to live near dad.' Unexpected, my eyes opened wide and my stomach twisted into a tight knot. 'It would not be a big deal as I can transfer to an English school in Germany.'

How to react? Should I overrule and say no? 'What's the attraction of Germany as you like your new sixth form.'

'I had a brill trip, made new friends, and spent time with Dad.'

A lump formed in my throat. 'How's his new girlfriend?' Paris screwed up her face because I'd been too direct. 'Did you meet her?'

'Anna's great, she's like an elder sister. Dynamic, full of life and energy. Clyde and I hit it off with her straight away.'

'Why is Germany better than England?' I guessed, 'Did you meet a boy?' Rubbing my hands together, my mind raced.

Paris gave me a strange sideways glance. Her face showed no recognition, 'I met several of them, but no one serious, if that's what you mean. Germany is exciting.'

Patience might pay off, 'What happened?'

'They're keen on protecting the environment. They've good ideas.'

The penny dropped and I gave a silent groan. Justin had connected with the environmental movement in Germany and had introduced Paris and Clyde. They'd taken their father's side in the past when it had come to green issues and supported his decision to buy the farm.

'Do you want to be a vet?'

'Yes, I do,' she nodded with enthusiasm, 'and I had a good chat with David.' At least that problem had calmed down, as Paris had accepted him.

'But if you studied in Munich, it would be difficult to be a vet.' The words didn't sound convincing, even to me.

'Come on, Mum, I'll study at the school in Germany for two years. By then I will have learnt the language so I would have a selection of English or German Universities, making a wider choice.'

'As we're talking about studying, I've had a phone call from Mrs Hastings.' I studied Paris's face.

To my surprise, the smile didn't waver.

'I'm sure you did. I suppose an apology is needed, but the teacher is annoying and petty.'

'Mrs Hastings mentioned your work had slipped.'

'Yes, I've decided on Germany, so it's better to make the move happen.' I had lost control of this conversation. 'I haven't been wasting my time. I've been studying.'

I straightened my back and twisted my fingers together, 'Studying what?'

'German, of course.' Paris stood up. 'Think about me moving to Germany. It's come as a surprise!'

'The answer is no, definitely not.' Would I get a tantrum response?

'In the summer I'm eighteen, then I can decide for myself.' She closed the door leaving me sitting on the bed. It had been the first time Paris had adopted a controlling attitude. I understood Justin's remarks about maturing. Throughout the conversation, she'd been in charge.

Paris's tantrums? I'd assumed adolescence and immaturity, but I needed to revise my views. In the fashion world, models threw frequent tantrums as they became a means of getting their own way. Tantrums would become part of her adult life. Paris had become manipulative.

44

Dinner became a noisy affair, but I sat in a quiet, reflective mood. The conversation between David and Paris took a new direction when they discovered he spoke German. Although I hadn't spoken to Clyde about his opinions, it became obvious.

Paris tried her German on David who responded with enthusiasm. When Clyde joined in with a more comprehensive German vocabulary, the situation became obvious, as he'd only studied French at school. When the dinner finished, Paris and David moved to the front room to carry on the conversation.

Clyde hovered at the end of the meal. As soon as we were alone, 'Has Paris asked you?'

'Yes. Are you moving to Germany?'

'No, I don't think so.'

'What does that mean?' Popping the condiments back into the larder, I waited for an answer. 'Finishing my degree is important, but I need to tell you, I've changed subjects.' I wanted no more bad news. 'I will major in Ecology, but I'll keep maths as a subsidiary subject.'

While growing up I'd encouraged my children to be independent and make their own decisions. Now they didn't want to talk to me before they decided. Sadness gripped me, my children had become independent and I would be a less important part of their life. How different to when they were young. The enthusiastic way they would greet me after their day at school. They would be so full of eagerness, they swept me off my feet and re-energised me.

I had seen the difference in Clyde during dinner. More self-assured and he'd contributed to the conversations, without being invited. 'I've made German friends which is why my language skills are better than Paris's.' What else hadn't my two children told me? Clyde leaned against the sink with his arms crossed. 'Dad suggested that we learn German as trips to see him would become easier, so I started months ago after speaking with him on the phone.'

I allowed silence to develop while I finished the jobs. 'What did you think of Anna?'

Clyde made a face. 'She's a wonderful woman and treated us well, but she's so much younger than Dad.' He put his arm around my shoulders. 'We haven't given up hope you and dad will get back together one day.'

'Clyde sit down a minute, it's time we had a serious chat as adults.' I'm not having Justin back regardless of what my children think.

In the past, Clyde would have shied away, 'Yes, mum.'

45

Paris shouted and squealed from the front room. 'Quick, quick! Planetgreen is on the news.' Clyde rushed past me.

'Who are Planetgreen?'

He shouted over his shoulder, 'It's where Dad works. Anna is the leader!'

I'd no time to think through Clyde's words before we reached the front room and focused on the television.

'Today in Berlin, the radical and extreme Green political group, Planetgreen, invaded the buildings of the German Energy Ministry and the international energy multinational, Deepoil. These buildings are adjacent in the heart of Berlin. Over to our correspondent outside the German Energy Ministry.'

In stunned silence I glued my eyes to the screen. A shiver ran through me. This wouldn't be good news.

'At midday today the Planetgreen political group took control of the two buildings. In a coordinated attack, and there is no doubt it was an attack, a group of approximately fifty led the invasion.

Posing as members of the public and maintenance staff, they gained access to various parts of the building, then set off alarms and ignited smoke bombs. Terrified staff evacuated the buildings. In the chaos, Planetgreen radicals attacked fire crews attending the incidents. They have sealed themselves in each of the buildings.'

A news helicopter zoomed into the tops of the buildings. 'That's Anna! That's Anna!' Paris screeched and pointed. She erupted in excitement.

The camera focused on a woman, with flowing blonde hair, dressed in camouflage clothing. She climbed across the roof of the Ministry building unfurling Planetgreen banners. Disbelief spread through me that Justin had become involved with this group.

Paris and Clyde bounced with excitement. Paris clapped her hands together as she watched the spectacle unfolding, 'If we'd stayed, we would've been part of it.'

An icy chill raced through my body.

'Good God!' David pointed, 'that man on the other roof. It's Justin.'

'Where, where?' squealed Paris.

'The man wearing the blue overalls.' The helicopter camera panned and zoomed as Justin unfurled a large banner over the side of the building. 'Brilliant, dad!' shouted Clyde becoming more animated. The children's enthusiasm terrified me. What had happened to them?

Justin's action broke the law and he would be punished. Would he go to jail? Thoughts and questions hurtled through my mind. What had tipped the sensible and steady man I married into a manic protester? His actions could only result from him having a mental breakdown.

Justin, no longer able to cope with his high-powered job, had collapsed into escapism. So many times in past years I sensed the stress he worked under. Tears rolled across my cheeks, but no one noticed as their entire concentration focused on the television screen. The breakdown must have occurred before he left the country, but he'd hidden it from me. I'd opposed his wish to buy this isolated farm.

Perhaps he subconsciously tried to escape from himself. I opposed every action he attempted. I sobbed, and muttered, 'It's my fault.'

46

By Sunday evening Clyde and Paris were keen to return to their friends to show off their father's exploits. While they didn't want to leave the television screen, they returned to London. The protesters still occupied the two buildings that had been placed under passive siege. The German authorities wished to avoid violence and would await a peaceful outcome. The weekend had passed in a blur.

A sense of disbelief had enveloped me, as I hadn't spotted Justin's breakdown coming, and I'd confided this view only to David. Although he'd offered no opinion, he'd listened sympathetically. My mind had been so disturbed by the perceived breakdown and my children's enthusiasm for the siege, that concentration on designing my collection became impossible.

'Why don't we drive to the village for a drink at The Jaggers?' David suggested as he sat in his favourite chair next to the Aga. 'There's been no mention of Justin's name, so the news won't have any meaning in the village.'

'Are you feeling up to it?'

'Despite the trauma the news has brought on you. I've been fussed over and cared for, so I feel stronger.'

I wanted to refuse but moping around the house would not solve my predicament. 'If they know its Justin, then I won't stay.'

'Agreed, but I'm convinced they will be unaware. Justin rarely visited the village and they would not expect to see him in Berlin. As far as the news is concerned, the villagers will take no notice because it is about German militants.'

'What brings you two here together?' asked Cate, with a glint in her eye as we entered The Jaggers.

'Behave, Cate, you know he's been ill. David's been with my family for a few days to help him recuperate.'

Dressed up for the evening she wore smart black trousers inside her knee-length leather boots. A thick off the shoulder loose-fitting jumper exposed a glitter trimmed black bra strap. While not as slim as in her youth, she still caught the eye of men. Cate told anyone who would listen that she and I had struck up a wonderful friendship. I couldn't be sure, but I enjoyed talking about fashion again. As Cate talked of little else, we had established a good atmosphere between us.

'I'm glad you've come, David, as I wanted to ask you a couple of questions about our dog.' I frowned. Cate wanted to be the centre of attention and didn't appreciate a vet had off-duty time, especially as he'd been ill.

Sensing my irritation, David gently squeezed my arm, 'Don't worry, I'll only be a couple of minutes.' With a reassuring smile, 'Come on Cate, let's see the brute.' They left through the door marked Private.

Michael approached down the bar, 'How's life? You're pale and seem preoccupied?' Had he guessed? Perhaps I'm not at my best after the weekend.

Giving a flap of my hand, 'I'm fine, but I wouldn't say no to a large G&T.'

'What a pity you've put the farm on the market, we

were hoping you enjoyed life in the village.'

Why I weakened my stance as I spoke, I couldn't be sure. 'It's on the market, but I don't expect it to sell so I'll be around for a long time.' After sipping my drink, 'Justin has left me so putting it up for sale gives a valuation for the divorce.' Why had I told Michael those details which weren't strictly true? I owned the farm, although my bank account had been emptied by my deceitful husband.

George, my farming neighbour, came into the bar, with a toothy grin and his usual chuckle as he crossed the bar. 'Tis a pity you're leaving, we're used to each other now.'

We shared the same farm track from the lane. About a quarter of a mile along the track, it forked to the left which led to George's farm, and the right fork led to mine.

George, in his late sixties, wore a thick green jumper, baggy corduroy trousers and had tucked his woolly hat in his pocket. His weather-beaten face smiled, showing only two teeth at the front. He smoothed down the thin, grey strands left of his hair and leaned on the bar near me. He upheld the village tradition by referring to incidents which had amused him.

George often started a conversation with a chuckle, 'You'll remember when you first came. You moaned when your bicycle became muddy on the track.'

'Yes, I remember. You laughed, pointed at me and said, Silly arse, the countryside is made of mud.'

George chuckled again, 'I hope you'll stay,' then he waddled back across the bar. I had sympathy for him and the pain he had to endure in his knees.

Sitting quietly with my drink I resolved I would deal with what life threw at me. David returned with Cate. The dog had only a minor problem. Leaving them talking and laughing together I bought another round. I guessed they'd known each other for many years.

The image of Justin on the rooftop haunted me as I no longer knew the man, he'd become a stranger. Perhaps his Planetgreen activities had prompted the phone call. If I knew for certain that his breakdown had been my fault, then I might have a smidgen of compassion for him.

47

The volume of the television caught my attention as it came on. The young farmers, including Liam, had arrived to watch the Sunday version of Match of the Day. "We apologise to those waiting for the football, but we have an extended news tonight to cover the siege in Germany, now we know that one leader came from England."

I gripped David's arm and froze. Surely it wouldn't be Justin. The news flashed a close-up taken from the helicopter. Justin's face filled the screen. Pressing my lips together, I stifled an involuntary squeal and my throat went dry.

The newscaster continued, "German police have named one ringleader to be Justin Southwick, from the village of Mossmoor, in Central England." As the people in the bar registered that their small village was on the international news, silence fell. Rain beating on the windows became the only sound. The silence was broken when George called out, 'Bloody hell!' All eyes in the bar turned in my direction and a flame of shame spread across my cheeks.

The newscaster continued, "We only have sketchy details of Justin Southwick. We know he lived in the moorland village of Mossmoor and had been a head of department at Twitchard Management Consultancy in the City of London. We will update you as more news comes in."

'You poor woman.' An elderly lady sitting on the table next to me gave me a worried stare. It brought me back to my senses and I grabbed my coat to go.

A stranger came into the bar. In a loud voice which everyone heard, 'Bloody hell the news has broken already.'

He directed his next comment to Michael behind the bar, 'I'm from the Daily Chronicle, do you know where Jessica Southwick lives?'

'No!' Michael crossed his arms and stared.

'Thanks,' I mouthed. Everyone else in the bar turned away from the man and ignored his presence.

George approached him, 'Why do you want Jessica?'

The reporter gave George a disparaging stare, 'She might be part of her husband's plot.'

George's chuckles had gone. He studied the reporter up and down, 'You city types have a fanciful imagination.'

'You must know Jessica,' a smirk sprang to his mouth, 'let me buy you a drink.'

'Oh, aye, I know her.' I held my breath. The bar became silent, 'but I wouldn't tell you anything about her for a million pounds.'

The reporter snarled, 'When the rest of the reporters and the television crews arrive then we'll find someone who'll talk.'

'Will there be many of you?' George would keep the man talking allowing us to slip away unobserved.

'Yes, we'll be everywhere in this village.' His stentorian voice boomed across the crowded bar and his mouth compressed into a hard line. 'I'm first and I have money for the right story.' His words made my heart hammer and a swirl of knots twisted and writhed around in my stomach.

In one swift but silent movement I grabbed my coat and moved towards the door, trying to keep my actions calm so I didn't bring attention to myself. As we passed the reporter, George called David's name and joined us walking to the door. George called over his shoulder, 'Liam, lad, come over here, and you, Josh.' Although I didn't want to stay longer, I had to wait for David. Shuffling from foot to foot I pulled my jacket tighter.

David whispered, 'George is a wily old bugger. He's planning something.'

George whispered, 'David, take Jessica back to the farm, but don't go the normal way. Go down Gully Lane and then across the top fields.' David nodded, but it confused me. The old man continued, 'Liam you go with them and open the gates. When they're safely back in the house. Padlock all your gates and mine.' Liam nodded. I understood what he meant, no one was coming on to the farms. All routes and entrances were being secured.

I stood in amazement as George with a mischievous twinkle in his eye, 'Josh, give my son a ring and tell him to block the bottom of the track with the thirty tons of straw bales that are on the trailer. Then switch on the electric fences to full power.'

'Will do.'

'See you tomorrow, Jessica,' he whispered with the toothy smile.

I kissed him, 'You are so kind.' Tears flowed down my cheeks.

'Take her back, David. I've more words for the reporter.' Even though I cried from the tension, I had to smile.

We hesitated as George addressed the reporter in a loud voice, 'By way of apology, let me buy you a drink.'

'You have nothing to apologise for.'

The reporter propped up the bar and surveyed the scene, no doubt plotting his next move.

George ignored the remark. 'First thing in the morning I'm muck spreading in Brookfield.' Everyone in the bar knew it was the field where the track met the lane, and where they expected the press corps to be waiting. 'D'you know even after nearly sixty years, I'm hanged if I can drive one of those muck spreaders.' Despite the tension, everyone laughed.

The reporter muttered, 'Silly old fool.'

'The muck flies through the air, more will land in the lane rather than in the field.' Again, everyone smiled. He focused on the reporter, 'The apology is for tomorrow when you get covered in cow shit raining from the skies!'

48

I shook like a leaf as I walked into the kitchen. David settled me with a large brandy and made several phone calls to prominent local people. While they might not know me, they would fight to prevent reporters and camera crews from disrupting their farms and the village. Liam had taken a tractor and gone home across the fields.

David and I talked about the best way of dealing with the next few days. I didn't want any more bad news, but were there any further developments? With trepidation, I switched on the television for the 24-hour news.

'Following the raid on the occupied buildings in Berlin, the majority of those holding the building have been arrested. This is the earlier picture of the Englishman, Justin Southwick, being led away in handcuffs.'

Justin's drawn and hollow-eyed face filled the screen. Pale and weak he had lost a lot of weight. As his face came into close-up, an icy shiver slipped down my spine and the knot in my stomach tightened. His eyes had lost their normal sharpness. The expression on his face troubled me. A stupid grin. Where had that come from? Didn't he realise he had been arrested? Serious trouble awaited him so why smile?

Justin's face confirmed to me he'd had a mental breakdown and I shouldered the blame as the major catalyst. My legs weakened as my pulse raced. Only the strong sweet taste of the brandy kept me from fainting.

We are going over live to listen to the German government spokesman.

The screen showed a man in a dark suit standing on a podium, with a huge number of the worlds' press microphones in front of the Government building.

Despite the Government's attempt to bring this illegal occupation to an end without violence, we have to report that in the operation to liberate the building, a person among the occupiers fell to her death while attempting to evade arrest. We can confirm that it was a twenty-five-year-old woman known as Anna. There will be a full enquiry into the circumstances surrounding her death.

David remained silent and sipped his whiskey. Over the weekend Paris and Clyde had let more slip about Justin and Anna. Justin had become infatuated with this younger woman. When I'd seen him taken from the building, did he know that his new girlfriend had been killed? I had no sympathy for her. She had stolen my husband. My mind raced. If I'd spotted Justin's breakdown coming, then he wouldn't have thrown himself at another woman.

49

Ten days later, I travelled on a Pendolino train with Cate, which pulled into Euston station, five minutes late on a cold and crisp day. As everyone had feared, the press had arrived in droves after the announcement that Justin lived in the village of Mossmoor. The camera crews, reporters and photographers had set up at the bottom of the track.

Miles tried to persuade me to come to London, but I chose to stay at the farm. He'd been helpful by giving me the name of a leading publicist who issued bland statements on my behalf. A smile appeared every time I thought of George and the young farmers as they'd had wonderful times baiting the press.

Liam had set up several bird scarers which sounded like a shotgun firing. He had set them off during a live broadcast and watched them diving for cover. George had a herd of milking cows which he insisted on putting in a field far from the farm buildings. Twice a day his lads would drive the cattle through the press corps on the narrow lane and then back again after the milking had been completed.

During the first week, besieged in my own home, I

suffered agonies about the failure of my marriage. I wrestled with my conscience. Should I go to see Justin? I'd made enquiries. While he resided in jail awaiting trial, visitors were permitted, but I kept this information to myself. Paris's and Clyde's enthusiasm for their father's situation had waned through exhaustion and lack of information as the siege disappeared from the television news, and the German authorities prepared various court cases.

Although they knew about Anna's death, neither of them mentioned it. David had stayed with me through the encirclement by the press corps.

I'd been surprised at Cate's interest and energy in helping us. She'd come over the fields in her Land Rover on many occasions, bringing us items from the village and various snippets of information, and had spent a lot of time at the farm for which I'd been grateful. It gave David someone to talk to and allowed me to start on designing my collection.

The project had given me a mental focus, as I became lost in the world of fashion once I started work. The dark thoughts and my guilt resurfaced when I stopped or relaxed.

Euston station thronged with people as we stepped from the train. Miles approached us with an enthusiastic wave and a dazzling smile on his handsome face. 'You've kept him a secret,' muttered Cate eyeing him with interest.

As the press had drifted away, I had taken the opportunity to come to London to meet up with him. Cate had dropped the odd hint about meeting people from the fashion industry and shopping in London, so I'd invited her along.

Miles hugged and kissed me on the lips, 'Lovely to see you, Jesse darling. It seems ages since we last met.' I introduced Cate and he gave a smile and a brief nod before turning his attention back to me. Cate's face showed disappointment, no doubt wishing to hold the handsome man's interest for longer. Miles bundled us into a taxi to take us to a business meeting but would give no details about the agenda.

50

Arriving at the tall grey building on the south bank, Miles took us through the large reception area with its gentle music, comfortable seats and trickling fountains. Within a few minutes, we were shown into the office of his boss, Robert Murchison, Managing Director of the Environment Division.

A tall, slender man in his mid-fifties, he wore a smart business suit with a white shirt and a bright floral tie. Cate had kept her eye on a man in the outer office. Robert acknowledging the glint in Cate's eye, asked the man to take her for a coffee.

'The meeting concerns a private business matter.' Offering me a low leather chair at the coffee table in the corner of the large office, Miles sat to one side and Robert opposite.

The soft cream leather matched the thick pile carpet. The only colour in the office came from large square abstract paintings on each wall. Why had Miles whisked me here? What business?

With my design ideas buzzing I could lose concentration. Perhaps I'd missed something that Miles had mentioned, so I concentrated on Robert and cleared my mind. After opening a file, he looked at me, 'I won't beat about the bush, we want to buy your farm at the market rate.'

Elation coursed through me, but I needed a good dose of reality. 'Why would a large multinational want to buy a sheep farm in the middle of nowhere?'

'Miles visited you when employed by his last firm.' I moved to face Miles because I suspected a renewable energy issue. 'We ordered a full survey of your property.'

'Who gave permission, Miles?' With a questioning stare, I folded my arms and waited. Robert flapped his hands in a placatory manner, 'Jessica, Jessica, we're all friends, we want to give you facts and information then help by purchasing your farm.'

'You didn't mention this.' Once again, I focused my attention on Miles who shifted in his seat.

'Jesse, it's complicated. We had to compile the full picture before revealing any information. You want to sell the farm so you can move back to London, therefore we can all win.'

Robert took control again, 'We're a reputable company and do not sneak on to people's property uninvited, we completed the survey from a helicopter.' Robert placed a file in front of me, 'This is a planning application to build a wind farm on the top fields of your farm.'

'Can you seek planning permission when you don't own the land?' My voice sounded sharp as I needed answers. What had been happening behind my back? Investigations had taken place without my knowledge or permission. A frisson of anxiety niggled in the back of my mind, coupled with disappointment at Miles's underhand tactics.

'Yes, we can request planning permission although we don't own the land, but on submission, the planning authorities will inform you and your neighbours. It's likely to lead to a public enquiry which would be easier for us if we own the farm. That's the reason why we want to buy it from you, as soon as possible.'

'Selling and buying take time.' I pressed my lips together in a firm straight line and my breath caught in my throat.

Robert pushed another document in front of me, 'We've drawn up a pre-contract agreement. If you sign it, the rest is a formality.' He pushed a folder towards me. This appeared too simple. 'We would then give you a significant advance on the purchase.'

My mind raced. Selling the farm had become a priority but would Robert's proposals cut corners.

'We are bombarding you, but time is of the essence for us, so we want to be transparent with you.'

I thought fast. 'What about George's farm? Half of the upper fields belong to him.'

'That's where we need your help as we would like both farms.' Placing the flat of his hands on the desk he gave me a disarming smile. 'Can you persuade him to sell?'

'I can't imagine him selling as he's worked it all his life.'

'I believe he has four sons who will find little work in the area.'

I leaned back in my seat and folded my arms, 'You've been doing your homework.' For some reason it annoyed me. What else had they found out? I disapproved that the lives of the people in Mossmoor were being investigated without their knowledge, and then being discussed in a London office. They didn't seem to notice my discomfort as they were focused on what they wanted to achieve.

'As part of any purchase and a project of this scale, we commission an impact assessment. I won't reveal it all to you, but we consider the village and countryside around our proposed development.'

I frowned, 'The village would be opposed to it.'

'Of course, it will come as a shock, but visible pollution is limited in the village because of the rise of the intermediate land.'

The words rattled from Robert's mouth as he'd planned the conversation and had all the information at his fingertips. Apprehension and uneasiness coursed through me.

'Think of the positives,' Miles leaned towards me and patted my knee. 'It will help the locals.'

Did his voice have a wheedling edge to it? Stalling for time to organise my jumbled thoughts I stared out over the rooftops and concrete tower blocks of London. The two men waited. 'I'm not sure there are many positives about a huge wind farm near to the village.'

Robert gave a smug smile, 'We want to help the villagers so we would expect to contribute.'

'Such as?'

'A new village community centre, which would be bigger and better than the village hall they've had planned for years, it would also incorporate a health centre.'

'You would pay for that?'

'Yes, and much more. For example, I'm sure we could do a deal to extend the village shop.'

I shuffled the papers, reading none of them as I needed time to think. Their research had been thorough, if they knew about the village hall and Maureen's shop. What else had they uncovered in the course of their investigations?

Robert, one step ahead of me, continued, 'Jessica, please don't think we are pressurising you to sign today. You're in London for a few days. Think it through. But please keep this meeting confidential, it's in your interest and ours not to spread the news.'

'This is a big surprise, I'm confused.'

Not taking much notice of my comments he continued to reveal his plan, 'Next door's farm is crucial. We are prepared to talk about a substantial bonus payment, if you can engineer us the sale of both farms.' Resting his elbows on his knees he steepled his fingers and his eyes searched my face with an intense scrutiny. 'Confidentiality is of the utmost importance at this stage. If the news leaks out, we will review our approach. We might even withdraw.'

Robert's last words hung in the air like a threat, leaving me with an even deeper sense of unease and confusion.

51

Cate and I had been left to relax with a post-dinner drink at a Michelin restaurant. Robert and Miles chatted on the far side of the bar with business colleagues.

Needing someone to confide in, I had risked telling Cate the news about the proposal to sell my farm to Robert's company, and the planned installation of wind turbines on the top pastures. From the pub, and a large part of the countryside to the south of the village, the masts wouldn't be visible. The little tourist trade that existed wouldn't be affected. The wind farm would bring the village more activity, meaning more money for the pub, and the income from the extra business would benefit The Jaggers.

Cate had promised not to tell Michael or anyone else until I'd decided. Placing her drink on the low marble table, she gave a mischievous smile, 'Converting our large barn on the other side of the pub car park into holiday lets, is a possibility. It could make eight bedroom units, with their own facilities. That would be profitable.'

I paused, holding my glass in mid-air as I listened to Cate's positive comments as it hadn't been what I'd expected. In desperate need of reassurance and to find out more about Cate's opinion, I pursued the conversation, 'Do you think Maureen in the village shop would oppose it?'

'Darling, Jessica, Maureen has little initiative, she'll wait to see what happens, but she'd be in favour as she's hankered after a shop extension for years. The extension would give her a comfortable retirement. The village hall has always been her project and so she'd be delighted with a centre.'

To have a wind farm, the village would have to sell its soul. A tight knit community where life in the village had barely changed over several decades. Would they allow such a huge change to the environment in exchange for a new village hall and an extension to the village shop? Money wouldn't be persuasive. Would the village oppose the idea?

Robert returned to join us and placed his empty glass on the table, 'Our business friends have invited us to a club. I understand if you don't want to come, Jessica, as it's been a long and tiring day.'

Robert had given me a perfect excuse. 'Yes, I am tired so I will give it a miss.'

'Miles isn't joining us, but what about you Cate? Would you like to come?' Cate's smile stretched from ear to ear, and her face lit up.

Leaning forward she kissed me on the cheek and whispered, 'Don't wait up, I won't be back until the morning.' Cate put her hand through Robert's arm in a proprietorial manner, 'Come on, introduce me to your friends.' She'd taken an extra interest in Robert during dinner, after he revealed he had recently divorced. As they left in a whirl of noisy chatter and laughter, I pursed my lips as perhaps bringing her to London had been a mistake. Cate's flirtatious behaviour gave me grave concerns.

Miles sat down next to me on the huge comfortable

sofa and placed his hand gently on my arm. 'You're cross with me, but I wanted to help you sell the farm.' A small smile quivered across his lips and for a few moments a heavy silence settled between us. A whole barrage of questions filled my mind which needed answering. Without a shadow of doubt, he'd set me up.

'Miles.' The single word had a hint of disappointment in my tone. Any further words failed me, and my lips thinned with displeasure. The voice inside my head screamed about duplicity, secrecy and invasion of privacy. It would be a big risk telling him to get lost because I needed to keep the fashion contacts, as his aunt might be my salvation.

A momentary look of discomfort crossed his face and the hand which still rested on my arm gave me a small squeeze. 'I am a caring person and I've tried to be genuine, although you won't realise.' His voice had dropped to a whisper and he removed his hand and placed it on his heart.

With a wide stare his innocent eyes focused on me. No doubt this expression had won over many women. Well, not this one. I still hadn't recovered from the amount of private information they knew about the villagers. Without doubt Miles had kept the knowledge from me. They wanted a quick decision and I didn't like it.

'Tell me,' I huffed out a long slow breath, 'how completing business behind my back, is showing you care?' My breath grew thin and ragged as I awaited his reply. Would he be able to wriggle out of my accusation?

'Jessica, you're an attractive woman who I'm finding more desirable each time we meet.' My heart thumped as I hadn't expected that response to my question. With a disarming smile he caught hold of my hand, 'You wanted a fashion commission and to sell the farm, I've helped with both.'

He released my hand and gave an expansive gesture with his arms giving the impression of simplicity. Did he think a few words of flattery would allow him to wriggle out of a tricky situation? What about the questions that needed asking and answering?

I rolled my eyes and folded my arms across my chest, 'I'm grateful for the design job, but I'm not sure I approve of this cloak and dagger approach about the farm.' I didn't smile and a ball of anxiety settled in my stomach. Once again, I'd lost control.

Miles' brow tightened, 'It's our business method. The outcome is important. The money from the farm would buy you a good flat in the Barbican and you'd be back at the heart of the fashion world.'

Miles made it sound so easy and straightforward. I didn't want George being hassled at his age. When the television crews had descended on Mossmoor he had been brilliant, a true friend and the support of the villagers had been superb. They'd rallied together to support me.

Circumstances had changed. Admitting that I might now have doubts, didn't seem possible and filled me with dread. I reflected on his comment about finding me desirable. He stood out as a handsome and vivacious man, and I found him physically attractive. I enjoyed his company. Would I like to know him better? Uncertainty gripped me.

Miles sipped his drink. 'I don't want to hurt or betray you, I'm caring.' It hadn't been what I'd expected, and I mulled over whether a pushy salesman might have a caring side. Hesitation invaded my mind.

'Caring?' I tilted my head to one side and narrowed my eyes hoping for an explanation.

'You'll remember we dined out together after you won the commission?'

'Yes.' I gave a brief nod.

'I wanted to ask you back to my place. We'd had such an exciting day. I wanted to finish it well.'

'Why didn't you?' A sudden note of confusion crept into my voice. 'At worst, I would have refused.'

He puffed out his cheeks with a long slow breath before replying, 'The plan to allow you to sell the farm had already been set in motion. It didn't feel right sorting it out behind your back. I would've felt guilty, if we had gone to bed together and not been able to discuss it with you.'

Oh, God! He's genuine. I had him down as a womaniser. 'I do like you, but I'm not coming back with you tonight. Not after the revelations of today.'

Miles' words had sent a shiver through me, I'd never expected so much from him. Although I'd made the decision not to go to his flat this evening, would I say yes in the future?

'Darling, as much as I would like you to, I understand. I'll take you back to your hotel. We can have a night-cap, then I'll get a taxi home.' In the chaos that surrounded my life, I'd found a wonderful spark of kindness.

52

I sat a few minutes after Miles had left me in the hotel lounge to collect my thoughts. In a daydream I wandered to the lift in the entrance foyer. Whether I would be able to sleep would be another matter.

Alone in the lift I leant against the wall waiting for the doors to close. A female voice called, 'Hold the lift please.' Automatically, I pushed the open-door button to wait for the person who stepped in, 'Thank you.'

The one person in London who I did not want to meet stood in front of me. The smile dropped from Caroline Darken's face. I closed my eyes at the inevitable confrontation, but the frown on her face changed to a smirk, 'Did you see my article about you?'

Although I didn't want to talk to her, I had no option but to respond, 'Are you still whittering on about what happened all those years ago.'

'Your underhand methods were despicable and dishonest, it made your career and stopped mine.'

'That's an exaggeration and you know it. Get a life, Caroline.'

The doors opened, her finger pressed on the hold door button, 'I'm seeing John Mantle in the morning.

Have you been to see him? He decides promotion and rejection in the world of fashion. No matter what it takes I want to make sure you never get a fashion job again.' She swished out of the lift and strode along the corridor without a backward glance.

Typical Caroline, as vitriolic as usual.

53

David and Cate had advised me against travelling to Germany. Pulling my coat tight I gave darting glances around the unfamiliar environment as I walked through customs at Berlin Airport.

Paris and Clyde had been delighted when I asked them if they wanted to accompany me to Germany. They had flown from London and I'd travelled from Manchester. As I walked into the arrivals' lounge, they rushed to greet me.

For some time, they had been pleading with me for permission to travel to Germany, but I'd refused. Not wanting another stand-off with them, along with the associated ill-feeling it caused, I'd conceded and contacted the German authorities.

The authorities had been tracking the Planetgreen group. After their earlier visit to their father, Paris and Clyde had been picked up on their radar. The German authorities maintained they would refuse entry to them, so I'd been relieved it hadn't been my decision.

My conscience nagged at me as I'd failed to prevent Justin's breakdown. My opposition to his plans had been the last straw and had tipped him over the edge, making him pursue some idealistic fantasy in Germany. While he'd been impressionable, he'd fallen for Anna. No amount of reason would shake it from my mind that the breakdown had been my fault.

One night when I lay awake crying, I made the decision that the only way to discover if his breakdown had been caused by me, would be to meet him. A surprise call from the Foreign Office explained that Justin wanted to talk to me, so I informed them about the children and the Planetgreen group.

Dismissing the exclusion they suggested if the children wanted to accompany me, it could be organised. Without further thought I asked them to arrange a visit for the three of us.

I greeted Henry Manning, a Foreign Office official waiting in the Arrivals' lounge, who would escort us to the prison. Did Henry want to help or keep an eye on us? Leading us to a diplomatic car, parked outside with a driver, we set off for the prison.

Henry explained, the children would visit first for thirty minutes, then I would have an hour if I wished, but the thought made me shiver. My anxiety increased when Henry asked if I spoke German.

With shaking hands, I twisted my fingers together and explained I had no knowledge of the language. Henry pointed out if Justin and I spoke in English there would be restrictions, a recording would be made of the conversation and a prison-approved interpreter would be present.

I'd wanted a private and personal conversation. My stomach tightened and nausea welled, but as I had no option, I nodded my agreement as I had nothing to hide. Before the arranged trip I'd spoken at length with Paris and Clyde about restricting their conversations and tried to impress upon them the importance of not asking questions about the raid. Inappropriate remarks might result in trouble.

I sat alone with my thoughts in a drab room when, after lengthy delays and checks, Paris and Clyde were taken to visit their father. No sounds emanated from the building. A table and four black plastic chairs. The bare floor tiles shone. Henry had left me to see a senior prison officer.

What would I say to Justin? I'd rehearsed a variety of approaches. Could I complete the interview without breaking down? I resolved to stay strong, but that only brought tension and tears. The minutes ticked away. Nothing happened. Only the sound of distant footsteps on the hard corridor floors broke the silence. Then a tall, well-built prison guard entered. In perfect English, 'It is your turn, Mrs Southwick.'

54

A cold sweat ran through me. 'What about the children?'

'Please relax, they have left a different way, they are with the British official. Please come this way.' The guard led me along the corridor, outside one of the many doors that lined the route, a middle-aged woman waited, we shook hands.

'I am the translator,' she had a faint trace of a German accent and a serious expression. 'Please do not be embarrassed during the conversation, I must listen, but I'm not interested in private matters. The conversation will be recorded. If you avoid talking about the charges and the crime, there will be no reason for anyone else to listen to the tape. However, the police will listen to the tape of the interview with your son and daughter.'

'What did they say?' My high-pitched voice rose, edged with anxiety.

'Calm down! They asked about your husband's role in the raid, but you shouldn't be worried about the conversation, it is a formality because he talked about the raid.' The warmth and calmness of the woman helped me to settle.

Justin sat at a large oblong table. With every muscle in my body tensed, I lowered onto the single chair opposite, as the interpreter settled in the corner and switched on the recording equipment. Justin remained silent.

I wanted him to speak first. The whiteness of his face and the dark sunken eyes made me shiver. Out of character, his hair hadn't been combed. Placing his elbows on the table, his hands displayed dirty fingernails with swollen and grazed knuckles. Had I played a part in making him like this? I shuddered at the thought.

The transformation from the handsome, smart man I'd married, to the person in front of me produced a shiver which travelled through my entire body. What had happened? He struggled to speak as tears rolled down his cheeks, I would have to speak first. 'You asked for this meeting?'

'Thanks for coming,' he stuttered, 'it must be difficult. I will not oppose a divorce.' A ball of dread formed in my stomach. Words failed me as I'd intended to tackle the issue of divorce, but not until I'd settled my future. It had been my assumption it would happen later rather than sooner. 'I'm sorry, you deserved better.'

Howling, he flung his head onto his arms and sobbed. The translator stood up to check nothing passed between us. With a sudden movement he wrapped his arms over his head and wailed even louder, like a small lost child. I leapt up and stepped back. Her calm voice served as a beacon in the charged emotion of the room. 'I thought it would be emotional. There's no harm done. Please sit down again, Jessica.' In an authoritative tone, 'Southwick, sit up.' He followed her instructions.

Justin whispered, 'Is there any hope that one day you might consider having me back?'

'Oh, Justin!' Tears rolled down my cheeks, but I fought them. 'You've no right to ask. When you first left,

I wondered if you would return.' I rubbed my hands over my face and eyes, 'After what you have done to me, what do you expect the answer to be?'

He regained a little of his composure, 'Do I have to earn the right to ask.' Pain hammered at the base of my skull as I struggled to form the words, 'Why did you leave? Had I been that bad to you?' My voice stayed strong.

'You've done nothing wrong, Jessica. Don't blame yourself.'

I didn't rush. 'A massive transformation took place in you. Everything about you changed! Appearance, attitude...' My voice trailed away. 'Did you have a breakdown?' I quivered, waiting for his reaction.

Justin squinted at the table, then at the translator, he shrugged, 'If you call a middle-aged, sensible man becoming infatuated with a woman young enough to be his daughter, then I had a breakdown, but it's not what you meant. Nothing else mattered apart from Anna.' I shuddered at the mention of her name. 'It started in a flash the first time I went to Munich.'

I held up my hand as I didn't want details, but he continued, 'When on top of that building with the helicopter circling overhead, I woke up and decided a life with Anna wouldn't be for me.'

'I don't want to know.' Hurt came into his face, but I'd no sympathy. I'd come to Germany to find out whether I could manage without him. When Justin arrived at breakfast that day, I'd had no warmth or love for him. The exhilaration of the years of our marriage had evaporated. Even if I hurt him today, I had no sympathy for him. My face warmed and I wrung my hands together.

55

'All I've learned so far is how wretched you feel. I don't give a damn! It's your fault! You walked out on me for another woman. You've been obstructive! Worst of all, you have indoctrinated my children against me with your ridiculous posturing! You also stole my money!'

Justin howled, sobbed and fell across the table, I thought he might attack me. The translator leapt to her feet to intervene. The frightful noise brought a prison guard into the room, but I hadn't finished. 'Whenever you contact the children. Tell them you've been an idiot!'

'I will, I will!' he wailed. The interpreter changed her mind about interfering. She stood near to me for protection, her eyes fixed on Justin. The guard left the room.

'If the children were younger, I would obtain a court order preventing you from speaking or having any contact. Justin, stop that wailing and lift your head!'

The noise stopped and he raised his head. With tears streaming down his face he stared open-mouthed and bewildered. His eyes were flat and glazed. I shouted, 'There is one thing you can do for me!'

'Anything, anything! Give me some form of hope.'

'There is no hope. You owe me! Not only money but

the way you have treated me.'

'What is it?'

'Persuade Paris and Clyde your environmental pursuits are total rubbish. Get Clyde back to studying maths and Paris behaving herself at school.'

'I'm not sure I can.'

'Then I hope they lock you up for the rest of your life and throw away the key.' I rushed from the room.

As I slammed the door, I burst into tears. The guard, who had been sitting outside of the door offered his seat. I slumped onto it. A loud echoing wail came from inside the room. The interpreter emerged and signalled to the guard to enter. The guard's sharp, authoritative voice bellowed, 'Stop that noise and go back to the cell.'

The translator pulled up a chair next to me and caught hold of my hand. An act of pure kindness to a fellow female. It calmed me but I took a few minutes to regain my composure. 'Thank you for allowing me to say it all.'

'It is no more than he deserved,' her voice held a note of sympathy.

'I want to go home.' I squeezed the interpreter's hand, 'I assume you will pass on the tape to the police because he mentioned the incident and the woman.' I refused to utter her name.

'Yes, I'm sorry,' the interpreter gave me a reassuring smile, 'but I must.'

'There's nothing I'm ashamed of in the interview. Don't be sorry. Would you take me to my children?'

56

Two pale faces greeted me in reception. Clyde and Paris had been shaken by the experience. I hugged them but struggled with my own emotions. 'What did you talk about?'

Paris avoided my gaze, 'The office invasion and the people involved.'

That was not what I wanted to hear, but Paris became even paler, 'You seem shaken. Are you all right?'

'Yes, it's dad, he's unwell, I'm worried. He was nervous about meeting you again and hoped it would be a good meeting. Was it?' I decided not to reply.

As we left the prison, Paris did a little jig on receiving a text message and showed it to Clyde, who responded with a happy grin. She didn't offer to share it, but it gave me no concern as I hankered to travel home, relax, and return to my designs. I intended to have serious words on their next visit to the farm. They needed to change their ways. The time of acquiescence had passed, and I would be direct as to my expectations for my children.

Paris's eyes darted around as we entered the departure lounge. 'There they are!' She pointed and ran towards a group of three boys and a girl who appeared about her age. Clyde trotted over to join them. They shook hands. Paris kissed the young men. My heart sank, they must have met when they were in Germany before.

It was my intention to leave them with their friends for an hour while I had a peaceful stroll around the shops. As I reached them a deafening noise from a public address system blasted out in German. I recognised the word for police. Most people in the departure lounge stopped moving and raised their hands above their heads. With no hesitation I copied them. The message came in English, 'Police! Stand still and raise your hands above your heads. Everybody! Now!'

Paris and Clyde with their friends ignored the announcements and carried on talking. I snapped, 'Paris, Clyde follow the instructions!'

'Oh, mum, it's nothing,' Paris flapped her hand in a dismissive gesture.

Double doors nearby burst open. About twenty police, fully armed with sub-machine guns, piled into the area. I stared open-mouthed as my stomach contracted and my heart pounded. The hands above my head shook and my legs turned to jelly. 'Police, hands above head, now!'

I froze to the spot, expecting them to rush past, but they surrounded the young group and me. The bustling terminal became silent. Only the police instructions echoed through the hall. An officer shouted in English, 'Lie on the floor! Face down!' The nearest policeman to me waved his gun. Without hesitation I slumped onto the floor.

Paris shook her head to defy the police. I shouted, 'Paris!' It didn't matter. An officer stepped forward and with an expert movement flipped Paris off balance. The officer slammed her on to the ground and secured handcuffs.

'Face the floor!' came another command. Trembling I complied and pressed my forehead onto the hard-tiled surface. I expected handcuffs, but nothing happened.

Paris needed help, but fear clawed through me and I remained motionless. My heart pounded and my blood ran cold. Why has this happened? What had we done to be treated like this?

Why hadn't Paris followed the police instructions? What would happen to her? Is she crying? I listened hoping to pick up clues about what was happening. Is she scared? Where's Clyde? When will this nightmare end? Tears rolled down my cheeks.

57

Terrified, I closed my eyes and attempted to stop shaking. A gentle woman's voice close to my ear, 'You can get up.'

I lifted my head to see who'd spoken. A smiling dainty policewoman's face encased in a huge helmet stared at me. With surprising strength, she grabbed my hand and helped me to my feet. Paris and Clyde lay on the floor handcuffed. Paris's shoulders lurched as she sobbed.

With a mother's instinct, I stepped towards Paris, but the policewoman guided me away and led me across the foyer. 'As you English would say, it is only her pride that is hurt. A slight nosebleed, but it is not broken, I have checked. Because she intended to disobey us, she had to be manhandled to the floor.'

As Paris had defied the police, she had to accept the consequences. A multitude of thoughts raced through my mind. Why had this happened? What would happen next? Why had they disobeyed the police? On and on the questions formed in my mind with dizzying speed.

The policewoman led me away from the public area. Just before the door closed my eyes scanned the public space but Paris and Clyde remained on the floor in handcuffs. 'This way.' She removed her helmet. About thirty, with long hair in a bun, she appeared too petite for such a physical job. 'That door, go in.' Her gentle voice held no threat.

Henry, the Foreign Office official, sat with a smart middle-aged man in a blue suit. Henry indicated a chair, 'Please sit down. This is Ludwig, who is an Inspector in the German police. You have already met Heidi,' he motioned towards the officer who had escorted me from the foyer. Everyone appeared relaxed as though attending an informal party.

'Please accept our apologies for the dramatic behaviour,' the Inspector spoke in clear unbroken English. 'For some time, we have been trying to trace two of the young men who met your son and daughter. The other members of the group also interested us, so the decision was made to confront them in the main hall, before they dispersed. We were uncertain whether they would be armed, so we took no chance of an accident. Your son and daughter met the young Germans when they were in the country at the New Year. We knew your identity, but by including you when we encircled everyone, it made the operation easier to handle. I hope you weren't hurt.'

Amazed at the civility and concern, 'Only shaken.'

'Yes, understandable. They are pretty terrifying,' he smiled at the pretty blonde policewoman. Even I appreciated the humour in the remark and my lips curled at the ends.

Reality hit me, 'What about Paris and Clyde?'

'May we have your permission to ask them some questions about their time in Germany?'

Henry inclined his head, 'We would like to help the German police if we can.'

Without a moment's hesitation, I nodded, 'Of course, you may ask them questions. I can understand why it's necessary. As for myself, I had nothing to do with my husband's activities.'

The Police Inspector grinned, 'We have no doubt about that. Your tape confirmed what we already thought.' If they've listened to the tapes that quickly then they are exceptionally efficient. 'It is our intention to interview simultaneously.' I nodded. 'Perhaps as your daughter is under eighteen, you will oversee that interview.'

Although apprehensive about them being inter-viewed, maybe the experience would frighten them, and ensure they discarded their environmental ideas, and more particularly their German friends. 'When we have young people on the edge of serious matters, we try to frighten them off.'

Rubbing the back of my neck to ease the tension I frowned, 'I don't see what you mean.'

'It is essential to ask your son and daughter a few questions. In some circumstances, we would make it a friendly chat. Our alternative is to make it formal. Tak-ing fingerprints and giving them a sense of isolation for a short time, can frighten them, and hopefully deter any future involvement.'

Although I worried about them, the police approach sounded sensible and reasonable. Anguish in the short-term appeared to be a better solution than long-term problems. Taking a deep breath, 'Yes, I agree a formal approach is a good idea.'

58

An hour later, hot and sweating I left the interview room. The questioning had been gruelling for Paris. Even when she cried, she received no sympathy from the policeman conducting the interrogation. Using bullying tactics, he gained the upper hand by making Paris use German.

The interviewer switched to English when she became confused and back to German when complacency surfaced. Before the interview I instructed Paris to tell the truth. Because of the German, I didn't understand the main theme, apart from the meetings she'd attended with Justin.

Anna's name came up several times. At the end, the policewoman who had been sitting close to Paris took her away for fingerprinting and photographing. The policeman told me Clyde had undergone the same treatment.

'Did the German police conduct the interview fairly?' asked Henry as we sat with coffee in the departure lounge.

'Yes, they didn't have a gentle approach, but I didn't expect that. Although I became distressed during the worse part, I stayed quiet and have recovered. I can understand they need to find out what happened.'

'The German Police are not expecting either of them to have any useful information, but with the seriousness of the situation, they will explore all angles.' The departure lounge bustled with people and I surveyed the moving heads, desperate to glimpse Paris and Clyde.

I yearned to go back to the solitude of my isolated farmhouse and the friendly chatter of the villagers. I craved for the nightmare to end and I wanted to take my children home, 'Will they release them?'

'The authorities will release them into your custody.' Henry remained calm and detached as he leaned back in his chair and watched my face. They expect to have completed their enquiries in time for you to catch the flight this evening. It is only a formality in case they want to speak to them again.' My shoulders relaxed. By late this evening, we would be home.

'They will compare notes while the fingerprinting and photographs are completed. There is a possibility they may have further questions if their comments do not tally.' Hopefully poor Paris wouldn't have to endure more stress, but I would have to wait to find out.

Half an hour later we were summoned back to the interview room. Heidi, the woman police officer, drew up a chair and sat next to me. Why was she sitting so close to me? I wasn't going to run away. The Inspector entered and sat. The light manner of before had disappeared.

'We no longer need to detain Clyde and he will be released into your custody in case we wish to interview him again, he may leave the country.'

'What about Paris?' A knot formed in my stomach.

The Inspector's eyes narrowed. In perfect English, 'She attended two meetings that are critical to our inquiry. It came as a surprise to realise her presence. She accompanied your husband, and several others, including

Anna.'

'What's that mean?' I gasped and stuttered while my whole body trembled. Sickness welled up in the pit of my stomach. Glancing down he rearranged his paperwork with methodical precision before answering.

'What?' I squealed.

'Paris will be charged with conspiracy to commit high treason against the Government of Germany.' My heart thumped and my head whirled. A strange roaring sound filled my ears and the voices in the room faded away. Darkness encased me.

59

After putting Clyde on a plane back to London, I spent a disturbed night in a Berlin Hotel. The clean, minimalistic room with Scandinavian furniture did nothing to help me forget the clinical conditions of the prison and detention centre. It had been late when I'd left the police station after they had made sure I'd recovered from fainting, but I'd had such a shock.

Paris needed my concentrated support. The terror on her face when she'd been handcuffed and taken away, heightened my determination to take her back to England. Paris remained steadfast that she didn't understand why she'd been arrested, but the police had been adamant about her involvement.

It seemed unbelievable that only a few days ago I'd had dinner with Robert, Cate and Miles in a relaxed and carefree atmosphere. The decision to sell the farm hung over me, but it would have to wait until I resolved the arrest of Paris. The only clear decision had been to send Clyde home. Although he had been involved with Justin's group, he hadn't attended the meetings with Paris. It gave me a modicum of relief that he'd returned to England, away from the German authorities. If he'd remained, I feared he would be re-arrested.

Putting through a call on my mobile, 'David, can you come to Berlin?'

'Why, is there a problem?'

'Paris has been arrested and charged with high treason, she's in a detention centre awaiting further questioning.' I grimaced but spoke without my voice faltering. 'I can't explain the details over the phone.'

The sound of clicking travelled down the line, 'I'm on the Internet, there's a flight from Birmingham this afternoon, I'll be on it.' I closed the call.

The phone rang. Miles' name came onto the screen. Oh no! I would have preferred not to speak to him, but he'll pester for an answer about the farm. 'Hello, Miles.' I ignored his initial chatting and waited. 'I'm in Berlin. Paris is in trouble; she's been arrested so I can't talk.' I swallowed deeply to stop the shakiness in my voice. 'I haven't decided about the farm.'

'It's not important,' the concern in his voice was evident, 'I'll fly out to help you.'

'Miles, it's kind of you.' Touched by his spontaneity, it gave me momentary relaxation. 'David from the village is coming and he speaks German.'

'Two heads are better than one, I also speak German.' I raised my eyebrows. Miles had hidden talents, 'See you later today.' I went to speak, but he cut me short. 'Don't try to argue, I'm coming.'

I didn't want both men here. David had been my choice. Should it have been Miles who had a can-do attitude? But they're both coming. The only time they'd met before was at the ill-fated breakfast. Would they recognise each other?

60

Henry had arranged another meeting with Justin. The bare interview room hadn't changed. The only difference would be me. Unlike the previous time, when I'd planned the words, this time the questions would flow.

In no mood for his self-pitying talk, Justin would receive the full force of my anger. The result would be important, as I intended to dig down to the root of the problem, and make him face the realities of his actions, as it had been his fault that Paris had been arrested.

The same interpreter came into the room, she greeted me with a smile, 'Have you remembered that I must record the interview?'

'Yes, please make sure nothing is missed. Listen carefully and make a note of any facial expressions or body language.' The interpreter raised her eyebrows but didn't reply.

I didn't wait for Justin to sit, 'Have you heard about Paris?' I spat the words out with a venomous sneer.

'No, what's happened?

The interpreter pointed to the seats.

'Paris has been arrested and charged with treason because she accompanied you to the critical meetings.'

'Oh, no! She knows nothing,' Justin opened the palms of his hands and shrugged. 'Why have they arrested her?'

'Justin!' I screeched, 'Stop being so bloody stupid, I've not come for your benefit and have no intention of explaining anything. Paris is in jail because of you and that German tart!' Holding up my hand with the palm directed at his face, 'I will tell the police to interview you again. This time you will tell them the whole truth and what happened at those meetings with Paris.'

'But I...'

'Don't give me any crap, Justin!' My voice rose to an alarming level, 'You will give names, dates and everything they ask. Is that clear?' Justin's eyes and mouth opened wide. 'Is that clear!' I shook my fist at him as I screamed. My anger bubbled and boiled like a volcano ready to spew hot ash.

He stuttered, 'I'll do....'

But I hadn't finished with him as he wouldn't tell the truth, his expression gave him away and he'd given in too readily. Slumping on to the table as he had done in the previous meeting, he buried his head in his arms and sobbed.

'Not good enough!' I yelled, at the top of my voice. Leaping from my seat I grabbed his hair then twisted it in my fingers and yanked as hard as possible. He yelped in pain. Good! I wanted him to hurt and beg for mercy.

The interpreter shouted, 'No touching!'

Without taking my eyes from Justin, I let go of his hair but threatened to do it again. 'My daughter's in jail because of you! She's a terrified, frightened little girl. I can't stand seeing her like that and it's your bloody fault!' I stared up at the ceiling, clenched my fists then opened my mouth and screamed. Long and loud. My fist thumped the table with astonishing speed and force.

Justin cowered, 'I'll tell them! I'll tell them!' he squealed but I still had a nagging doubt. Would he give information but not enough? Would he leave Paris implicated? I slumped onto the hard chair.

Sweat poured from every pore in my body, my heart pounded, and fury still coursed through me. I counted slowly in my head from one to ten, attempting to regain some composure. When I was ready to continue, I leaned forward resting on my elbows.

In a calm, low voice, 'Justin, look at me.' He fidgeted but kept his head on his arms.

'Sit up!' snapped the interpreter, he jolted, then raised his head. Tears streamed down his face.

My low voice continued, 'On Saturday before she came home, did Paris go to a meeting with you at Anna's apartment?' I amazed myself as I managed to control my emotions and voice.

'Why do you want to know? I'll tell the police.' He wiped the back of his hand across his face to remove the tears.

'When I've finished with you, I'm visiting Paris in the detention centre. The police questioned her last night at the airport. They conducted the interview in German, and I didn't understand.' Justin wouldn't catch my eye. 'I want to help her.' He groaned and moaned but didn't speak.

I wouldn't be deflected, 'Don't you think I'm entitled to know what you did with my underage daughter!'

Justin's head shot up and his eyes widened, 'Nothing happened! Nothing at all, no one touched her! The meeting wasn't like that! Why did you say underage?' he squealed and stared at the recorder, 'Underage is recorded now!'

Keeping my elbows on the table I leaned further forward until a few inches from Justin's face. 'Tell me what happened when she came to visit you in Germany, I want every detail of those meetings.'

Justin leaned back in his chair trying to get away from me and put his hands on the table as though intending to stand. 'Stay!' barked the interpreter.

His eyes flicked between us, 'Do you believe I would do anything to harm her?'

I mustn't falter, my voice remained calm, 'The truth. Every single piece.'

Justin had one final glance at the interpreter then his voice, slow and ponderous at the beginning, gained momentum and he didn't stop. I kept my eyes trained on him and wouldn't allow eye contact to be lost, and I prompted when he slowed.

61

Two hours later I left the prison where I'd been ruthless but had achieved my aim. Or I hoped I had.

At the juvenile detention centre, I had to agree to the restrictions about no physical contact and the length of the interview. Although a modern institution, the interview room had the same cold layout. Four chairs and a table with recording equipment. The interpreter showed me into the room then sat by the machine without saying a word.

A guard led Paris, dressed in standard-issue grey sweat top and trousers, into the room. The greyness of the clothes accentuated her pale face, with eyes red from constant crying. The guard caught her before we could hug. The interpreter snapped, 'No touching or I shall stop the interview.'

My eyes watered as I wanted to hug my little girl, who shook from fright.

'How are you?' My voice trembled with emotion. Paris burst out crying, gulped several times, 'I'm so scared, they will lock me up forever when I've done nothing, but they won't believe me.'

I swallowed to gain strength, 'Calm down, darling,

I'm doing everything possible. Tell the truth. I'm meeting a lawyer this afternoon who will help you.' I shook with anxiety and rubbed my hand across my face. 'Paris, you are my golden girl and will be coming home before long.'

Paris sobbed, 'But they will lock me up forever.'

I tried to sound reassuring, but I understood Justin's explanation, and the prospects didn't sound good for Paris.

For the rest of the meeting, I tried to calm her, despite the rambling conversation punctuated by Paris repeating the same words. It was heart-wrenching to leave her without a kiss, but the silent officials enforced the time restriction.

62

David strode from the customs hall into the Arrivals' Lounge. A lifeline from the normal world and not the current nightmare of Germany. I threw my arms around him and cried on his shoulder, but relief engulfed me at his presence.

A foreign country where I didn't speak the language accentuated the isolation and terror. Even the hotel staff appeared threatening as they spoke in German. David's embrace gave me confidence and calmed my wildest fears, I sensed he would be a tower of strength.

After spending hours at the solicitors, we returned to the hotel and met Miles in reception. 'Jessica, you poor woman,' he gripped my hand in a comforting way. How would they react? Would they recognise each other from the infamous breakfast?

'Will you update me on what's happened, Jesse?' asked Miles. We found a quiet table in the corner of the lounge and I gave them a full history of events. Earlier I'd only given David brief information. At the end of the lengthy conversation, the Police Inspector appeared in the doorway and then approached the table.

With a solemn face, 'I've good news, it's not perfect

for you, but it might give you relief.' The Inspector studied David and Miles as I introduced them. They greeted him in German and chatted for a few minutes.

'I have taken them into my confidence so they may hear any information you have.'

The Police Inspector joined us at the table but spoke to Miles and David in German.

Miles replied, 'Masterful'.

'You conducted a masterful interrogation of your husband this morning and are a brilliant lady to go down that route. We are still interviewing him about matters on the tape but that will take several days.'

One thought that twirled repeatedly, would it release Paris from the accusations? 'At the current stage of our investigations we believe your daughter to be an innocent visitor to these meetings.' I raised my head, gazed at the ceiling and my shoulders relaxed. 'The investigation has not been completed.'

'I understand.'

David interrupted, 'Will you release Paris?'

'We are working on it, but we must leave the charge, as you English say, lying on the books as it is difficult in Germany to release someone charged with high treason, but we have a plan.'

'How can we help?' asked Miles.

'We have a suggestion to make to you and we think it's better than your daughter staying in the detention centre. As part of our enquiries, English detectives visited Paris's boarding school. We propose to release Paris, who will be tagged by the English police, into the custody of Mrs Hastings. Paris will be accompanied during the day and will share a bedroom, and she may not use phones or computers for communication.'

'Has Mrs Hastings agreed?' I had doubts whether the school would welcome Paris back after what had happened.

'Yes,' the Inspector nodded, 'I spoke with her earlier, she is a formidable woman who speaks fluent German.'

'She terrifies me.'

The Inspector laughed, 'Before I outlined my idea, she itemised her strategies to prevent Paris contacting the outside world and had a far better list than I had prepared. And when I raised the possibility of her sending messages through other girls, she told me off.' We laughed. 'Can you imagine an English headmistress telling off a German police officer?' The Inspector grinned.

'I've met Mrs Hastings and I can well believe it.'

'Mrs Hastings will address the whole school and make it clear that punishment would be severe for anyone trying to smuggle a message out. She also added before I asked, There will be none of this heroic nonsense about saving the world.' She further added that your daughter will have her nose in a book and her friends will be doing the same.'

The news that Paris could return to school gave me immense relief. Perhaps the episode in the detention centre had frightened her enough to push the silly ideas from her head. More than anything else I wanted to give my little girl a huge cuddle and take her home. Would my life ever calm down? I appeared to be lurching from one crisis to the next.

The Police Inspector showed no sign of leaving and chatted away to David and Miles. Their words became background noise as I focused on my own anxieties. I wanted time to order my thoughts. As I made my excuses and rose to leave, the Inspector addressed Miles and David, 'You asked if you can be of any help. If we let Mrs Southwick go to her room, perhaps the three of us may exchange ideas.'

What ideas did the Inspector wish to pursue? How

would Miles and David be able to assist him?

63

Sitting alone in the kitchen I relaxed, safe in the knowledge that Paris had been transferred into Mrs Hastings' care. Within the next week, I would see a solicitor to draw up the divorce papers. To my surprise, neither David nor Miles had returned to England with me. They had bonded and were conspiratorial about the Inspector's request for help, refusing to give me details.

Life had to return to normal, so the sale of the farm needed addressing. But would my conscience allow me to let the village down? I liked the people, and they had been so supportive when the television crews and the press descended.

David had a passion for the village and its people. If I sold out for wind turbines, it would be the end of our relationship. Nothing had started, but he had been kind and considerate, I liked him, so it would be a pity to lose him as a friend.

I also had a soft spot for Miles and had reversed my initial opinion of him. Without being asked he'd attempted to help, first with the design contract, and second with selling the farm. The big question is how to decide. A knock came on the door and I caught my breath as I wanted no more surprises.

Liam's tall, slender and wiry figure wrapped in many layers of jumpers and a jacket loped into the kitchen. His solid taciturn face remained unchanged, it didn't show happiness nor sadness, only his everyday view on life. After the traumas of the past few days, Liam's calm manner came as a great comfort.

'I'm sorry to hear Paris has been in a spot of bother.' A typical expression of the local people, understated with no mention of specifics.

'Thank you, Liam.'

'If I can help the next time she comes home, let me know.' This was a longer speech than Liam normally managed.

'Did you have anything in mind?'

Screwing up his brow. 'No, but I'll think of something.' Liam was moving between his feet with his eyes focused on the floor. 'I don't want to offend you, or your family.'

'I promise I will not take offence.'

After a deep breath, 'I don't like Paris.' His voice held a note of finality, but then he added, 'In case you thought I wanted to ask her out.' I would have smiled at his approach, but he was serious. 'Mossmoor people help each other.' I didn't want to stop him talking now he'd started, 'On the farm in every flock or herd there is often a willful animal.'

'Yes?' I understood his meaning and wanted him to continue.

'The behaviour of the animal must be broken otherwise it will create chaos in the herd or flock, but you don't cure them by cruelty, that never works so it has to be a kind and disciplined approach by showing the animals the proper way to behave.'

'You think that Paris is willful.'

He blushed but muttered, 'Yes.'

'Liam, you're right, it's a good description of her.' He appeared relieved. 'You have caused me no offence and I understand why you don't like her. That's fine by me, and I shall ask for your help the next time Paris is at home.' His eyes came up from the floor. The ends of his lips curled, and a small smile appeared.

Even a small smile was an achievement when Liam spoke to me, perhaps he didn't like me.

'I'll attend to the animals.'

'Thanks, Liam.'

'I met George on the way here, he wants you to pop over when you have a minute.'

If George wants to see me, then it's an ideal opportunity to talk about selling the farms. Ten minutes later clad in wellington boots, I walked up to the door of George's farmhouse.

64

The old stone farmhouse had a neglected air. The paint peeled around the windows and ivy scrambled unheeded up the walls. One of the dogs, too old to work, came to meet me. I liked a man who allowed the dogs, after retirement, to spend their last years in the warmth of the farmhouse.

'Come in,' he gestured, opening the door, 'Aggy's gone into Braxton, tis market day. Kettle's on.'

The kitchen stepped back in time. The range had an old metal kettle with a whistle. After making the tea he sat in his usual blanket covered seat by the range. Aggy, his wife of many decades, a pleasant and cheerful woman, only left the farmhouse for shopping and to visit relatives. I would give the information at a slow pace and stop before upsetting him.

'I expect you are anticipating a well-earned retirement in this lovely old farmhouse.'

He chuckled, 'I understand your sense of humour now, you're trying to wind me up. The place is falling down, it's freezing cold throughout the year and look at the kitchen!' He waved his arm in an expansive arc around the ancient room. 'It's out of Dickens. We haven't those newfangled gadgets you use.' He put more sugar into his tea. 'We've been thinking about the future.' He stirred the tea in a slow methodical movement and a small frown creased his forehead.

'Some time ago we investigated moving, as we hoped we might have a small bungalow, that is warm with central heating. It would be good for Aggy's rheumatism.' Clenching the mug of tea, he gave a sorrowful shake of his head, 'If we sold, it would leave the boys without a farm and we can't do that.'

'George I've something to tell you. It's between you and me, about our farms.'

He topped up our teas and pulled his chair closer. I took him through the conversation I'd had with Robert and Miles. Did he understand? Keeping my eyes focused on his face I searched for an expression, but he gave nothing away. As I explained my throat muscles tightened and my hands shook, forcing me to place my mug of tea on the table. I liked George and didn't want to upset him. Finally, I stumbled to a halt. 'What do you think?'

'Well, I'll be jiggered! So, let me get this clear, they will buy the farm and give me 25,000 pounds.'

Robert had indicated the incentive for me to persuade George to sell would be 50,000 pounds, which I would split with him. George thought out loud, 'We would buy that much bigger farm on the other side of Mossmoor, but we'd never get planning permission to build a new bungalow.'

'Don't worry, their legal team would help.' The noise of a car distracted us as it pulled into the front of the old farmhouse.

'That'll be Aggie and Liz, our granddaughter. Not a word, I'll speak to Aggie later and I'll give you our answer tomorrow.' Sipping his lukewarm tea, he settled back in his chair, 'I've clean forgotten why I wanted to speak to you.'

'Never mind,' my mouth twitched with amusement, 'we can chat again tomorrow.'

Liz moved backwards and forwards after the introduction. 'What is it?' asked George.

'Do you want me on the farm today, grandad?'

Aggie smiled and patted her granddaughter's arm, 'She wants to finish the dress she's making. We bought a few bits and bobs in the market to help.'

'Yes, run along Liz, do your dress. I'm sure you'll look pretty in it.'

'Thanks, grandad.'

Anything to do with fashion interested me, so filled with curiosity I asked, 'Are you making your own dress?'

'Yes, all the local girls do.'

'Can I see it?' She raised her eyebrows, but within a few minutes, she presented me with the half-made dress. Even though a poor design, no doubt from a cheap magazine, I gave praise. There were also good additions that Liz had added.

'Have you thought about finishing the bottom with a scalloped edge?'

'No, I hadn't,' Liz grinned and gave a quizzical glance, 'it's a good idea, but I don't know how. Neither would my friends?'

'Bring your friends over and I'll explain.'

Liz bubbled with excitement. George winked at me as I left, but he looked a worried man.

65

Six o'clock the following morning I crawled from my bed, but with a smile on my face. Working late into the night I'd made progress on my designs. Tiredness had overcome me, but I would make another big effort today. Wrapping a towel around me I set about firing up the Aga before showering. As I struggled to ignite the system, my towel dropped away just as Liam came through the back door.

I screamed, not because I worried about Liam, but he'd caught me by surprise. With a mumbled apology he sped out of the kitchen. He had arrived earlier than normal this morning. I must have frightened him by screaming. After I'd showered, dressed and put on wellington boots, accompanied by my thick anorak, I set off to find him. The heavy rain of the past few days had reduced everywhere to thick mud.

The cows in one building made more noise than usual and I guessed he would be in there. With my lantern torch, I approached the main door and called his name. The cavernous barn, full of cattle movement and deafening bellowing, provided shelter from the strong wind and driving rain.

Although lit by fluorescent tubes they cast shadows and didn't reach the dark dusty far corners of the barn. The pitted and uneven floor had become an ice-rink of slippery mud. Being so close to the large animals terrified me and my heart hammered in double time. The steam from the animals gave a fog which hung in the air. Trying to find the best place to stand I didn't notice the cow backing up. Liam shouted, but too late, the huge backside of the cow cannoned into me.

My precarious footing gave way, I slithered then fell face down into the mud behind the cows. Agitated by my scream one of them kicked out. The glancing blow ripped the sleeve of my anorak. Before I gained any sense of what had happened, Liam arrived and stood between me and the animals. With a wave of his arm he shouted at them, and they moved away. Shaking and shivering I lay on the floor, scared to move from the shock of the pounding hoofs so close to me.

Panic gripped me, 'Help me, help me!' I grabbed at Liam. From under the woolly hat and hood of his anorak his bright beaming face appeared.

'Are you hurt,' came his strong but gentle voice.

'I don't know but get me out of here, it's a nightmare, help me up.'

'No, I'll carry you.' I tried to say he wouldn't manage it. Kneeling beside me he put one arm under my back, and the other under my thighs, and lifted me from the floor in one easy movement. While I had slipped and slid, Liam crossed the mud in the farmyard with ease.

The warmth and safety of the boot room soon revived me. The waterproofs had protected me from the wet mud. Once inside, apart from a cut arm and a graze I hadn't been hurt, so I took some deep breaths to calm. Liam fussed by removing the waterproofs.

As he took off my boots, a wonderful smile appeared. 'I'm sorry about earlier I had no idea you would be up so early.'

'There's no harm done.' I returned his smile, 'I'm sorry I screamed at you, but you took me by surprise.'

'I'll knock and wait next time.'

'Liam, don't be so ridiculous. You will do no such thing. Come in as you always do. Whatever the time! It's not a problem, but why were you so early this morning?'

'Blizzards are forecast for tonight. After I've finished here, I need to help take the scaffolding down at home.'

66

An hour later, David, back from Germany walked into the kitchen, but with no hug or kiss of welcome. 'Are you okay, David? Has the illness returned?'

'No, I'm better and that's thanks to your kindness and hospitality, but I've come to pick up my things as I'm going home.' Frowning he focused on the table.

'Oh, David, you're welcome to stay, as I've enjoyed your company.' But there was no movement in his face which remained emotionless. I hoped for a smile and a positive answer as my words had been clear and encouraging. If he asked whether the arrangements were changeable, I would have not let him down. The blank expression on his face never altered.

'What did the German police want?' I made my voice sound bright and cheerful hoping to shake him out of his strange mood.

'Nothing much, they wanted me to talk to some vets about Planetearth. So, I visited surgeries and then passed on information which the police thought useful. That's all.' His sparkling eyes were dull and lifeless, and a disgruntled frown pulled at his mouth. 'How's Paris?'

'As fine as she can be in the circumstances.' With

no smile and no further comment, he stomped off to pack. Why had he changed? What had happened? Why wouldn't he talk about it?

Ten minutes later he came in with his bags, 'Thanks again,' but the words held no sincerity.

Tension gripped me, 'For goodness' sake David, what is the matter?'

Stoutly setting his jaw and scrunching his face, 'I don't want to stay here.'

The sharp words tore straight through me, I clutched the kitchen table for support and treated him to a look of unmitigated fury. The stress and tension of the past few days overflowed, 'You bloody ungrateful man, get out of my house! And never come back again.'

Slumping in the chair as the Range Rover pulled out of the yard, tears welled, I shouldn't have ranted. Since our first unfortunate encounter he had been kind and helpful. Perhaps he hadn't recovered from his illness, and I had added to his difficult circumstances. As a knock came at the door, I wiped away the tears and composed myself.

As George hobbled into the kitchen, I expected that lovely toothy grin, but he had a serious expression and only muttered, 'Hello, luv.' What's wrong with everyone today? Sitting at the table, his face held no glimmer of a smile, 'I won't beat about the bush, poor Aggy cried herself to sleep last night.'

'Why what's happened?'

'We'd talked about what thee told me yesterday.'

'Oh dear,' I moved uncomfortably in my chair.

'Aggie and I chatted yesterday afternoon, and we discussed your proposal with the boys in the evening.'

'Didn't Aggie want to move?'

'She would love to move.'

'I'm confused.'

'A new farm and a bungalow would fulfill our dreams, but we cannot let the village down for our gain. A hard decision, but it's our final one as a family, we won't sell!'

'Yes, I can understand,' I smiled hoping to lift the old man's spirits.

'But there's something else,' he lifted his head and stared with intense scrutiny, 'and this is the difficult bit.' I took a deep breath and tried to quell my anxiety. It wouldn't be good news, I could tell by the serious expression spreading across George's face, but I needed to know the worst. 'We'll support the village if you try to build the wind farm, even if it costs your friendship.' Taking a deep breath, he let out a long low sigh, 'I've blurted it all out. It's been a difficult chat, but I had to be straight and honest with you. We like you, but it can't happen to our village.' He gulped and twisted his hat around in his hands.

'I don't know what I want to do,' I moaned as a great sadness settled on me, 'because I've become fond of the village and its people.'

'Jesse, we'll make a villager out of you yet,' he stood up, winced as his knees gave pain and shoved his flat cap onto his head. Since our first meeting he had called me Jesse, the villagers used Jessica, but George always referred to people by some shortened name. I kissed him on the forehead as he left.

He swiped at his brow and gave a toothy smile, 'We don't want all that London kissing malarkey here.'

'But you're such a sweet man.'

'Ugh.' He closed the door with a smile, and I gave a small chuckle.

67

As George left so Miles pulled into the yard, leapt out of the car, ran across the yard and hugged me. 'I've just flown back from Germany. Landed in Manchester this morning so thought I'd pop in before heading back to London.' Grabbing my hands, he squeezed. 'Great to see you again, Jesse,' he kissed me on both cheeks.

Moving into the kitchen he made a beeline for the rocking chair next to the Aga, 'How's Paris?'

'In a safe place. Mrs Hastings is a formidable woman. The school has handled the situation with extreme thoroughness, but I'm also grateful for your help.'

Miles waved a dismissive hand, 'What are friends for?' Chatting with enthusiasm about his time in Germany, he praised me for handling such a difficult ordeal. The German police were concerned that some of the Planetgreen members were infiltrating major companies and becoming "sleepers", waiting to be awakened for the cause. He had helped the German police identify two possible sleepers. Despite his outward appearance, as a flash salesman, he had a kind and thoughtful approach.

Fixing his eyes on me, 'Have you decided to sell the farm to my company?'

It was inevitable that he would want my decision. Before answering, I huffed out a sigh, 'George, has refused the offer.'

'That doesn't matter,' his voice had an edge of irritation, 'others in the company will bribe him out.' The word bribe made me catch my breath, it suggested underhand dealing and corruption. Miles didn't notice my discomfort and had a smug expression. The brief but honest chat with George earlier sprang into my mind.

How do you explain to a salesman like Miles that George has principles and loyalties, so his life is not governed by greed or money? 'Money won't make him change his mind, as he wants to support the village.' The brief explanation didn't begin to explain the complexities behind George and his decision not to sell.

'Don't worry about George, it's more important to hear what you have decided? The Barbican flat?' Rubbing his hands together, his eyes sparkled with mischief. 'We'd be near each other.'

The dismissal and disinterest in George rankled me, so I allowed a long pause as my mind whirled through the dilemma. It had been my priority to sell up and return to London after Justin had left me, but times and ideas change. Attempting to keep my voice steady, I let out a long slow breath, 'Miles, I have thought long and hard.'

'You're going to say no, aren't you? I don't believe it.' Words weren't necessary, he'd understood the expression on my face.

'You desperately needed a new job and to sell the farm,' he scoffed, and the corners of his mouth turned into a sneer. 'I solve both and you change your mind.' Sweat clung to his brow and his face reddened.

'I will not sell the farm to your company. So, the answer is no.' The decision tipped him over the edge.

'Won't you agree to please me? Come to London!

Let's be together!'

I hated the connection between selling the farm and having a relationship, as they were separate issues. While an attractive and desirable man, I wouldn't be pushed into selling the farm, so I shook my head, but that only referred to the farm.

Miles leapt from his seat and shouted, 'You teased me along, got what you wanted, and now it's goodbye Miles.'

'Believe me, it's nothing...' I didn't manage to finish the sentence as the redness on his face deepened and the knuckles of his clenched fists turned white.

'You use men and give nothing in return.' As he opened the door, 'I think you will become a tight old spinster living on past glories and not able to keep a man.'

The car bounced along the track while I stood open-mouthed in the kitchen doorway. I'd dismissed him as a foolish man when we'd first met, but since then he had been charming and helpful. He had a temper, a less favourable side, but I had provoked him. Did I have anyone left to argue with?

68

Settling to my designs in the spare bedroom, I couldn't concentrate, as Miles' words came back to haunt me. Did I want everyone running around after me? Since Justin had left, did I demand my own way regardless of the consequences? Perhaps I'd adopted a less favourable side. Would I become the tight old spinster Miles suggested? The thought made me shudder.

David had been in a strange mood when he arrived this morning, but I showed him little sympathy. Then I argued with him rather than being supportive. Had I changed? Did I subconsciously plan to become a vet's wife or did the London fashion scene prove a magnet too strong to resist?

Why hadn't I been kinder to Miles, as there were worst ideas than moving to the Barbican with him? Tears formed in my eyes at my own frustration. I shook my head. Concentration for my designs eluded me. No one else had caused the alienation of two good men, the responsibility lay solely with me. Snap out of it, make life happen.

I needed an excuse to see David to apologise for my outburst. I phoned the pub. 'Jaggers Inn,' a man's voice grunted.

'Hi, Michael, it's Jessica, can I speak with Cate? Perhaps she fancies popping into Braxton this afternoon.' If Cate had no plans, she would be pleased to go. A wander around the shops, a coffee and then I would suggest visiting David on the way home.

'Sorry, Jessica. She's gone to Ashbourne.'

'Never mind.'

'But if it's any help, I'm driving to Braxton, if you want to come along. I'm going to the Cash and Carry, but after that, I'll take you into town.' Normally I would have rejected the offer, but my keenness to see David won the day.

'That's perfect! It's a pain not being able to drive and there aren't too many tube trains in Mossmoor.'

He laughed, 'I'll pick you up in fifteen minutes.'

'Are you in a rush?' I asked as we settled back in the car. Michael had picked up his goods from the Cash and Carry warehouse while I'd popped to the market.

'No, where do you want to go?'

'David has moved back home, and he didn't seem his normal self this morning, could we pop in to make sure he's okay?'

'Yes, of course. He's a good man I like him.'

'Do you know where he lives?'

'Yes, I've been there many times, especially before his wife died. Cate and I often went to dinner.'

'It's huge.' Michael brought his Nissan 4x4 skidding to a halt on the gravel at the front of the old Elizabethan house, which had small metal windows, large limestone mullions and dark gritstone blocks.

The magnificent building had various extensions which must have been added during the intervening centuries. 'This way,' Michael marched towards the building. 'Over there, that door,' he pointed.

'He needs a good front doorbell.' I stopped at the huge oak door.

'No need.' Michael lifted a small wooden flap and punched a number on the entry keypad. 'David has told us if no one responds, to go straight through to the surgery. Here we go!' Michael pushed the door open and we stepped into an antique-filled hall, with a thick red carpet and a large chandelier.

'This is magnificent!'

'Anyone home?'

As he received no reply, he opened one of the doors from the hall and I followed him into the huge lounge, which had an inglenook fireplace, wall tapestries and a lush patterned carpet. I stood uncertain of my next move. Perhaps he was in the surgery attending to a sick animal.

'Oh, shit!' A female voice exclaimed from a corner alcove. I opened my mouth in astonishment as Cate, wearing only a pair of lacy black knickers, stood at the cocktail bar in the alcove with a cocktail shaker in her hand.

The situation worsened when David appeared around the corner wearing his boxer shorts, 'What's the matter, Cate?'

Michael swore and sprinted from the house. Moving with speed he crashed through the doors slamming them and leaving me behind. Not wanting to stay I rushed after him reaching the front of the house as he roared out of the drive. Closing the door behind me I strode away from the house as fast as I could. The option of remaining didn't appeal.

The wind howled and an icy blast permeated the thin fashionable coat selected for browsing around the shops in Braxton. However, it was unsuitable for the high moors outside David's house and gave me little protection from the strong chilly wind which buffeted me.

The main road had one car coming towards me en route for Braxton. I relaxed a little as the car had a female driver. Would she stop if I flagged her down? The car slowed and I stood upright to show that I had nothing to hide. As the car pulled over the driver opened the window, 'Have you broken down?'

With a little exaggeration to make my cause more interesting, 'I had a lift to my boyfriend's house to give him a surprise.' I pointed to the building. 'When I arrived, I found him wearing only his boxers with his arm around a naked woman.'

The driver grinned, 'Get in, I want the sordid details.'

69

The stranger who picked me up in her car dropped me at the edge of the village, and I sauntered up the track to the farm. With no distractions other than the wild moorland scenery my mind returned to the lounge at David's. What a shock it must have been for poor Michael.

Cate's car must have been hidden away and nothing had prepared him for what he found. Tension gripped my stomach, but I didn't know why. David had made no effort to take me out and our only outing had been the annual village bash.

Nothing had happened between us, not even a goodnight kiss when he dropped me back at the farm, but I'd been confident we would get together. We'd developed a good rapport, and he often popped into the farm when nearby. Our relationship had finished before it started. David and Cate, who would have believed it?

I'd been conned by Cate, I screwed up my face and pressed my lips together. Unbelievably it had happened right under my nose. The evening that David had taken me to the pub, Cate had wanted to get him alone and made up the story about the dog being unwell. Now I understood why Cate had been so willing to volunteer to bring supplies and news over the fields during the press siege.

I'd left Cate and David on their own for hours because I wanted to work on my designs. No one suspected, least of all me. What would happen at the pub? Would Cate leave? What would David do?

I became cross with myself, the obvious answer, Cate would move in with David. How would the village react? They must have had scandals before. To be blunt, I fancied David and in my wilder daydreams had envisaged myself as a vet's wife. What a silly idea!

My deliberations were interrupted by someone calling my name. Liz, George's granddaughter, trotted up to me. Well wrapped in a thick anorak, jeans and wellington boots she took no notice of the howling wind. Without indulging in any preamble about the weather as most villagers she came straight to the point. 'When we met before, you offered to help us with our dressmaking?'

'Yes.'

'Amy is stuck with her dress. My other friend Sarah doesn't know what to do either. Is there any chance you could help us?'

It would be a relief to have a normal conversation. 'Yes, of course,' I smiled with enthusiasm, 'Why don't you come over to the farm this afternoon.'

What a contrast between the girls. Liz, Sarah, Amy and Paris were about the same age. None of the three in front of me wore makeup but were pretty in different ways. Also, there were no designer labels only standard supermarket cheap clothes.

But their presence lit up the room and the laughter and giggles lightened my mood. We sat at the dining room table as they showed me their work and the problems they were having.

They had the potential to become good designers, especially Liz, who showed me more additions to magazine designs and some small accessories she had designed and made herself.

Two hours of chatting and laughter flew past. When Paris had been at home, she'd made no local friends in Mossmoor. Now I understood why. Paris would throw a tantrum and insist on being the centre of attention. These girls enjoyed each other's company with no dominant one.

The first splattering of snow on the windows came as twilight arrived and it became the signal to end the session. The girls tramped off down the track buffeted by the strong gusty winds and the first swirls of snow.

Despite the happenings earlier in the day, the afternoon with the three girls had lifted my spirits, and with a positive frame of mind I settled down to my designs. With luck, if I worked through the evening and into the night, I could complete my portfolio.

Today had seen David and Miles recede into the distance. There were no immediate prospects of selling the farm. It would be lonely here, but if my design portfolio became successful, I would cope. I remained confident the people who worked for Camilla would approve the collection.

But would it bring my name back into the limelight of the fashion industry? Picking up my coffee, I ambled up to the makeshift studio and settled down to work.

70

The snow continued throughout the evening and had piled into drifts by the dry-stone walls, the wind roared, the gates rattled, and wire fences whistled. The gale buffeted the old farmhouse. As I descended the stairs, the pounding reached a new level and I checked the front door. Plenty of draughts but secure.

I'd left a fire burning in the front room and had stacked in the logs. The embers glowed red, so I put another two large logs on the wide-open fire and listened to the wind screaming in the chimney. Moving into the kitchen, I shuddered as the blizzard attacked the building and the farmyard.

The studio faced the leeward side of the current storm. The kitchen windows and door took the full force. The kitchen had become cold and damp because the Aga hadn't been working for a couple of days. Scared of the storm's constant pounding it would be a bleak introduction of what life would be like here on my own.

Being alone is a frightening thought and while making my sandwich I shivered. It would be cosier to have my food and drink by the log fire in the front room. The electric heater kept the studio warm, but I preferred the flickering flames and the glow that emanated from a real fire. Such a wild night would prevent me from sleeping so I'd work through after I'd finished my food.

A mighty crack from outside shook the whole house. The lights flickered and darkness descended; I screamed. Stay calm shouted a voice inside my head. Electricity goes off in storms, it might come back on!

I kept a lantern torch on the windowsill in the kitchen in case I had to go outside during darkness. So, I groped my way along the hall to locate it and my shoulders relaxed a little as the kitchen glowed in the weak light. The doors and windows shook in their frames. A howling preceded a violent gust of the wind. The solid oak door moved as the loud blast hit the house. A split second of eerie silence, then a huge crack which sounded like splitting wood. Had a tree come down? I rushed into the boot room to peer through the windows to see the damage.

Shadows crept over the outside of the buildings. Then the snow blinded my view again. Something or someone moved in the farmyard, I screamed. The outline of a cow appeared. Another terror gripped me. Liam had locked the animals in the barns so they would be secure and out of danger. Rushing into the hall I picked up the phone, but it didn't work.

My stomach heaved and my hands shook. What would happen to the animals? Can I do anything? I returned to the kitchen. Outside the snow and wind blew even harder. Panic bubbled up inside me. What shall I do? Too frightened to go outside I shook from fear of the next disaster.

When the swirl of snow cleared two headlights of a tractor pierced the darkness. Oh, my God! Someone has come out in this weather. I unbolted the door but dare not open it. Then it opened as Liam held on to it with all his strength. 'Help close it,' he shouted.

Together we pushed the door closed as the snow whistled around the kitchen. 'This is worse than we expected! I've come to check on the animals!'

'There is no electricity.'

'I'll see what's happened outside,' he grabbed the door handle, 'stand by the door I shall need help to close it.'

Shouting to get above the noise of the storm, 'You can't go out there!'

'No option,' he yanked the door open. As soon as we closed it with Liam on the outside and me on the inside, I rushed into the boot room and grabbed the thickest anorak and waterproof trousers to deal with the cold and wet of the kitchen. I had no intention of venturing outside, but I needed to keep warm.

A drift had been forming on the outside of the door, and it had collapsed inwards when he first arrived, so I put on the weatherproof clothes and returned to the door. I used my strength to help hold it as Liam slipped back in and we pushed it shut again.

'The main barn door has been ripped off, so the cows are wandering seeking shelter. The roof of the tractor shed has blown away, but the sheep barn is holding, so I've put a tractor against the door to prevent them escaping. We must secure the cows, or they will be killed if they wander off. A couple are already dead as they were caught by the electricity lines as they came down.'

'We can't do anything, it's wild out there.'

'Yes, we can, and we must, but I need your help.' My eyes opened wide and the little strength I had seeped away. Liam smiled, 'Come on, say you will give it a go, then we can get the cows to safety.'

'I'm no good with them.' My whole body shook.

'Let them know who's boss. Give them a hard whack

on the backside with the flat of your hand or pull their horns. They will move, even in the snow. Come on, let's do it, I can't do it on my own.'

Determination spread across Liam's stern face, but his eyes flashed. I can't let him down. 'What can I do? I don't know what to do!'

'There are three gaps between the buildings into the farmyard.'

Terrified about going outside in this weather, the fear doubled by the thought of trying to manage cows. They were huge beasts and I'd been convinced since I'd arrived on the farm that they didn't like me.

'We'll move the cattle into the yard and then block it off. It's too dangerous to put them back into the barn. I'll block one side with the tractor as the cows are milling and staggering around the other two gaps. You take the small entrance and I'll do the big gap.'

'What do I do?' This will be the end of me.

'Go past them, find the one furthest away and drive her back to the gap.' He nipped into the utility room and returned with two walking sticks. 'Use these, they will help you stand, and you can poke the cows with them, but only smack them with your hand, not the stick, is that clear!'

My thoughts swirled with the disasters that might befall me. The cows might kill me, I'll be trampled to death by the enormous beasts.

71

Liam tightened the straps on my hood for me, 'Ready?' I nodded, and we took the full force of the wind as the door inched open. We pulled it closed behind us. Liam pointed, and I understood what I needed to do, but achieving it would be another matter. A few cows had taken shelter in the yard, so I slipped and slithered past them. The brightness of the snow allowed me to see without the torch.

Staggering through the snow and battling against the strong wind I aimed for the furthest cow and I closed on her. The driving snow stung my face, my eyes watered, everything became a blur. Its black eyes stared at the approaching red anorak. The cow shook its head. 'It's facing the wrong way,' I shouted to myself. 'Well, it's now or never.'

My stomach quivered and terror welled up in a sickening wave, my face ached as I struggled to stand in the wind and snow. I grabbed the short horn on one side of its head, 'Come on dear, this way!'

The cow with a nonchalant flick of her head sent me flying into the snow face first. The cow wouldn't win, I had to do everything to help Liam. Struggling to my feet

I discarded my stick and staggered back towards the cow.

'You and I will fall out unless you do what you're told.' I moved past the head and leaned with all my might against the shoulder of the beast, keeping clear of the legs and hoofs. 'Move!'

The wind and snow blew in my face, coldness seeped through the anorak and fleece. Icy tingles crept into my fingers and toes. 'Move!' I screamed, as I pushed again.

With the third push and shout the animal turned. The cows coped with the snow even though I found it treacherous. The cow stopped after a few paces and I shouted against the wind and smacked it with the flat of my hand on the rear, it ambled forward. Elation rushed through me as the others followed.

72

'You were brilliant, Jessica.' Liam checked the door had been secured, he beamed at me. Extreme tiredness only allowed me a weak smile back. 'They are safely penned.'

The weather roared as another strong gust hit the house. The splintering of glass followed a thunderous noise. Liam peered through the kitchen window, 'I can't see the damage!'

The door from the hall flew open and a violent icy wind flowed into the kitchen. The cold blast hit me across my face. 'Come on!' Liam raced into the hall and up the stairs. Snow blew along the top landing and down the stairs.

'Oh, God.' I rushed up the stairs. The bedroom doors slammed back on their hinges in the gale. The hall table had overturned and paper, flowers and tissues swirled in the air. Liam shouted back to me, 'A window has gone!'

I didn't care about the window. What had happened to my collection? I reached the top landing. The hall window had blown in. The landing floor had glass and mangled wood strewn throughout its length.

'I must reach my collection!' I rushed into the room

near to the burst window. The drawings swirled in the air as I tried frantically to grab them, but some blew out the door on to the landing. I shouted and cried in despair as I tried to catch the papers. The strong arm of Liam grabbed me and dragged me from the room.

'My collection!' I screamed.

Liam pulled the door closed, 'Hold it closed, then nothing can blow away. Stand there and hold it!' He sprinted along the hall and down the stairs. The wind and the snow howled through the house. The bedroom doors flapped and slammed in the wind, I held tight to my studio door.

The icy blast had taken the feeling from my hands. I'd taken off my gloves when I'd come back into the house, so the full force of the wind bit into them. I struggled to hold on, my fingers numb and stiff with the cold. How much longer? I gritted my teeth and willed myself to continue. Liam appeared with a toolbox and several large tools.

He darted into the nearest bedroom and crowbarred off two of the wardrobe doors. He picked up one, and battling against the wind, put it down on the floor near the broken window and told me to stand on it. The second he placed half over the window, so it overlapped the wall.

'Leave that now. Come and hold this!' I hesitated, and he shouted, 'It's the best way!' The studio door flew back on its hinges.

I put the force of my body against the wardrobe door and tried to hold it in place against the wind and snow. As soon as I did that, Liam picked up the other door and placed it over the remaining gap. He forced it against the wall, and as he did so the gale in the hall disappeared.

'I can't hold it for long!' Liam held on with one hand and then by leaning against it, he hammered in the nails. He finished the first door and helped me to hold the second while he buried the nails in place. As the last one bedded in, I slumped down the wall onto the floor.

Liam grinned, 'That proved difficult.' I gave a short laugh, another typical understatement. Liam helped me up, and we went into the studio to survey the damage. While odd pieces would need to be done again, my collection had been unharmed. Relief swept over me and then I realised how cold I'd become.

73

The bedrooms had been devastated, and both the carpet and bedding were sodden and unusable, but the clothes in the main wardrobes had remained protected. Even the scale of the problem didn't daunt me. Alive and safe, the farm had remained intact and so were the animals. The wind sounded as though it had eased a little. A full list of the damage would wait until tomorrow as we needed to get warm.

The log fire in the front room flamed under the blast of air down the chimney.

'The room is dry and warm, so you'll be all right.'

'We'll be okay here, you're not travelling in this weather, we'll stay here, try to sleep and see what's happened at first light.' He went to protest. 'You're staying.'

'Thanks, I'm tired and cold.'

I threw him Justin's tracksuit. He hesitated. 'Now's not the time for modesty.'

Liam stoked up the fire and waited for the old tin kettle he'd placed on a fire trivet, to boil, and he made the tea. I struggled to stay awake but wanted a hot drink and to warm up. I spread Liam's clothes out close to the fire so they would dry by morning. Then we toasted bread and sat on the floor in front of the grate in our tracksuits. As I moved the blankets around, Liam pointed, 'You lay near the fire, I'll have the couch.'

'No, it's still too cold away from the fire, we'll share the blankets on the floor here.' As I lay, the scene of the blizzard came back to me, I'd never been so frightened in my life.

Now exhilaration ran through me as I'd been out there in a blizzard and helped secure the animals. Proudness pulsated through me and I had a satisfied smile plastered across my face. And to top it all my collection remained safe. As I relaxed, my other worries drifted away. The crackling of the log fire helped to drown out the howling storm.

I moved under the blankets to get warm, my eyes closed, and Liam move closer to my side, I didn't move away. My body relaxed, and he rolled on to his side facing me, I slid closer to him. Tiredness took second place. Despite all that had happened I'd become warm and content. Silence lingered. I moved a little closer.

He placed his hand gently on my stomach. The touch awakened my senses. Longing whispered through me. I pushed his damp hair away from his forehead and gently explored his face with my fingertips. I wanted more from him. Would he need some encouragement?

As our lips met, he groaned and pulled me closer. My body sizzled with expectation as the kiss deepened and desire radiated between us.

74

Wrapping a blanket around my naked body I moved to the fire, which still smouldered. Liam had gone and so had his clothes. I placed logs on the wide grate and waited for them to catch. The chimney made no noise, so the wind had calmed, and the morning sun gave a watery light across the snow.

The logs caught, crackled and roared, the sound which I'd liked so much last night. I'd been so cold and tired, but the tea, toast and roaring logs had revived me. Liam had been so brave and self-assured in such terrible conditions.

He had been a good lover, gentle and sensitive, I'd enjoyed the passion that had existed between us. Last night his taciturn face had been replaced with smiles as he'd sat by the fire. At last, I'd seen him relax. I liked the relaxed and passionate side of his character. Would it ever happen again? I hoped so. Perhaps I'd seen the true Liam.

I enjoyed the fire for a few minutes, but as I moved every muscle in my body hurt, although the exhilaration hadn't left me. I'd played my part in making the animals safe. Although I'd been so scared when Liam explained I had to go out to help him, I'd succeeded in something I never thought possible.

The thrill of what I'd achieved last night gave me the courage to open the doors and still wrapped in my blanket search for dry and warm clothes.

The house and farm buildings had been devastated, so I steeled myself for the destruction, but I had an inner determination to overcome the difficulties. The log fire kept the front room warm, but when I opened the door to the hall, then the icy damp blast hit me. I rushed up the sodden staircase and along the landing and picked my way amongst the debris that had blown around.

The temporary fixing of the wardrobe doors, across the blown-out window, had held during the rest of the night, preventing even more catastrophic damage.

My bedroom, the nearest to the blown window in the hall had been covered in driving snow. The carpets and bed were sopping wet. The big heavy wardrobes had substantial doors, and some of my clothes had survived unharmed except for being cold. I took jeans, tee-shirt and jumper and dressed in front of the fire downstairs. A full inspection of upstairs I would leave until later.

After putting the kettle to boil over the logs, I returned to the kitchen, and through the window could make out Liam and his brother working on the roof of the cattle barn. The cattle still pinned in the farmyard had been fed, so moved around contentedly. Jackie came across between the cows and into the kitchen.

'Hi, Mrs Southwick are you all right? Liam says you did a magnificent job last night with the cows,' she grinned and added, 'we'll make a farmer of you yet.'

I laughed, 'Have you eaten this morning?'

'No, we were up early to help Liam and so we've come straight over.'

'Is there three of you?'

'Yes.'

'I'll see what I can rustle up.'

'Liam mentioned you will need to contact the insurance people as soon as possible.'

'Food first, then insurance, and after that I'll take pictures of the damage, in case I need evidence, and then I'll start on the devastation inside.'

Normally I'd have given up at the thought of preparing breakfast for three hungry workers without the normal kitchen cooker. But my new feel-good factor from last night made me determined to solve the problem, so I rooted around in the utility room and found another fire trivet, which I placed over the end of the log fire.

Thank goodness it was such a huge old-fashioned fireplace. I picked up one of the cast iron frying pans from the kitchen and prepared one of the strangest breakfasts I'd ever cooked. The sausages, bacon, mushrooms and eggs were nearing the end of cooking, so I called Jackie and the men. A strange wave of nervousness swept over me as they entered the kitchen.

How would Liam react? It would be muted because of the others but I hoped to capture a hint of meaning from his face. 'Smells great, Mrs Southwick.' Liam's younger brother led them into the room. Liam came last. He's apprehensive and it shows in his face. He avoided eye contact, 'Come in Liam, help yourself to a good breakfast.'

The words made him look at me and I gave him a gentle smile which he returned. It would be all right, but to my surprise, I was nervous now I'd seen him again. A handsome man with hidden depths. A warm glow spread through me as I remembered the lovemaking. I had instigated it, but his response had been enthusiastic. What did he think of me? Had he enjoyed the passion as much as I had?

75

Gasping in amazement at the scene, I walked around the side of the barn. The hills and moors covered with thick snow, sparkled like tiny twinkling diamonds in the low sun, which shone brightly in a clear blue sky. The countryside replicated a Christmas card. In the foreground, the snow clung to the trees, and in the background, the blue-tinged snow drifts spread into the distance. One of the most beautiful landscapes I'd ever seen. Breathtaking. A winter wonderland.

The devastation of the farm saddened me. The cow barn door, blown to pieces, had been strewn over a wide area. Liam and his brother were repairing a gaping hole in the roof. Little remained of the tractor shed and the roof had finished in the ditch. The gales had weakened the whole structure enough that one wall had fallen. Fences had collapsed, gates torn from their posts, cables lay on the ground and debris whipped up by the storm littered everywhere. When I'd finished in the house, I would come out to help. Jackie would tell me what to do.

Today life had changed, I took a deep breath and pushed my way past the cows which would have been impossible before last night. They took no notice of me.

As I reached the edge of the herd, I recognised my cow from the storm, so I picked up a handful of hay, and fed it to a rough and grasping tongue. 'Thanks, old girl, you did me proud.'

After a quick visit to the village on the back of the tractor driven by Jackie to contact the insurance company, I prepared to tackle the mess in the house.

If the assessor didn't come immediately, I had evidence from the pictures I had taken. I surprised myself by taking the damage so calmly, and with a clipboard in hand, I made a list of what needed doing. I wouldn't be daunted, but I had no one to help. I would salvage clothes that remained dry and bring them downstairs. But first I lit the fire in the dining room as it would make a haven for drying clothes.

The answer machine light flashed as the batteries had continued to work. The message had been left yesterday afternoon and I assumed I hadn't heard the phone ring because of the noise of the storm. 'Hi, Jessica, this is Felix from FCI, it's about your designs. It's crucial you send them to us tomorrow otherwise they will miss out on the money needed for their development.'

My heart sank, I hadn't finished last night and now several pieces needed re-drawing because of the damage. And with the chaos in the house, posting them today had become impossible. Having coped with the damage, I was now deflated. I sat down and sobbed.

'Jessica?' Liam's strong but quiet voice penetrated my sobs as he approached. 'Has the shock overwhelmed you?'

'Oh, Liam.' I stood up and a nervous twinge swept through me at seeing him again, 'There is something that can't happen because of the storm, but I'm an over-emotional female about it.' I wiped my face. 'There I'm fine now.'

'There's nothing wrong with showing emotions, everyone does it differently.'

I waited for what he would say next, but a young girl's voice called out, 'Mrs Southwick.'

'Thanks, Liam, and I mean it, you have been magnificent!' Liam blushed as he left.

Liz led her two friends into the hall, 'We're not needed on our own farms and we've come to help you.'

'It's a terrible mess.' I led them upstairs and showed them the chaos.

'Oh, my God,' Sarah waved her arm around, 'so much is ruined.'

Liz gave her friend a poke, 'She wants to be in drama school. Don't say things like that, it will upset Mrs Southwick.'

'Thanks, Liz, but I'm all right and coping with it. Just!' Liz impressed me, as Paris would never have thought of someone else's feelings.

Amy stood deep in thought, Liz pointed at her, 'Amy is the bright one of us, she's had an idea.'

'The wardrobe doors over the broken window are only just about holding.'

'What do you suggest?'

'Providing you are happy with just a single sheet of glass then I will re-glaze it.' I stood in amazement.

'Do you know how to do it?'

'I'm always doing bits of glazing around the farm and outbuildings, it's not a heavy job, so I can do it with ease. Liam will have materials, or I'll get them from Liz's granddad.'

'That would be excellent, please.'

Amy continued, 'In that room, the wardrobes have come from flat packs, why don't we move them down to the dining room, rebuild them, and then we can hang up the clothes with ease.'

'That would be brilliant.' I decided not to question their capabilities. The four of us set to the tasks. Within an hour, the wardrobes were erected in the dining room.

My heart sank as I caught sight of The Jaggers Nissan 4x4 coming along the track. What did Michael want? After yesterday's scene with his wife and David, I had sympathy for him, but would have preferred not to speak with him. I won't know what to say. As I opened the door my chin dropped and my mouth flew open, 'Cate, what are you doing here?'

'Can I come in?' Lost for words I stepped back. Cate held up her hand, 'Don't say a word! I will not talk about it. Not a word. Your farm has been badly hit, including the farmhouse, so I've come to help. Shall I stay or go? The choice is yours, but my lips are sealed about yesterday.' Cate stood in the doorway. 'Stay or go!'

I had no hold on David as we were only friends and not lovers, so I made a snap decision, 'Stay.'

'What do you want me to do? I'll help, but I'm useless at anything practical.' Her work clothes consisted of jeans and a rugby shirt, covered by a body warmer. They were immaculate and had been recently ironed. An idea struck me, and hope returned. I called for the three girls to come into the kitchen and we sat at the table along with Cate. 'What's up?' Liz gazed questioningly, 'Do you want us to do something different?'

'I want to gauge your reaction and for you to decide.' They appeared confused. 'I used to be a designer in a leading fashion house in London.'

Liz's eyes opened wide, 'Wow!'

'I have been commissioned to design a new collection, but I have a problem.'

'What is it?'

'I've a few hours more work before I complete my designs, but I must post them off today.'

Cate snapped her fingers, 'That's an easy decision, you do your designs and the four of us will clear up the house.'

76

The fate of the Rustic Realism Collection would be decided at the meeting today. I took a deep breath as the tube train pulled away from Euston Square station. Would FCI like the collection? I'd done my best, but would it be appreciated?

Whenever I returned to the capital, I thought of friends old and new. I'd reflected long and hard about whether to ring Miles, but in the end, decided not to contact him. A tinge of ungratefulness formed because he'd helped me, but after our last furious row, the wound between us had become too big to heal.

Leaving Barbican station, I had a spring in my step as I walked the short distance to the FCI building. My confidence had returned, it would be a good day.

A meeting with about a dozen people had already started. My security escort shepherded me in. Felix, the chair of the meeting indicated a vacant chair, but as some-one had asked a question, he continued with the meeting.

Another five minutes passed before he pointed to-wards the screen, 'Let's move on to the last item on the agenda, it is the review of the Rustic Realism Collection by Jessica who has joined us.' The butterflies would ease when I started my presentation. FCI already had my slides. 'Can you introduce yourselves for Jessica's benefit.'

The boredom of the routine showed through as the introductions around the table were completed at lightning speed. I didn't remember a single name. 'Do you want me to present my portfolio?'

'No, thanks, I circulated it two days ago. Everyone will have seen it. Presentations are too time-consuming.' I had no alternative but to wait. Felix flicked at the laptop in front of him, 'I've jotted down points from your slides that we need to discuss.'

A long list appeared on a screen above his head. The points were a mixture of design issues, business matters and several I didn't understand. 'Jessica, let me begin with the first question.'

I'd been worn to a frazzle over the past hour and performed poorly. The intense high-level questions left no stone unturned. If I'd tried to gloss over anything, they spotted it and wouldn't let it go. Many times, I didn't know the answer.

'What do we recommend ladies and gentlemen? I see there are three possibilities. First, accept it in its entirety and make a collection from it.' Many shook their heads so it wouldn't be a full-scale collection. Felix continued, 'Scale it back considerably and put it in one of our various designer's themes.' Only two nodded. 'Take a few pieces to add to our general range and ask Jessica to think about it for another year.'

'Sorry, Jessica,' one woman at the far end of the table spoke, 'but I don't think it's creative or original, I would recommend reject.' She gave a small shake of her head. No one disagreed. Felix appeared unmoved.

For him, one of many decisions he had to make on a regular basis, 'One last point, Camilla referred it to us, so someone needs to report back.' Silence fell. Felix then added with a laugh, 'No volunteers I see. Rotten lot! I'll brief her after this meeting.'

I sat in utter dejection. No one took any notice of me. A hand touched my shoulder. At last, someone to talk to me about my work, 'As you met Camilla before you'd better come along too.' Felix checked his schedule. 'We have an appointment with her at two o'clock. I'll see you then. Can you find your own way out?'

It had been a terrible meeting, I wandered around the City of London in a daze. In an hour, I had to meet a ferocious woman whose company had rejected my designs. Also, I'd severed contact with Miles, Camilla's nephew. It wouldn't be good. Should I pull out? I shook my head as I didn't have the courage.

My phone vibrated with a text message, 'What hotel are you in? Cate.' Why did Cate want to know? After the storm, she'd been superb in sorting out my wardrobe and ironing my clothes. I didn't want to see Cate in London. In a more confident mood, I would have tackled her. But with my confidence in a fragile state after the meeting, I opted for the easy answer. Same as last time. A return message popped up. See you tonight. I will tell you everything!

Too early for the pointless meeting with Camilla, I dumped myself on a bench outside the FCI building. Lost in my own world I took no notice of the person who dropped onto the seat next to me.

'Fancy meeting you at FCI Headquarters, I wonder what you are up to.'

I tensed as I recognised the voice, 'I haven't got anything to say to you Caroline unless you want to patch up the past, then I'd be willing to talk to you.'

The smirk returned, 'I tried to talk to you in those days and you didn't want to listen. Why would I wish to chat with a has-been designer who used treachery and betrayal?'

I stood up and strode towards the FCI building with Caroline walking alongside, 'I'm attending a press briefing by Camilla this afternoon. I'll find out why you're here, then I feel another article coming on.' She quickened her pace and flew through the door, showed her press pass and disappeared down a corridor. Would Caroline get her way? Camilla never showed sympathy to the press but with the rejection of my designs, her company had no reason to support me.

77

Close to two o'clock Felix and I entered Camilla's luxury office with its thick carpet, highly polished desk and leather chairs. A man who I hadn't seen before sat next to Camilla. 'Sit down,' she nodded but with no recognition.

Felix opened his briefcase, 'I've put this meeting...'

'Stop waffling. What have you come to tell me? Adrian and I are trying to finish a report.'

'You referred the Rustic Realism Collection by Jessica to the design group, but they have rejected it.' He pushed a copy of the portfolio to Camilla who ignored it.

Camilla peered as though seeing me for the first time, 'I remember. Was the meeting unanimous?'

Adrian leaned across the desk and without making any comment to Camilla or Felix he picked up the portfolio and flicked through the papers.

Felix nodded, 'Yes, unanimous to reject the designs.'

Camilla switched her gaze, 'Is that true?'

'Yes.' My eyes were downcast.

'You asked for a chance. In the end, it didn't meet the criteria we require in this company.'

'What is this?' Adrian asked.

'Adrian, try to keep up,' snapped Camilla, 'A commissioned collection that has been rejected by the design department.' Adrian flicked through more pages. Camilla regarded him quizzically, 'Are you interested?'

'Give me a minute.'

'Oh, very well,' Camilla started typing on her laptop.

I whispered to Felix, 'Who's that?'

'Adrian Greenside, he's the director in charge of budget clothes.'

My heart sank. Camilla gave him two minutes. 'What do you think?'

'Yes, it's worth a go,'

'Who for?' Camilla stopped typing and showed a greater interest.

'Batemans, the supermarket chain. If we can remove several obstacles, it's worth a punt.'

'Why them?'

'I had dinner with the Purchasing Director yesterday in Paris, he wants to brand his own practical style of clothing.' My name wouldn't be on the cheap supermarket clothing, I fought back the tears.

'You've rejected everything design have offered you, what's different about this?'

'It's nothing like the creative stuff with floating chiffon that the design department produce, which is useless for a practical world. Are you, Jesse James?'

'Yes.' But I lacked enthusiasm for budget clothes and supermarkets.

'Bloody stupid name, use your real one, I suppose you thought up the title?'

'Rustic Realism.'

'That will have to go.' I'd been so excited and had worked hard on the designs. Why were these people so rude? I tried to convince myself that budget clothes would be better than nothing, but it didn't work.

Camilla picked up the portfolio, flicked through it, 'Good idea, Adrian, what are the obstacles.'

'As a company, we have no green credentials and no community support programmes.'

Camilla frowned, 'Tricky.'

'Bateman's prefer integrated working with their suppliers and would want a thorough input to the final designs. Also, they insist their suppliers work with them within reach of their head office in Manchester.'

'We've no office or any design shops in the north of England,' Camilla flapped her hand at him in dismissal, 'anything else?'

For me, the list of obstacles seemed endless. 'We need to make samples but can't afford to pay a lot. Felix's team cost a fortune, which is fine for the catwalks of Paris and Milan, but I'm talking cheap Manchester.'

Camilla turned to me, 'Any ideas?'

I shook my head, which irritated Camilla and Adrian. 'So, the final decision is no, your designs are rejected.'

They were unfriendly, patronising and rude. I'd spent all day at FCI being ignored or insulted. Adrian pushed the folder back across the table, 'Okay, we'll bin it, pity there wasn't more business thought.'

Adrian's comment tipped me over the edge. I sprang to my feet, 'You are so patronising and unfriendly! You asked me to do a clothes design, not re-design your bloody business for you. It's not my job to sort out your green and community policies. If you'd even hinted at that, I wouldn't have wasted weeks on trying my best. It might not be good enough but...' Tears flowed, but I hadn't finished. I carried on despite Camilla holding up her hand, 'If you wanted green ideas why talk to me? What's wrong with your own bloody nephew? I've travelled from Staffordshire and...'

Camilla's bright eyes stared intently, I hesitated. She

reached into her bag, 'Here's a tissue. We've put you under pressure today.' At least she'll finish with an apology. 'Miles introduced you, didn't he?'

'Yes,' I calmed as I hadn't helped myself.

'I remember now. Didn't Miles say you lived on a farm in the middle of nowhere?'

'Yes, the nearest village is Mossmoor.'

'Is it thriving?'

'No, it's a declining sheep farming village.'

The faintest of smiles passed between Camilla and Adrian. 'There are green issues,' Adrian reminded them.

Camilla focused, 'Can you contact Miles? I want proposals for making FCI a green and eco-friendly company? I see a way forward, Jessica, I want you here tomorrow morning at eight-thirty.' Words failed me, I stood and gaped. 'Adrian, can you do a plan?' He nodded. 'Let's close it there.' Within minutes I stood outside the FCI building not knowing what to think.

If Camilla and Adrian were supporting my ideas, then they could become a reality, even if I didn't like either of them. Should I do what Camilla had asked? Miles? Contacting him will be difficult. But I had hope for my designs, although they wouldn't carry my name and would be cheap supermarket clothes.

With a struggle I attempted to remain positive. I would have to swallow my pride and ring him. Leaving a message on his voicemail I attempted to sound bright and breezy, 'Hi, Miles, it's Jessica. Don't hang up, I need help and there might be business, and I mean serious business, for you. Explain all when you ring, I'm in London in the same hotel as before. Call me as soon as possible, it's urgent. Bye.'

78

Not wanting to become involved with Cate, I decided to have a quick drink, and then wait for a call from Miles to pass on the business opportunity. The initial optimism about Camilla and Adrian had dwindled as they would find a reason it wouldn't work. With luck, I would be back home by tomorrow afternoon.

Mixed emotions swept over me as Miles stood in the doorway, I'd expected a phone call. A handsome man, immaculate in a business suit, white shirt and sober tie, smiled at all the nearby females as he entered the lounge. How would he react?

Miles kissed me on the cheek. 'Jessica, you are exquisite.' He hung his head, 'I'm sorry about the scene at the farm. Will you forgive me? Selling is your choice not mine.' Holding my hands, he gazed with a wonderful glint in his eye.

I weakened on the spot, 'It's forgotten,' and I didn't know why but added, 'I'm sorry I haven't been in touch.' Kissing me on the cheek again, he suggested we sat down, then he ordered drinks from a waiter.

'I need...'

'Can we wait for Robert?' I closed my eyes. Robert

and Cate again. Oh no! Miles oblivious to my reaction stood to welcome his boss, who greeted me like a long-lost friend. I contrasted Robert's approach with the cold business attitude of Camilla and Adrian. I had rejected his proposal to buy the farm, but he greeted me in a friendly and charming manner.

A movement by the door caught the men's attention. Cate appeared and sashayed across the room towards us looking every inch a model in her classy clothes. No matter what I thought of her morals, with stunning grace she strutted with poise and confidence, across the bar. 'Darling, so wonderful to see you,' she threw her arms around Robert and kissed him on the lips. As they parted, he stroked her hair and caught hold of her hand. Robert's smile widened as his eyes met Cate's.

I sat with my mouth wide open and didn't manage to utter a single word. Cate in a smooth movement took a tissue from her bag, bent down to me and grinned, 'Lipstick smudge.' Placing her finger under my chin she closed my mouth. Then she rubbed away the imaginary lipstick mark and whispered, 'Tell all tomorrow, we're an item.'

How would I cope with the evening? As Cate moved away, I picked up my glass, and took long slow sips to regain my composure.

Cate refused a drink, 'Shall we go Robert?'

'Yes, I'm sure Miles can cope with the business.'

'Yes, have a good time.' They made a striking couple as they walked arm in arm towards the exit.

I held up my hand, 'Don't say a word, let's talk business.'

79

The reception held no nerves for me as I'd convinced myself Adrian's ideas would fall through. Miles strolled across the entrance atrium, we'd had a good evening together, with him at his most witty. He made no hint or suggestions about a relationship and we kept the whole evening on a business footing. I liked Miles and a fling with him would be great fun, but is it a reaction to my single status?

As we waited, 'There will be Adrian and Camilla, you and me.'

'There will be more.'

'How do you know?'

'About eleven o'clock last night I had an email conversation with Robert and Camilla. Adrian has a plan. All the relevant people will be there, they started at seven-thirty but don't want us until eight-thirty.' He caught my hand, 'Jessica, do you realise how important this is?'

I shook my head as I thought gloomily about cheap supermarket clothing. It would be a hard tag to shake off and my name would not appear. 'Camilla has gone over my head to Robert, don't you see?'

'No, half the time I don't understand what they are

talking about.'

'Camilla wants the Batemans Supermarkets' business. It will be huge.' The word huge made me think about the scale of supermarket clothes. 'But to win the business FCI must show it's a green, eco-friendly company and that's where Robert and I come in.'

'Okay, I understand that you will help FCI to become eco-friendly.'

'FCI need to prove they support local communities, and they will need to set up a design centre not far from Manchester.' Although I understood his words, I didn't understand why he bubbled with enthusiasm at the proposals. 'I don't know for certain, but do you want my guess?'

'Yes,' as I realised he was still holding my hand.

'For the design centre, they will go for Mossmoor as it is within easy reach of Manchester.'

'Oh, they didn't say that.'

Miles smiled, 'They probably hinted, but you missed it.'

My phone rang. 'Hello, David.'

'What the hell do you think you are doing?'

'David, I have no idea what you are talking about?'

'How can you let the village down after their unqualified support?'

'Do what David? I don't understand.'

'Where are you now?'

'In London...'

'That proves it then.'

'For goodness' sake proves what?'

'The regional news on television this morning announced you are in London to sign a pre-contract agreement on the sale of your farm to a wind turbine company.' Then the line went dead.

The silent phone hung limply in my hand, and I

stared at it, expecting it to give me answers to the questions that circled in my mind. I hadn't signed anything.

80

As I entered the meeting room, déjà vu swept over me. A dozen people had crammed into the room with computers, papers and wall charts everywhere. Camilla waved a hand in our direction, 'There is no time for introductions, Jessica.'

The only other woman apart from Camilla, shuffled her chair to make space, 'Pull up that chair, you can squeeze in here next to me.' She made nearby men move, 'You look terrified.'

'I am,' but I appreciated a friendly face.

Miles spoke above the gentle hubbub, 'The regional news have a leak on the wind turbines and they think Jessica is in London to sign.'

To my amazement, no one appeared bothered. Camilla snapped her fingers, 'Can you deal with that Robert? We must keep Jessica out of it.' Everyone else appeared to know what was happening. I hadn't a clue. I sat and listened as though in a whirling fog.

'Jessica used a publicist when the press invaded Mossmoor.'

'Contact the same one. Can you get on with it, Miles?' He nodded and left the room.

Camilla's eyes checked around the room, 'I will take Jessica through what we've decided. Anyone else can join in. Then if Jessica agrees, we go for it.'

After about five minutes of explaining she summarised, 'So we would base the design centre in the village using local labour, which we would train ourselves.' I immediately thought of three young women who would make ideal trainees.

'Is there a community project to support?'

'They've wanted to build a village hall for years but never have enough money.'

'Perfect, we'll do it for them,' Camilla's eyes lit up, 'Miles and Robert will investigate the green issues in your village. 'What do you think?'

I tried to sound strong. 'And there are no wind turbines.'

'Definitely not.' I had listened carefully but didn't understand many aspects, but those that I did I thought were brilliant. 'So, Jessica do you agree with what we've proposed?' asked Camilla.

'Yes, I agree,' My voice wavered with tension hoping I'd made the right decision for both me and the village.

'Will you go personally, Robert?'

'No,' he continued to collect the papers from the table and put them in a folder, 'I might have domestic problems in visiting Mossmoor, I'll send Miles.'

'OK, it's crucial you go, Deryn.' She nodded at the woman seated next to me.

'Yes, I'll rearrange and go this afternoon.'

Camilla sat back in her chair with a satisfied smile, 'Let's close it there and make a success of it everyone.'

81

At midday I waited nervously at a wine bar in St Pancras station, 'Darling', a voice came from behind. Cate had been insistent about having lunch together. With a radiant smile she hugged me and brushed both of my cheeks. 'Isn't Robert a darling?

She hadn't allowed me anytime to hedge around my reservations, as she settled on the next bar stool, and took a glass of wine from the waiter.

As always, her immaculate appearance coupled with confidence and poise were to be admired. Without hesitation Cate chattered, 'We had such a delightful few days in Paris and only arrived back yesterday.'

Not wanting to know the details, I tried to interrupt the flow, 'Cate?'

'Darling, forgive me. We're here to talk about you.'

'Are we?'

'I'm sorry about David as I know you're sweet on him, and he likes you.' She glanced at a group of businessmen settling themselves at a nearby table, 'It's my fault that I've buggered it up between you, please forgive me.'

'Cate, you are not making any sense.' I concentrated

on making my voice stern as I found Cate's full flowing manner irritating. Although she bubbled with excitement, she reduced the level of her voice, 'David and I go back a long way.'

For some reason I didn't want to hear the details, I sipped my wine and studied her animated face. 'We were childhood sweethearts and nearly married. David backed out a couple of times and I met Michael, but that was twenty years ago.'

I had no idea about the background between them, but she didn't give me a chance to respond. Now that she'd started talking, she wouldn't stop. 'When David married. The four of us were often together. Then tragedy struck, David's wife died.' I would not interrupt as the tension on her face had become obvious, her smile had disappeared, and her eyes glazed. 'In the same week she died in the accident, I found out Michael had been having an affair.'

I didn't know how to react to the information from Cate.

'Michael and I split for a while, and during that time David and I were thrown together, and we became lovers.'

I shuffled around on the bar stool, 'I'm not sure why you are telling me this?'

'Please hear me out,' Cate twirled her hair around her finger, 'please, it's important.' Tears welled up in her eyes. I nodded. 'David and I drifted apart as I tried to get my marriage back together. Then Michael did it again. Michael and I have stayed together for the sake of the business. Corny and pathetic, isn't it? But we haven't slept together for years.' I had information overload but still had no idea why Cate had related the details.

'David and I have remained friends and occasionally have finished up in bed together. On the afternoon you found us together I didn't go to Ashbourne. As it was the anniversary of when we first met, he invited me over for lunch. That's when I told him I intended leaving Michael and relocating to live in London. I'd met another man, which I hoped would be a success, and that we were going away together the next day.'

Sitting forward on my stool I attempted to interrupt her as I didn't want to hear any more. But Cate would not be stopped, 'You haven't given David any encouragement although he likes you.'

Cate's words were direct and hit home, she took a large sip of her wine and then took a deep breath, 'And now the bit I'm ashamed about. When I met David for lunch to celebrate the anniversary, it was also to say goodbye. We'd been friends and lovers over the years, and I would never see him again...' Her voice trailed off and I remained silent.

Cate downed the remains of her wine in one swift gulp, 'I can tell by your expression what you think of me.' Cate had tears in her eyes, 'You think that I'm a whore who will jump into bed with any man. I'm not, but you won't believe me.' She suddenly stood up, 'Goodbye, Jessica, it was important to explain the circumstances. David's a good man, give him another chance, please.'

As I strolled along the Euston Road, Cate's words replayed in my mind, but uncertainty floated to the forefront. Because I liked David, I wanted to believe her. But Miles had been charming, and I'd forgotten how much I liked him. But my mind kept drifting back to Liam.

I reprimanded myself, he's several years younger than me. Having a lover that young didn't seem feasible. The night by the fire flashed into my mind, he'd been a passionate lover, but I pushed it away as I had instigated it. Being too young ruled out both Miles and Liam.

82

I wanted to have the train journey alone, but it wouldn't happen. Deryn, who had sat next to me in the meeting, had already texted explaining she would be on the same train and suggested travelling together. She had been the one welcoming face at FCI. However, Deryn's job remained a mystery.

Why had Camilla been so adamant that she travelled to Mossmoor immediately? Deryn insisted on travelling in First Class and paid the excess on my ticket. As we settled on the train, I had the first chance to study her.

Deryn arrived wrapped up in a thick coat with a scarf around her head and wore large designer sunglasses against the bright winter sun. She removed her coat, scarf and sunglasses to reveal a blue business suit with a knee-length skirt. Her figure and beauty suggested a model in the fashion industry.

The men's eyes in the carriage focused on her. Then she loosened the wooden pin and let the jet-black hair cascade down her back. Flicking at it she became satisfied with her appearance and settled herself on the seat. Even I had to admit that Deryn had the 'wow' factor.

'Thanks for letting me travel up with you, I will need

your help to complete my job.'

'What do you do?'

'FCI is so bad at introducing people, I thought Camilla might have explained.' I shook my head. 'I'm the Facilities Director responsible for the buildings and those exciting things like drains.' She smiled and gave a little giggle. 'Aren't you surprised?'

'No, there are some young lasses on the local farms who are immensely practical, and they put me to shame, so now I don't question people's ability.'

'That's excellent news, I want to meet them.' The refreshment trolley arrived, and our conversation lapsed while we organised coffee and biscuits. Once we were settled, my curiosity prompted me once again.

'What will you do in Mossmoor?'

'I will change Mossmoor into an eco-friendly FCI design centre which has first-rate community facilities.'

'The whole village?' My eyes widened in amazement.

'Yes,' she smiled with confidence, 'and the villagers will love it.'

'How do I say something diplomatic without offending you?'

'Go ahead, I've got a thick skin, don't forget I work with Camilla.'

I laughed, 'London thinking differs greatly from a small remote village and I'm not so sure they'll like your ideas. Especially as you come from the big city.'

Deryn laughed at my concerns and nibbled on a biscuit, 'Have you ever been to Llangollen?'

'Yes, it's in the Welsh Mountains.'

'I'm one of five girls, and my father is a sheep farmer on the edge of the nearby hills.'

83

I surveyed my farmhouse with pride. With my chin raised and a satisfied smile, I pushed my shoulders back as I strolled through the house, revelling in the transformation. Within ten days of the storm, the redecoration of the rooms had been completed and I'd chosen the styles and colours with care.

I'd been able to select the décor which suited me, and had made the house warmer and more welcoming, with a wide range of stunning colours. Even the kitchen had been finished, and although modern, it suited the farmhouse with its cheery bright red décor, and of course the Aga still had pride of place.

The windows had been replaced in the original style but were double glazed and draughtproof.

Deryn had accepted an invitation to stay at the farm. On the journey from London, I learned a lot about her, especially her aptitude at dealing with people.

The low spot had been when we stopped at The Jaggers. Deryn had wanted an early feel of the village. I hadn't known whether it would be open, but it had been business as usual and there had been no mention of Cate. It had been the first time since finding David and Cate together that I'd met Michael, who carried on as though the incident had never happened. Several locals nodded, but didn't speak, and had not been as welcoming as usual. They had turned their backs and their eyes avoided me. Even Deryn noted the frosty attitude.

A couple of people had made comments about me letting down the village by wanting to make quick money out of wind turbines. When I had denied it, the regulars remained silent and found someone else to talk to. It had been obvious they didn't believe me. Perhaps this morning's news might make a difference, as it would include a weak apology about the wind turbine project, which had been withdrawn.

Big companies like FCI and the one for which Robert and Miles worked were coming to a small village. Success appeared a slim possibility, but I would give Deryn a chance. We had sipped our wine in the corner of The Jaggers' bar and ignored the frosty glances from many of the villagers. After a couple of glasses, we had giggled like teenagers. The evening left me feeling regenerated and hopeful.

Deryn sauntered into the kitchen for her breakfast. Slim and elegant even though she wore black work clothes, her trousers with multiple pockets were not just for show. A tee-shirt and fleece completed her practical outfit, and she held a black padded jacket for outdoors. The only contrast to the black were the cream steel toe-capped boots. Her long hair was tied in a bunch and hung down her back. 'It will be a good day,' her eyes were bright and full of enthusiasm, but I wasn't sure.

Liam arrived and his eyes zoomed in on Deryn. No doubt throughout the day Deryn would put on her best charm offensive. 'Good morning,' and with a little girlish giggle, she added, 'I'm guessing you are Liam.'

Liam's eyes flashed in my direction, but Deryn moved

into his line of sight, 'You have hay caught in your hair.'

Liam a little embarrassed swiped at it, 'Here let me,' and Deryn extracted two small pieces of hay from his wind tousled hair.

'Will you stay for some toast?' I twisted a loose curl on my neck and heat rose in my cheeks. Nervousness gripped me when I met Liam.

'Thanks, Jessica, I will.'

'Liam if you have time this morning can you show me the farm and its buildings. Deryn grinned. 'Don't be worried, I'll explain what I'm doing as I go around the farm with you.' She munched her toast. 'Jessica, will you come?'

'Liam knows more about the farm than I do.' He sat at the table concentrating his gaze on anything except me. 'I'll leave you in his accomplished hands.'

Deryn shook hands with Jackie as she arrived, 'I've heard about you, I believe you are a capable young woman.' Jackie beamed as she wasn't used to compliments. After finishing their toast Liam and Jackie took Deryn on a tour of the farm.

The postman arrived with a parcel for me, which contained several documents and a note from Adrian, 'I've been through your design for Bateman Supermarkets and given the main buyer a quick preview. There are a lot of comments. Give them a read through and ring me later today, Adrian. PS Good to have you on board, I like your work.'

The postscript took me by surprise, I hadn't liked Adrian when I'd met him, he'd been bullish and rude. Did he have a different side? At least his note made me happier.

I put my parcel to one side at the unmistakable sound of a tractor arriving. George clambered down and made his way towards the house. I greeted him with a cheery good morning and settled him in the chair next to the Aga.

There was no chuckle from him as I handed him a strong cup of tea with plenty of sugar, 'Come on George, why aren't you happy? Is it something I've done?'

'It's this talk of wind turbines. If they've been scrapped, why do you have a woman from London with you, who's interested in the village.'

As he finished talking, so the door opened and Deryn appeared. 'This is George from the neighbouring farm, he is concerned about what you're doing here.'

'Please don't stand, Mr...'.

As George struggled to stand. 'Everyone calls me George, young and old alike.'

She shook his hand, 'You remind me of my father. His name is Sior, it's Welsh for George and has its origins in the word, 'farmer', but I expect you know that.'

'Is your father a farmer?'

'Just like you George, a sheep farmer, and like you, has poor knees from decades of hard work, I'm the youngest of five daughters.'

'Do you know much about farming? All the lasses around here do.'

'Oh, yes, I was excited for my parents the other day when we picked up that new EU grant for yearlings.'

'I haven't seen that.'

'Shall I come over to your farm and explain, then I can meet your family, especially Liz, who is highly praised by Jessica. Also, I'll tell you what I'm doing here and put your mind at rest.'

'I've got the tractor,' George pointed to the yard, accepting the invitation. 'That's fine, I'll stand on the back, I've been doing that since I was a little girl.'

As they left, a doubt about Deryn crept into my mind. Is she too good to be true?

84

As the tractor chugged along the track which led up to George's farm, a Range Rover swung off the lane and bounced along. Another visitor, I recognised the distinctive maroon colour. Why had David come?

Fear and dread mixed with a frisson of excitement. What would I say? Cate had encouraged another chance. Since I'd walked in on David and Cate, the only contact had been when he had rung to shout about the wind turbines. Standing in the farmyard I waited as the Range Rover pulled in, but he didn't rush to get out and I guessed he needed to compose himself.

'Hello, David.' He stood next to his car as though reluctant to move closer, and opened his mouth to speak, but stopped, as though he struggled for words. His low voice had a noticeable quiver, 'May I apologise.'

The lines etched on his face deepened as his jaw tightened. A proud man, a local pillar of the rural society and well respected for his knowledge, behaviour and his capabilities.

The relationship with Cate was none of my business and he was entitled to jump into bed with any woman he chose. A stalwart of village life, why had he jumped to incorrect conclusions? Why hadn't he found out the facts before shouting accusations?

'David, I don't feel there's a need for an apology, although it's good of you to visit, come in.'

We sat in the front room, but I decided that the sombre atmosphere had to be lifted.

'Your appearance has improved as you have some colour in your face and no longer need your walking stick for support. Have you recovered?'

'Yes, thank you,' he hesitated again, 'How's Paris?'

'Coping and in reasonable spirits considering she must have someone with her twenty-four hours a day. Also, there must be someone listening when she calls, but the school is better than staying in a detention centre. I hope the experience has scared her enough. As someone observed the other day, she is willful, and I can't disagree.'

'I like Paris, she's lively and full of enthusiasm, so I'm confident she will stay on the straight and narrow.' An uneasy pause lengthened between us, so I attempted to make my voice sound cheerful.

'You seemed to get on well with Miles when you were in Germany?'

'Yes, a good man, I liked him.'

'As he's coming to stay today, and should be here by this afternoon, why not come to dinner and meet him again.'

David weighed up the invitation, 'Yes, thank you, I would like that.'

'I've someone else staying, she's from the fashion company who have accepted my work.' A slight rise in his eyebrows followed my announcement, but he didn't speak. 'Deryn will be at dinner tonight, and she'll explain her reason for being in the village, because half of it is beyond me.' As he appeared skeptical, 'Hear her out first before you jump to conclusions, she believes her work will be superb for Mossmoor and the people. Please listen to her.'

'Yes okay, I will listen without prejudice.'

'Everything has returned to normal after the storm.' He didn't appear to be listening and had a blank expression in his eyes. He won't let this conversation end without saying something.

'Jessica, I need...'

I cut him short, 'David, let me stop this before it starts. That you had sex with Cate is none of my business. Beyond the obvious total embarrassment of being caught as you were, the matter is a private affair. We both know you have a temper which rises to the surface at times. The first time we met, when you were cross because I fed Angela chocolate cake, and then the other morning on the phone. Your call resulted from you being misinformed, you should have asked me for an explanation first, but your temper got the better of you and you sounded off. But I had done nothing wrong. I don't wish to discuss either of the incidents ever again.'

'Thank you, Jessica, you are a special woman, and your positive attitude is a real tribute to you.' His words jolted me, as he didn't give compliments easily.

'Come on, David, let's get on with the day, I've work to do, and I'll see you at eight o'clock for dinner.'

I returned to my studio and settled into the large armchair I'd placed in the corner of the room. Light streamed in through the windows and the distant moors with varying shades of greens, browns and shadows held my attention.

85

I brought my mind back to focus and settled to work on Adrian's comments; he knew a great deal about fashion and his notes were helpful.

To my surprise, the call went straight through, 'Hello, Jessica, I'm pleased you rang.' The cheerfulness in his voice made my mouth drop open, 'We treated you badly the other day. We will get along fine if you accept my apologies for my abruptness.'

'Yes, of course. I'm still concerned about why Bateman Supermarkets would want the designs.'

'Yes, I can understand, but they are keen and have already signed documents to show they are committed, so it's full steam ahead, you will be famous.'

'Hang on, Adrian, you were adamant they wanted to re-badge the designs as their own clothes.'

'No, I was wrong, they not only want your name on it, but they have asked for a picture of the designer, so I sent them one.'

'And?'

'They loved the photograph and it will be at the top of their displays in every one of their supermarkets. Within months your face will be known throughout the country.'

I shook when the call ended. Everything had moved so quickly.

86

'Is the room okay?'

Miles put down a suitcase and stared around absent-mindedly, 'Yes, thank you.' Then he grabbed my hand, 'Jessica, we've had a rather up and down time since we met. Although you have many male admirers, might I be allowed to know you better. Nothing heavy, you call the tune. Please have a think about a few evenings out.' Giving a wonderful smile he set about unpacking.

Deryn with the three girls, Liz, Sarah and Amy sat at the large kitchen table drinking coffee. 'Look who I've found. Aren't they wonderful? They have been telling me about their dressmaking and Amy about re-glazing the window. They are talented, capable young women.' Enthusiasm shone from their faces. A tear filled my eye as the contrast to Paris had become so evident.

'Yes, they are super. Sarah, I believe you have another talent.' She blushed.

Deryn put her head on one side, 'What is it?'

'I like cooking,' she glanced down at the table as a slight flush rose to her cheeks.

'Would you be prepared to cook dinner tonight?'

'Yes.'

'That's settled then,' I rubbed my hands together with enthusiasm. 'Let's go through the menu later. There's someone else I want to invite for dinner.'

Liam drilled into the rough stone walls of the main store to put up new shelves. The one small grubby window only let in a little light. Dust and cobwebs covered the single light bulb. I waited for the deafening noise of the drill to stop.

'Liam,' he turned around and smiled.

But he took me by surprise, 'I want to talk with you if I may.'

'Yes, of course.' I closed the door and sat on a bag of potatoes. Liam dropped on to an old crate and studied his feet. His rough workman's hands were tense with white knuckles which rested on his knees.

'I know I'm younger than you...'

I smiled and interrupted, 'Let's not talk about ages.'

'I would like to take you out, perhaps to a pub in a nearby village, but it's difficult because you're my boss.' I hadn't expected him to be so direct.

'Before I answer, can I ask you a question?' He nodded then shuffled around on the crate and studied his hands. 'Are you asking me out because you feel guilty about having sex with me?'

He blushed. 'No, I've wanted to ask since the first day I arrived on the farm but haven't had the courage.'

'An evening out together sounds a great idea. But it might have to wait a few days because I've guests staying.'

'I don't mind,' a shy smile spread across his face.

'Will you come to dinner tonight and bring Jackie with you?'

He rubbed his hands together, 'I'm not great...'

I cut him short, 'Liam Drinkwater you are an intelligent and bright man, who can come to an informal dinner party. As can Jackie. Please, I would like you to come.' He hesitated. 'The evening is not formal, and I will not be dressing up. Miles and Deryn will be sensational in whatever they wear, but I will wear jeans and a tee-shirt. It is not a fashion parade. Please say you will come.'

'Yes, we will come.'

87

I spent the rest of the day preparing for the evening. As I changed, the conversation with Liam came to mind so I put on a pair of jeans with a plain white tee shirt. With a flourish I selected a colourful scarf, one of my own designs, to finish off my outfit.

I would be quiet and observant at dinner as Deryn would be the centre of attention. It will be interesting to have David, Miles and Liam together.

My mind wandered over the three, but they were so different. David had confidence, almost the country gent. Miles bubbled with enthusiasm and enjoyed the fun. Liam is quiet and shy but with hidden depths, and a passionate man once you break through the reserved exterior.

A small flush passed across my face as I remembered the intimate scene by the crackling fire. Did I want another man? I didn't know the answer.

88

The grandfather clock struck one. 'Come on Deryn, let's finish the wine.'

'I shall regret it in the morning, but top me up, please.' We lazed by the fire in the front room. I'd never known a week like it. The requests arrived in a torrent, and I struggled to keep up, but I had received a great deal of encouragement and help from Adrian. My confidence with the designs had grown and reminded me of the old days before my marriage, but much busier.

Deryn had been working throughout the village during the week and had submitted a plan to Camilla for her approval. Tonight's dinner had been a celebration for the completion of the planning stage.

That first evening around the dinner table, she had explained the project and organised them to complete a variety of tasks around the village, which involved measuring and taking photographs. The group also talked to local people who had been curious. After the separate tasks, she would bring them altogether in a meeting and then they moved on to the next phase.

I had been too busy with clothes design to even think about what they were doing, but David, seen as the protector of the village interest, declared himself delighted with the project. Miles had gone to bed, David and Liam had returned home which left the two of us.

'You enjoy your work, don't you?'

'Yes, but life is more than work.' Deryn lazed back on the carpet with a dreamy expression.

'Such as?'

'Men and babies.'

I giggled, 'Let's start with babies, men might take longer.'

'I'm thirty-five and have been working for FCI for fourteen years. By the time I reached twenty-five I had international responsibilities, as I'd risen quickly through the ranks. It's no secret that I'm well paid, and I have sufficient money in the bank from various share options, but I don't have a family and I'm getting old for having even one baby.'

Tears filled her eyes and streamed down her face. An unexpected side of Deryn that she'd kept hidden. She had appeared a career girl to me, but I'd been mistaken.

'I'm sorry I didn't mean to upset you.' I leaned across and patted her on the shoulder.

'It's not you, it's my lifestyle. During the last week, I have realised how much I miss the countryside and its people. Jet-setting seems an attractive life until you've done it for a few years, I yearn to settle down.'

'Back in Wales?'

'Not particularly, I like it here. Running this project and taking maternity leave, would be easy. But I can't take it in my current job as Camilla sends me anywhere at a moment's notice.'

'Would you be a single mum?'

'Coming from a traditional family, it would be marriage, otherwise I couldn't look them in the eye.'

'Well, you won't have a problem finding a man.' We

giggled and sipped our wine in companionable silence as the flickering flames of the fire formed dancing shadows across the room.

Whenever I stared at the fire in this room, my thoughts returned to Liam and the passionate night together, my cheeks glowed as the memory returned.

Deryn topped up our glasses, 'There's been a lot of men chasing me over the years, but how can I decide? No one has leapt at me as Mr Right. If it's not too painful, how did you pick your husband?'

A lump formed in my throat. Oh! What a question! Thinking about Justin made me tense. I shivered and a knot tightened in my stomach, his departure clouded my memories of him, but the early years of our relationship had been perfect. 'I didn't pick Justin; I fell in love with him.' I shivered as I mentioned his name, his presence in one form or another never left me.

Deryn rolled over on to her stomach, 'Falling in love, at first sight, hasn't happened yet and I'm running out of time.'

'Do you like men?'

Deryn had a fit of the giggles which took time to shake off, 'I'm not gay if that's what you mean.' But she stopped smiling and appeared thoughtful.

'What is it?' I was curious to find out what was on her mind.

'Do you want to help?'

'Finding you a man?'

'Not finding one, choosing one, there's a difference.'

'What type of man do you like?'

'Regarding appearance and intellect, I'm not fussed providing he is not the hunchback of Notre Dame. During this week, I've been with three men, Liam, David and Miles, they are different. At a stretch, they fit into my age range and all are charming and delightful men. How do

264

you choose between them?' My face must have given me away.

89

'Oh, Jessica, I've jumped in with two left feet, one of them must be yours.' I shook my head. 'They are besotted with you,' Deryn put her head on one side and her eyes searched my face as though trying to read my thoughts.

'You're exaggerating!'

'Not at all, tell me which one, then I won't choose him.'

'Are you serious?'

'None of them would have me otherwise I'd stay here.'

'Don't be so ridiculous, you're beautiful and brilliant, any man would be proud to be with you.'

'Take Liam, he's terrified of me as he always thinks he will make a mistake.'

'Liam is shy, but I like him and he's coming out of his shell a little more.' The mention of his name reminded me of the conversation in the storage shed, as he'd been so worried about asking me for a date. We hadn't managed an evening out together, but I must make sure it isn't forgotten.

'Is he your man?' asked Deryn. I became flustered,

spilt my drink and my face warmed. Deryn gave me a wink and added, 'Say no more.' I wanted to move attention away from me.

'What about David, he's confident, he wouldn't be frightened of you?'

'A lovely man, and a pillar of the community, who has a successful vet's business and is willing to take command. He's delightful, I think the physical side would be good, but he would still steer clear of me as he believes I'm bossy.' We both laughed, 'Yes, I know, that's because I am bossy, but it would put him off.'

'Miles?'

'Jealousy is a difficult trait. He is kind and sincere, but men notice me. Although I'm used to the attention, Miles would never cope.'

I attempted to get up from my chair, but Deryn's eyes flickered with amusement, 'Oh no you don't! You haven't decided which man yet?'

'For you or for me.' I relaxed back into the chair again.

'Both, who's best for you?'

The image of the young Justin flashed into my mind. I would only marry again for love, and although I was interested, I didn't love any of the existing men. I enjoyed their company and I found them all physically attractive.

'I'm sure you are weighing them up.' Deryn's mouth twitched, 'I remember at the first dinner party the day after I arrived, you were silent and let me do the talking, while you were eyeing them up.'

I laughed, 'You've caught me out.'

'So, which one, I can't stand the suspense anymore?' Deryn's voice bubbled with excitement.

'All right, I will tell you what I think of them, but you must never repeat it.'

'Promise!'

'David became one of my first encounters when Justin left and helped me a great deal. He organised everything and employed Liam for me. He's a good handsome man and is well respected, but...'

'No buts. Next.'

'In the dark, I knocked Miles down while riding my bike along the lane without lights.' This brought on a fit of giggles in Deryn, but she encouraged me to finish. I recounted the story in detail which made her laugh even more. 'His pathetic behavior irritated me, but when I met him in London, he showed a completely different side and that's how I obtained this design job.'

'Liam, why leave him to last?' Deryn's eyes gleamed.

'A man of few words, but I've got to know him better and I like him.'

'Will you stay on your own?'

'I keep thinking I will, but whenever the house is empty, loneliness rears its head.'

Deryn patted away a tear, 'We're both in the thick of things and yet we are two poor lonely souls.' We hugged each other, and tears ran down our cheeks, 'You're good company.'

'I've never had a friend like you.' We hugged again, and more tears flowed. 'Go to bed, you've got a long day tomorrow.'

90

With my mind buzzing after the heart to heart with Deryn, I wouldn't be able to sleep, so I tidied the kitchen. Despite the hour, the noise of a car engine caught my attention as it pulled into the yard. A pang of worry shot through me. It can't be anything wrong with the animals because it wasn't Liam or Jackie.

The sharp knock on the door jolted me and I froze. The knock sounded again, but no other noise accompanied it.

'Who is it?' I hoped for a familiar voice.

'Police Sergeant Ibbotson, if you have a chain, I will show my warrant card.'

'No, I don't.'

'We'll put the car lights on.' Uncertainty gripped me, but the farmyard and windows of the kitchen were lit by blue flashing lights. I opened the door and the uniformed Sergeant Ibbotson stepped into the kitchen.

'What's happened, is it Paris or Clyde?'

'No, Mrs Southwick, your son and daughter are fine. I am here about your husband.'

'Justin? He's in jail in Germany.'

'Please sit down, Mrs Southwick.'

'What has happened?' I slumped down at the kitchen table.

'I'm sorry to tell you that Mr Southwick has attempted to take his own life.'

I hadn't expected him to do that, even though he had been at a low ebb. The image of Justin in jail burst into my mind. Whether it was anguish about the children being involved or the death of his lover, I had no idea. In a way, I had no sympathy for his misery as he had brought it on himself. But attempted suicide meant he must have sunk low. 'Oh, dear.' It sounded inadequate.

I lowered my gaze and then gulped, 'You might know we are separated.'

'Yes, I do. The details have been shared with me by our German colleagues, but as you are still his wife and next of kin, we must inform you.'

'You mentioned attempted?'

'Yes, he is seriously ill in hospital.'

The shock sent a shiver through me. The good times flashed through my mind, 'Poor man.' While I no longer loved or needed him, sorrow engulfed me.

91

During the night images of Justin kept swirling around my mind. The memories of the good times came flooding back when we were young, fresh and career hungry in London. As I'd experienced such a fitful sleep, I rose early and made ready for a busy day. I'd rung Clyde earlier and woken him to explain about his father. When I ran the school, Mrs Hastings, already in her office, volunteered to break the news to Paris.

David, Miles, Liam and Deryn sat around the kitchen table with the remnants of coffee and toast. 'Can you join us?' asked Deryn showing no signs of a hangover. She had returned to her confident, bubbly self. So far, I hadn't told anyone about Justin, but I would when the opportunity arose.

'Camilla has accepted the plan, so it's full steam ahead.'

'Is the village meeting taking place this evening?'

'Yes,' she tapped the papers spread on the table with her pencil, 'but there is a lot to do beforehand and I'll need your assistance. Preparation is essential as its planned to be a large event. The location has changed, and we are meeting in the big barn behind the pub.' There were dubious faces, but Deryn smiled, 'Trust me, it will work.'

'If you say so,' David pursed his lips, 'but apart from

us I can't see anyone else coming.'

'Camilla wants us to confirm that the arrangements in the village are okay, and no one has changed their mind. If everyone here agrees, I'll divide up the tasks and we will complete them.' The others nodded, and Deryn handed me two envelopes.

'These are essential documents. Can you deliver them?'

One addressed to George and the other to Maureen at the shop. Please let it be good news. As I scooped the envelopes from the table, I metaphorically crossed my fingers.

Within ten minutes I strode into the yard at George's farm. Aggie had seen me coming and we soon settled in the kitchen. With a flourish I placed the envelope in front of George.

'George and Aggie, I hope this is okay. Deryn is a lovely woman and has become a valued friend, but I don't know about big business and a little village like us.'

George opened the envelope, scrabbled in his pocket for his reading glasses, which he then perched on the end of his nose and steadily read through the document. Aggie and I waited in silence and I held my breath. As he reached the end, he smiled, which afforded me some relief, but apprehension remained.

'It's exactly as she explained, she's a canny lass, that Deryn. Has that important woman in London agreed?' He tapped the letter and gave a toothy grin.

'Do you mean Camilla?'

His eyes fixed on my face. 'Aye, that's the one.'

'Yes,' I nodded, 'she has agreed.'

'Well, I'll be jiggered. It's going to happen.' Aggie burst into tears and put her head in her hands.

'What's the matter? Are you all right, Aggie?' George flapped the paper, 'This says our dream is coming true.'

My mind whirled in confusion and I didn't know whether to laugh or cry, 'I don't know what it says. You'll have to explain, George. Oh, Aggie don't cry. Is it a new bungalow?'

'Yes, FCI are buying this farm and we will then buy the other one I told you about, which is much bigger and will suit our sons. Also, they have agreed to build a bungalow for us.' Worry coursed through me, as it sounded too good to be true, so I tried to put in a little caution. 'What do they want with your farm and when is it all set to happen?'

George chuckled, 'They are under your roof and you don't know what they're doing.'

'I've been working hard on the designs.'

'They are converting this building into the Design centre, that's what the lassie explained.'

'Oh, my. I never realised it would be this big.'

Aggie dabbed at her eyes with a tissue, 'Deryn told us we would be living in our bungalow within three months.'

'There is a condition,' George laughed. 'We must have energy devices, panels on the roof and they will use the brook for additional electricity. I asked how much it would cost.'

'How much?'

'That city boy in the flash clothes.'

'You mean Miles.'

'That's him,' he rubbed his hands together and gave his usual chuckle. 'It would be free and the normal electricity bills would be small.'

'It's wonderful.' The news made laughter bubble up and I giggled with excitement.

'All thanks to you, lass. Deryn explained it was all down to you.'

I hugged them both before I left, and I walked down

towards the village with a spring in my step, sploshing through the puddles like an enthusiastic child.

'Hello, Jessica,' Maureen greeted me in her quiet manner, but a slight smile tugged at her lips.

'I think you already know, don't you Maureen?'

'Yes, a man called here yesterday from Batemans Supermarkets. He rang me this morning to say it's all settled and that they would buy the shop and the contents.'

'That's fantastic news,' but I worried about the deal that had been offered, 'Did they give you a good price?'

'Generous, considering the state of the business these days and they offered something else.'

'Yes?'

'They want our flat above the shop and as they were building a bungalow for George, they've offered us one next door, in payment for the flat. It's marvellous Jessica and all thanks to you. I'm so excited.'

92

Adrian had arrived for his first visit to Mossmoor and I found him sat by the Aga in the kitchen when I returned. He waved a hand in greeting, 'Are you excited?'

'Yes, but will it happen?'

'Yes, definitely.' He opened his briefcase and extracted a folder emblazoned with my name. 'And now I've two matters for your approval.'

'These are the photos taken by the photographer who visited last week.' Adrian moved across to the table and spread out the pictures. I'd thought the photographer hopeless. First, he'd combed my hair a slightly different way, and then changed my makeup, after which he told me to ignore him and carry on with my work. Most of the day he sat around and sometimes started taking pictures.

'They are amazing.' They were the best ones ever, and I appeared relaxed and happy. 'Are they for publicity? When are you using them? When does it all start? Adrian, we haven't any samples yet.' The questions fired from me in rapid succession.

'Calm down, yes we have samples,' he picked up a suitcase and opened it, 'the team in London have made them.'

It had always thrilled me to see my designs become a reality. I spread them out on the table. There were men's, women's and children's outfits. Taking my time, I examined them with care. When I had finished my eyes gleamed, I allowed my hand to stroke the fabric of one of the outfits.

'All okay?' Adrian watched me with a huge smile, then left to find Deryn.

As soon as I was alone, my mind drifted and Justin crept to the fore, but I buried myself in my work, and sent out thank you notes to the team that had made the samples.

It had surprised me they left me there in peace and quiet, when there were so many jobs that needed doing. I worked diligently in my makeshift studio through the afternoon. The village meeting was due to take place at five o'clock in the barn. Time to get ready. I'll wear some thick clothes and jeans as it will be cold and draughty.

I left my studio and bumped into Deryn who had already changed. The work clothes had gone, and she was immaculately dressed in a thin white blouse and black trousers. As usual, her hair and make-up were perfect. 'You'll freeze in that, it's a draughty old barn.'

'It won't be I can assure you.'

I revised my intended clothes and chose smart bottle green trousers, teamed with a patterned mohair and cashmere sweater in shades of green and pink, but made a mental note to take a thick wrap with me. Just as I finished getting ready Deryn called, 'They will be here in a minute, let's go and meet them.'

'Who's coming?'

'Here they come,' Deryn walked into the yard and pointed skyward. I stared in the direction indicated by her finger as a helicopter appeared.

'Who is it?'

'Camilla, of course.'

'Camilla's coming here?' My voice rose in surprise and my eyes widened.

'Yes, with Ron Bateman who is the Chief Executive of Bateman Supermarkets.'

The helicopter circled over a nearby field where a waiting Range Rover had parked. 'Deryn, what's happening? This isn't a small village meeting is it?'

'No, we have been keeping it a secret, wait and see. You'll love it.' Despite her reassurances my stomach somersaulted. 'Now they've landed, the Range Rover will bring them to the farmhouse.' A few minutes later it rumbled into the farmyard. 'Let's meet them.'

Camilla wore her fearsome expression, except this time she recognised me and introduced Ron. I followed in a daze as they entered the kitchen away from the wind. As usual everyone headed for the Aga. Ron asked questions about the farm, animals and the village.

In the car on our way to the village Deryn explained the arrangements to Camilla, 'There are three seats on the stage for, you, Ron and Jessica.'

'You are the star, Jessica, so you can sit in the middle. Okay with you Ron?'

'Definitely, I'm looking forward to the show.'

I picked up on the word, "show", Deryn grinned.

A stage? Why did they need a stage? What show?

93

As the Range Rover swung around the corner to The Jaggers and its barn, so my mouth opened wide and I blinked rapidly at the sight before me. The red carpet and the television cameras gave the appearance of a film premiere.

The car pulled up alongside the red carpet. 'You go first, Jessica, then Ron and I'll bring up the rear,' Camilla smiled for the first time.

Nervousness swept over me, but a gentle hand came on my arm from Deryn, who whispered, 'Follow the carpet it leads onto the stage.' With a huge intake of breath to calm my nerves, I followed the instructions.

Cameras flashed as I stepped from the car. A wooden floor and stage had transformed the barn. Warm air wafted over me. Huge banners hung from the old rafters. A two metre picture of my face stared down. The bold script under my picture read, Bateman's Supermarkets brings you the Mossmoor Collection inspirationally designed by Jessica James. I pulled my shoulders back as pride bubbled through me and a permanent grin appeared. The walls had been covered with banners featuring parts of the collection and more pictures of me.

'Please welcome, Jessica James, the designer of the Mossmoor Collection.' The compere's voice on the amplified system resonated in the barn. A spontaneous round of applause was accompanied by cheers and whistles. I recognised many villagers but in the crowded barn there were many faces I didn't know. With a flushed face and an enormous smile, I settled myself on the stage.

The transformation of this old building in a short space of time amazed me. Across the middle of the barn stretched a raised catwalk. It was like a dream as Ron took the microphone, paid compliments to me, and then announced the launch of the collection. The grin never left my face.

The samples I'd designed were brought to life by the models as they strutted on the catwalk. I was overwhelmed at the reception that took place afterwards, with everyone from the village and many strangers praising my portfolio. Camilla had disappeared during the early part of the reception to visit the proposed design centre, George's house, and Ron visited Maureen's shop.

After returning, they mingled and talked to the people of the village. As the reception neared the end, Ron took Camilla to one side. Their eyes swept the room and the people in it, and then they spoke to Deryn and started pointing at various people.

Deryn drifted away from them and chatted to George, Liam, David, Jackie and the three girls as well as a few others from the village including the landlord, Michael, and took them to join Camilla and Ron. I had been asked to join them for a private conversation. Camilla took charge, 'Ron and I want this collection to be different.'

'We want you to become the models for the clothes.' The colour drained from Liam's face, as he shook his head.

George spoke first, 'Now, Camilla, let me see if I understand you right?' Even Camilla smiled at George. 'Will I be on those banners?'

'Yes, George, what do you say?'

'Well, I'll be jiggered. It's a good job you have come to me in my prime,' and he gave them a wide grin with his two remaining teeth.

94

Back at the farm at the end of the evening fear gripped me as flashing blue lights approached down the track. Two police motorcycle riders preceded a police car. The bike riders led the way into the yard.

The black car swung towards the kitchen door and stopped nearby. The darkened windows hid the passengers inside from view. As the vehicle halted, all three passenger doors swung open and three men stepped out.

Sergeant Ibbotson clambered from the front passenger seat. Henry, the Foreign Office official, opened one of the rear doors and to my surprise, the German Police Inspector appeared from the other side.

My heart drummed, and my stomach knotted. Why had they come? What news did they bring? I plastered a false smile across my face, 'Come in, gentlemen,' I led them through the house to the front room.

After they were seated, I perched on the edge of an armchair. Sergeant Ibbotson spoke first, 'To ease your apprehension, there is little change in Mr Southwick's condition, except that he has been released from intensive care but remains in hospital. He is still weak and in poor overall health.'

Tension gripped me and sweat trickled down my spine.

'Why are you here?' I hoped they didn't intend to re-arrest Paris.

Henry's eyes never left my face, 'The British government wish to do everything possible to help the German authorities. As the circumstances are most unusual, I have come from London to answer any questions which arise. Sergeant Ibbotson will also do the same. Let me ask Inspector Brandt to explain why we are here.'

'You and your friends were a magnificent help when in Germany and assisted us beyond all expectations. But we find ourselves in a dilemma and realise we need your assistance. I am afraid you will not like what we ask, but we believe it's the best solution to a difficult problem.'

Whatever did they want?

'During the police operation to regain the buildings a young woman called Anna fell to her death. The press are asking questions about why the authorities did not prevent the death.'

I made no acknowledgement and waited.

'Unfortunately, although we knew Mr Southwick had a poor state of mental health, we failed to prevent him attempting to take his own life. The news of Mr Southwick's action and current condition will be released to the press tomorrow. Mr Southwick keeps asking for his son and daughter.'

'Do you know why?'

'He says that he must change them back to their old ways that they followed before that first visit to Germany. It is what you asked him in your interviews.'

'Yes, I did.'

'To be brief our whole case is unravelling. Our lawyers have advised us that charges of treason will not be sustainable in court. Also, given they were minor assaults, and minimal amounts of criminal damage, we must consider far lesser charges. However, as Mr Southwick became a ringleader, we will press for a prison sentence for him.'

'Why does his case affect me?'

'We already have a bad press in Germany for our handling of the case, and it will intensify when we announce Mr Southwick's attempted suicide. The press will ask why we didn't manage to prevent it.'

'So, what are you proposing?'

'Given that it will be lesser charges and Mr Southwick is in poor health, and nothing has yet been proven in court, we are proposing releasing him.'

'Really!' The surprise leapt into my voice.

'We wish to release him to a similar situation as we did with your daughter.'

'But where will he be based?'

The Inspector paused and leaned forward, 'We would wish to release him into your house.'

'Absolutely no!'

Henry's expression dulled, 'We were prepared for that answer, but before we confirm it, will you listen to the Inspector?'

'I will, but I will not change my mind.'

'We have evidence that your daughter attended those critical meetings, and she spoke to encourage the plot that planned the taking of the building. As such we now wish to charge her, and we are convinced a prosecution would follow. While it would not be treason, we are keen that everyone in the group who wanted illegal action is charged with an offence that would result in some form of imprisonment.'

My heart sank, my lips trembled, and worry snaked through me. The worst possible news. Sergeant Ibbotson opened the folder on his lap and removed some papers.

'The German authorities have permitted me to see the evidence against your daughter and I would advise you that it would secure a conviction in an English court.'

I guessed what was coming next, but I leapt in first, 'So you want to do a deal?'

'A harsh way of putting it, but this is our proposal. We release Mr Southwick to house arrest here, where he will be tagged. We drop all charges against Paris, and she gets no criminal record. It will allow your son and daughter to speak with their father, and he can then persuade them to change their ways.'

I didn't want Paris to go to jail. 'Can Justin be trusted? What happens if he doesn't try to persuade Paris and Clyde?'

The Inspector grimaced, 'Then we will stick by our side of the bargain. No charges will be brought against Paris, and we will return Mr Southwick to Germany, and put him back in prison. The evidence from his current behaviour suggests he will comply.'

'Why are you doing this?'

The Inspector paused while he studied my face, 'I will be honest with you, we can say to the press tomorrow that in consideration of his poor health, he will be allowed temporarily to return to his family.'

'When will this happen?'

'If you approve, then he will be transferred from Germany when fit to travel, which we expect to be a few weeks. We will inform Mrs Hastings in the morning that Paris is free to come home.'

I suppressed a shudder, 'I have no option, do I?'

95

Furious with the authorities for manipulating me, I had no option but to comply and protect Paris from a criminal record. Justin, Paris and Clyde would arrive today. It had taken ten days for the final agreements to be made.

At some point, I would tell Paris how close she had come to a prison sentence, and I hoped it would shock her, and give her the push she needed to reform her views. She needed a wake-up call that her behaviour was unacceptable.

Standing on the landing of the house I made the final checks before Justin arrived. Although he might be based here, it didn't mean that I had to see him or have him wandering around the house. The blank end wall on the landing now had a door which I opened. The layout inside had been done to perfection.

Deryn's voice reached me from the stairs at the far end of the small self-contained flat, that had been created from old storerooms above the boot room and garages, 'What do you think of the flat?'

Amy climbed up the stairs, 'Hello, Mrs Southwick, I've come to finish tiling the kitchen.'

Deryn moved the last piece of furniture into place, 'The builder who is doing the other jobs for FCI in the village, wants the next phase of the work, which is the Design Centre. With that in mind he has put in every effort to complete this job on schedule, but was one person short, so Amy helped him.'

'Thank you, Amy, I will pay you.'

'No need, the builder is paying me.'

'He has offered Amy a job.'

Amy blushed, 'Deryn negotiated with him and the wages are brill. I can't believe I'll be paid that much for jobs I do around the farm. It's not difficult to hang a door and glaze a window is it?'

'Yes, it is!' I chuckled as I checked the small kitchenette which had been equipped with a kettle, toaster and microwave. 'As I am too busy with my designs and there are so many people staying, I've employed Sarah as my cook and housekeeper.'

Amy moved her weighty tool bag to the other hand, 'She is so pleased and is enjoying it.'

'That leaves Liz.'

'Oh no, it doesn't,' Deryn plumped the cushions on the sofa and adjusted the position of a small coffee table nearby. 'Adrian has offered her a job in the Design Centre.'

'You will be able to move into the temporary design centre tomorrow,' Deryn plugged in the small television.

'I can't believe you've done it so quickly.'

'George has been helpful and has allowed us to have one of his big barns.'

'So, it's a barn!'

'No, the local weather is harsh, so we have put temporary buildings inside the barn for protection. They are heated and have full facilities.'

A short walk to work in the design centre will be ideal as I shall be able to avoid Justin. Thinking about him coming filled me with tension and anxiety. I suppressed a shiver. If Justin is awkward or becomes a nuisance, I will have no qualms about sending him back to Germany.

96

All the time I moved around completing mundane and unnecessary tasks, I listened for the cars that would mark their arrival. Then the blue flashing lights appeared in the lane. A heavy sigh escaped my lips and my stomach churned, while I waited in the yard to meet the two police cars coming along the track.

'Please come in, Sergeant.'

'Hello, Jessica,' Justin climbed out of the far side of the car.

With the merest inclination of my head to acknowledge his greeting, I replied with one word in a calm, steady voice, 'Justin.'

The Sergeant watched his movements, I'd expected Justin to appear far worse. He was pale, but his appearance wasn't as bad as David's had been after his illness.

'Thank you for letting me come.' Justin sank into an armchair in the front room and despite his condition, his voice sounded firm and clear. He spoke without hesitancy, 'I will try not to interfere with your life.'

I wanted to release my tension, but I had to remain calm and composed. 'I agreed purely for the sake of Paris.' I intended to say our daughter but forming the first word became impossible. 'If they haven't told you, I will tell you about Paris later.'

The Sergeant opened a folder and passed me some papers, 'Mr Southwick has been advised by our German colleagues of the arrangements, and that you can request at any time for his return to prison in Germany.'

Justin had been staring at me, 'I intend doing exactly as I am directed by the police and instructed by you. I believe that you have agreed that I may see Paris and Clyde, so I am satisfied.'

'I hope you keep your word about reforming them.'

'Yes, I will do my best.'

The Sergeant waited for a pause, 'So that Mr Southwick's presence in this country has the same legal status as Germany, we have obtained a court order from a Crown Court judge. Mr Southwick is not allowed to make phone calls or send emails or texts or encourage anyone to send messages on his behalf. He may not meet any other person unless they are invited to the farm by yourself. Also, he will be tagged electronically to the phone line in this house, something you agreed on our last visit. Therefore, he will not be allowed under any circumstances to leave the farm. And finally, with your agreement, a police officer will visit Mr Southwick every day.'

'May I outline how I think this arrangement will work.' I led the way up the stairs and stopped at the top with my hand on the new door handle, and swiveled round because I wanted to observe Justin's face. His eyes were sharp, he went to speak but changed his mind.

The Sergeant methodically inspected each of the rooms in the new flat. It left Justin and me in a difficult silence. Having completed the inspection, the Sergeant spread his hand out indicating the area, 'This flat is completely new. Isn't it?'

'Yes, it will be allocated to the cook/housekeeper,

but Justin can use it on a temporary basis. If Sarah needs to stay over, she can share a room with my daughter.' Justin raised his eyebrows at the mention of the cook/housekeeper. 'I've had a full house for a while, but Justin only knows one of them, David, the local vet.'

The Sergeant nodded, 'Yes, I know David Hunstanton.'

'So, I will ask David if he wishes to visit Justin? Otherwise, I expect Justin to stay in his flat and none of my other guests will need to meet him. Paris and Clyde can come and go as they please. Sarah will clean the flat and cook his meals, which he will take here.' The Sergeant left Justin and me in the flat.

Alone with him, my mouth turned dry and a chill crept through my body. I'd been surprised by Justin's condition, while he appeared weak, his eyes were sharp and his voice strong and calm. The opposite of when I'd seen him in Germany.

'Will you come and see me sometimes, Jessica? I am here under your sufferance, I only suggest meetings between us, to discuss Paris and Clyde.'

'Justin, I will promise nothing.'

'Okay.'

'I'm returning to work until Paris arrives. Within the next hour you can go into our old bedroom and take any clothes and personal items you require.'

'You have started divorce proceedings,' Justin stared and didn't smile.

'Yes.' The tension rose, and a numbness infused my body, although I struggled not to show it. I wanted to scream and shout at him, but instead I walked calmly to the door, 'I shall come back later with Paris and Clyde and we can explain the regime to them.' He nodded.

With a pounding heart I walked along the landing and entered my studio. Closing the door with a soft click

I leant against it and with my face staring upwards, a stream of silent tears ran down my cheeks.

97

Clyde emerged first from the car, 'Hi, Mum, it's brilliant news about the designs.'

'Thank you, Clyde.'

'Mum, super to see you,' Paris hugged me.

'Welcome home, it's lovely to have you here, but there are several matters to talk about, they can't be delayed.' Paris made a face, but Clyde raised his chin and squared his shoulders, 'I would also like to talk to you as soon as possible.' Clyde taking the initiative took me by surprise.

'Paris, your father is here, turn left at the top of the stairs.'

'Mum, what are you talking about, it's a wall if you turn left?'

'Not now.' Paris scampered off to investigate.

As soon as the front room door had shut, Clyde hung his head and had a sheepish expression, 'Mum I've been stupid. I'm grateful that you have stuck with me.' I hugged him with tears in my eyes. 'I have dropped everything to do with Germany and moved back to studying maths. The University maintained it to be impossible, but when I explained the circumstances, they relented.'

'That's wonderful news.'

'Although I'm worried about Paris as she has a chip on her shoulder against the whole world.

The door of the front room burst open and Paris rushed in and blurted out, 'Someone else's clothes are in my room, and mine have gone.'

'Oh, yes, I've rearranged the rooms.'

'Can I move them back? I found my clothes in that little box room next to yours. Anyway, whose clothes are in my room?'

'Paris sit down.'

Reluctantly she dropped into the chair with a pout, 'I want my room back.'

'The house is full of guests.'

'Oh, yeah, your designs,' Paris yawned and gave a dismissive wave of her hand. Quivering with indignation at her attitude I suppressed the sarcastic comments on the tip of my tongue.

'You are in the room next to mine.'

'But it so small,' she pouted and rolled her eyes, 'why a second bed?'

'Just in case, Sarah, the new cook and housekeeper needs to stay over.' Paris glared at me open-mouthed. 'As she's nearly the same age as you, there shouldn't be a problem, but as you will be here only a short time, I don't expect she will stay.'

'It's so grossly unfair,' screeched Paris jumping up and slamming the door on leaving the room.

'There is something else, but it can wait,' Clyde moved towards the door. 'I'll go and calm Paris and then visit dad.'

Paris's attitude is wrong, but how do I change it? Is it my fault? Nothing convinced me otherwise as I had spoilt my daughter and so did Justin, but the problems had come home to roost. However painful it will be, Paris must change her attitude.

Deryn entered the kitchen from the yard with a flushed face and tight lips. 'Rude and arrogant young women annoy me.'

'What on earth has happened, you don't normally become so riled?'

'I was in the village shop making arrangements for the opening of the new store. A girl burst in and shouted for service. We argued, she swore at me, so I threatened to put her head in the water trough outside and wash her mouth out.'

'You okay with it? Did it upset you?'

'No, but what do their parents do? They must know their daughter is rude and has an attitude problem, I blame the parents.' A smile came to Deryn's lips.

'What's funny?'

'I've never been called an old bag before.'

The smile on our faces disappeared as Paris and Clyde sauntered into the kitchen.

Paris stopped and with hands on hips, glared, 'You! What are you doing here!'

'Deryn meet my daughter Paris and my son, Clyde.' Paris stared daggers at Deryn, 'Paris, Clyde please meet my good friend Deryn, who is currently staying in what used to be your room.' Paris burst into tears and stormed out of the room.

'Not again!' Clyde gave me a lop-sided smile, 'I'll go.'

Deryn had an anguished expression, 'I do apologise.'

'You've done nothing wrong, I'm afraid it's Paris.'

'I'll move out tonight, I can't possibly stay here now this has happened.'

I hugged her, 'You are staying, I've invited you to this house and I enjoy your company. It's distressing, but Paris is at fault. While I believe I'm losing control over her, I cannot and will not give in. Deryn, I might be upset, but it is not with you. I have a bad-tempered arrogant daughter that I must somehow reform, please do not go anywhere.'

I tapped on the door of the flat, 'Can we talk about Paris?'

Justin sat in the small armchair, reading the papers which the police had given him. He stood up and swayed slightly. 'Of course.'

Now I'd arrived, I didn't know where to begin.

The hesitation allowed Justin to speak, 'Paris believes the whole world is against her. The confinement at the school has not reformed her. She won't talk to me about serious issues. When I suggested talking to her about the current situation, she kissed me on the cheek, pouted, and announced she would unpack.'

'Paris had a tantrum about me changing her room, and another one because she was rude to someone in the shop, and I have found out. But I'm not giving in.'

Justin, who still hadn't taken his eyes off my face replied, 'I thoroughly agree, it's my actions that tipped her over the edge. I can't believe what I've done to you and the kids.' He leant his head away from me as the tears ran down his cheeks. I had no sympathy for his suffering. Finally, he stuttered, 'I will fully support you. Clyde is back on track. You have done well.'

I didn't want compliments, I'd come up expecting to argue with Justin, but it hadn't happened, and I didn't know what to do next.

Justin regained some of his composure although his hands shook, and he blinked rapidly. 'Thank you for the flat, it is beyond my expectations. I wanted to see Paris and Clyde and I'll appreciate it if I may stay for a few days, while they are here. My presence must cause you anguish. When it becomes overbearing, tell the German authorities.'

I didn't say another word and neither did I glance

back at Justin as I left. Once back on the landing I gave a huge sigh of relief. The stress of Justin's presence weighed heavily but winning around Paris had become my focus. I'd deal with his presence in my house later.

I found Paris and Clyde chatting normally in her new bedroom and suggested they come to the kitchen to meet my other guests. As we entered the kitchen, Deryn approached Paris, 'I'm sorry for being so short with you in the shop.'

Paris smiled a little and mumbled, 'Yeah well, I wasn't polite. Sorry.'

David approached Paris and caught her by the arm, 'How's your application to the Vet's school coming along? Come and talk to me.'

Miles introduced himself to Clyde and they chatted together with surprising ease. I suspected that Deryn had briefed the others.

I took David to one side after the evening meal, 'Justin is here, you are welcome to see him if you wish.'

'Do you want me to see him? If I do, I shall tell him what a bloody fool he has been in losing such a special woman as you.' I blushed a little at his compliment, 'Yes, I will go and tell him, he needs some straight talking.'

As the evening wound down, I picked up a bottle of unopened wine and two glasses and meandered up the stairs. I hesitated outside Deryn's door as I didn't want to disturb her. I knocked.

'Come in,' the usual bright voice responded immediately. Her main suitcase rested on the bed and had been half filled with clothes.

'Oh, no!'

She hugged me, 'It's for the best.'

'No, it's not! No, it's not!' My mood plummeted and tears formed in my eyes, 'I want and need you here.'

Shaking badly, I put the wine and glasses on the bedside table.

'Oh Jessica, it's a time for family first.'

At the end of my tether, I snapped, 'I've got a son who has settled down, a daughter who I love deeply but has gone completely off the rails, and I don't have a husband. There's no bloody family.'

I scooped up the clothes that were in the suitcase, took them out and hung them back in the wardrobe. 'You can't leave. I won't let you.' Deryn wrapped her arms around me.

98

'It gives me great pleasure to open the first of our ecologically friendly supermarkets,' announced Ron Bateman, chief Executive of Bateman Supermarkets, standing outside the enlarged village shop in Mossmoor. The small crowd, mainly the press, and villagers clapped. 'This store has for the past decades always been referred to as Maureen's and, although I am sure she will feel shy, I would like Maureen to come from the crowd to open it.'

I gently coaxed Maureen to the front and whispered, 'You don't have to say anything just pull the cord.' The curtain, hiding the storefront, dropped to one side to reveal an automatic door, and newly cut into the limestone lintel an inscription which read, 'Maureen's Store'. Maureen stared in open-mouthed astonishment at the lintel inscribed with her name.

A great cheer erupted but she didn't move, and her hand still held the cord as tears rolled down her cheeks. 'Thank you, Maureen, and may we all wish you a long and happy retirement.'

Ron led the crowd through the automatic doors into the shop, with the converted barn added to the old store, then he moved to one side where space had been cleared. 'It gives me great pleasure to launch the Mossmoor Collection. The clothes will be on sale from today in this store, and from tomorrow throughout the Bateman Supermarket chain of stores.' Huge posters that hung from the roof of the barn unfurled. George filled the first poster, with a toothy grin modelling the clothes. Ron, with a dramatic flourish of his arm, 'And now let's meet the man in person, come out please, George.'

George appeared, from behind the shelves, dressed in dark green denim jeans, with a green checked shirt, which he wore under the wool and cotton thick jumper with delicate green piping along the edges. On his head, he had a dark green flat cap. A spontaneous round of applause erupted as George appeared, with his grin as wide as ever.

I stepped forward into the centre of the new store to join Ron answering questions from the press. My heart sank as Caroline Darken stepped to the front of the few reporters. Would she attempt to be disruptive? Ron pointed to her for the first question, 'Ron, don't you think it's a bit of a risk choosing a designer who has been out of touch with the fashion world for several years.'

Ron flicked me a glance, he would be surprised at such an opening question. Usually press at a launch would ask for quotes. Frowning at Caroline, he waved an arm in my direction, 'Jessica brings our supermarket clothing a rich blend of fashion experience and practical living. Next question!'

As the ceremony ended, Miles appeared at my elbow, 'Fancy some lunch?'

'A sandwich from Bateman's Supermarket?'

'Why not indeed,' and he looped his arm in mine. Miles hadn't been in Mossmoor recently. Had he missed London? Miles opened his hand to indicate we should use a pile of old pallets as a seat to eat our sandwiches.

The warm sun took away the chill of the light breeze. 'Did you miss London as you haven't been around so much?'

'Not at all, I like Mossmoor, but my job is based in London, however, I didn't bring you out to lunch to talk about me.'

I feared this conversation would take a serious tone. 'I've given you plenty of space, to allow you to deal with your designs and the issues you have at home. I'm enchanted with you, Jessica, and I don't want to keep my distance anymore.'

I thought Miles' interest in me had gradually faded, but it hadn't. Work, Justin and Paris had focused my thoughts in recent months.

'It seems so unfair to have your husband in the house when Paris and Clyde are away.'

'It's a long story, Miles, but I haven't got the strength of conscience to send him back to prison. If he attempted suicide again and succeeded, then I wouldn't be able to live with myself, knowing that I'd sent him back.'

Miles took the empty sandwich packets, crossed to a skip that awaited collection and dropped them in, he didn't rush and took his time to stroll back. 'But the situation can't continue forever can it?' The irritation in Miles' voice rose to the surface.

'The court case is in a few weeks, then he will go back and serve his sentence.'

'When he finishes his time in prison will you have him back?'

The shock must have registered on my face, but either Miles didn't notice, or he chose to ignore my reaction. Perhaps it's a test as I had spent more time with him over the last month than I'd originally planned, as we tried to talk sense into Paris.

'I'm not having him back.'

Miles' dark eyes never left my face, 'You hesitated.'

'No, no, the divorce is progressing.'

'You wouldn't be the first person to start divorce proceedings and then let them drop.'

'That's unkind and untrue, I'm not getting back with Justin, I'm a free agent.'

'Let's enjoy the weekend together.'

'I can't, I must be available for Paris.'

'I thought you would say that, so I've an answer. Paris is staying at school this weekend, isn't she?'

'Yes.'

'Not far from Paris's school in Hertfordshire there is a five-star Spa Hotel. Let's spend the weekend together there and chill out.'

Panic engulfed me and my breathing quickened. Miles had it all worked out. What type of commitment did he expect? Part of me wanted to go as he's good company and I enjoy being with him. I wasn't put off by the thought of having a relationship with him, as I had no commitments either real or implied.

'It's time you thought about yourself, Jessica. A weekend away? What do you say?'

'Oh, Miles, I know you've given me time, but I still can't focus on what I want. I am fond of you, and wouldn't want to do anything to upset you, and give you false hopes or expectations.'

'So, the answer is no.'

I let out the breath I had been holding. 'You're right. The answer is no, as I'm too involved with myself and my life. You are a wonderful man and deserve someone better than me.' Miles went to speak. 'Please don't say anything else, it is hard to refuse you, but it is for the best.'

99

A turmoil of thoughts cascaded through my mind on arriving back at the farm. Why had life become so confusing? I'd been with Justin for lengthy periods, because we needed to focus on Paris. I no longer had any trepidation about meeting him.

Miles is handsome, fun, helpful and interested in starting a relationship. What had stopped me saying yes to him? I shook my head trying to clear the thoughts as I didn't know the answer, but something held me back.

Wanting to be alone, I retreated to my room, the only place where peace and quiet reigned. The future had become clouded. What did I want from it? Swirling thoughts led me nowhere and after ten minutes tears formed.

Snap out of it, become immersed in work and forget about men.

Then a flash of inspiration. Why not take a holiday? Paris and I could take a trip together, preferably somewhere exotic, to see whether some extravagant living would allow us to become close again. The next time I'm in London for a few days I'll pop in to see her, it would then be a double surprise. The thought cheered me up.

Should I tell Justin? Miles' comments returned.

Miles remained under the impression I would stop divorce proceedings and return to Justin, but he was mistaken. My marriage to Justin had ended. I wouldn't mention my plan for a holiday with Paris to anyone until I'd spoken to her. Quality time together we both needed. With a clear way forward, I had a spring in my step as I descended the stairs.

Liam didn't smile as I entered the kitchen. 'Hello, you look glum. What's the matter?'

'Nothing.' Staring at the Aga he chewed his bottom lip.

'Come on. Tell me, I might be able to help.'

'Jackie caught the train this morning to London.' His voice sounded flat and his eyes had a haunted look.

'The engineers from Miles' company have been impressed with her.' I moved towards the Aga, leaned against it to receive the warmth. 'They found her a course and a part-time job, it's a good opportunity.'

'Yes, I know,' he grimaced, 'but it's London.'

'Don't fret.' His concern for his sister's welfare touched me. This man had hidden depths. If only he would let them shine through more often. I smiled as the passion of our night by the fire came to my mind, sending a warm flush across my cheeks. 'Don't worry, she'll find it strange at first, but she'll be safe with friends of Miles.'

Deryn breezed in, 'Hi Liam, I've finished for the day, are you ready?'

'Yes,' he nodded, and a small smile appeared. I frowned pressing my lips tightly together. Why had Deryn received a smile?

With a quick glance at me one of her stunning grins lit up her face, 'Liam and I are planning the introduction of rare breed sheep onto the farm and how they can be managed to produce the best wool for your designs.'

I nodded in a half-hearted way. It had been Camilla's ideas to start farming sheep that would be uniquely incorporated into the designs.

'Liam mentioned he has never had a Chinese meal, so we are going to Braxton to have a working dinner in the Chinese Restaurant.'

My heart sank as they left, but I only had myself to blame as I'd never managed to arrange an evening out with Liam. I kept promising the following week, but it never happened. Had I left it too late?

My throat tightened and my mood plummeted as they crossed the yard towards Deryn's Range Rover. They would get on well, as Deryn always brought out the best in people, and I imagined them laughing together.

100

The evening hadn't been exciting as I'd attended the first meeting of the village hall committee. It had not been a riotous affair, and had been conducted with a serious approach, where everything had been discussed in minute detail. Many of the subjects didn't hold my interest and my thoughts wandered to Liam and Deryn. Did he fancy her?

Would this evening at the Chinese restaurant be the start of a budding romance? My jaw tightened at them together and I tried to push the thoughts from my mind. I blamed myself for not arranging an evening out with him after he'd plucked up the courage to ask.

Throughout the committee meeting David had been in a serious mood and kept glancing across to me. When the meeting ended, he offered me a glass of wine before I headed back to the farm.

After speaking to a few locals, I settled in the far corner of the pub. With a sombre expression, he returned from the bar with two glasses of red wine, 'Jessica'. The single word had been spoken in a low, pained voice.

Taking a long sip of my wine, I braced myself, 'Yes, David.' Clearing his throat, he fussed around placing a beer mat with extreme precision under his drink. When satisfied perfection had been achieved, he cast an anxious glance at me, 'I've found it difficult to speak to you apart from village matters. I made such a fool of myself and must appear ridiculous in your eyes.'

'Stop being so dramatic.' A bubble of laughter rose in my throat at his theatrical statement. 'I assume you are referring to Cate?'

'Yes.'

'For goodness' sake, it happened ages ago.' I gave a dismissive wave of my hand, 'we are still good friends. Let's forget the incident.'

Why had he dwelt on the matter? With a small laugh, I changed the subject. 'I believe you've taken Deryn to dinner several times.' I grinned, 'Is there a romance in the air?' He burst out laughing, not a normal characteristic for him. 'What's funny? She's an attractive woman.'

'I agree, she is stunning, but not for me.'

'Why ever not?' My eyebrows shot up. 'You enjoy each other's company.'

'But we wouldn't be compatible.'

'What's that mean?' I laughed.

'To be frank, she bosses everyone about, I can't imagine being married to her, I'd never get a moment's peace and quiet.' He shook his head and stared down at the drink. 'Every day would be organised.'

I gave him a wicked smile, 'She has many other assets.'

He took a sip of his wine, shook his head and his serious expression returned, 'Are you having Justin back?'

'No, I am not! Has he made suggestions when you've visited him?'

'No, we agreed to stay away from controversial subjects and confine our talk to rugby and motor racing.'

'Why would I have him back?'

'I don't know...' His voice trailed away. 'Sorry, it's none of my business, I shouldn't have mentioned him.'

101

Reluctantly, I answered my mobile as it rang one evening at a hotel in London. 'Mrs Southwick, this is Mrs Hastings, and I am afraid I have distressing news for you.'

Nausea churned in my stomach and overwhelmed me with weakness, I sank back on to the bed. 'What is it? What has happened to Paris? Is she hurt?'

'No, unfortunately your daughter appears to have run away from school.'

'Run away?'

'Yes, along with one of her friends.' Her tone was matter of fact and brisk but edged with a hint of irritation. 'Both are missing and have taken a small rucksack, money and other personal belongings.'

'Is there any reason?'

'The staff on duty this evening are trying to find out. And now I must ring Louise's parents and tell them. And after that, I shall inform the police.'

'Shall I come to the school?' My voice wavered and a sheen of sweat now covered my forehead.

'No, I don't think that will help,' her tone was sharp, 'several girls and staff have gone to nearby bus and railways stations to search for them. As soon as there is news, I will ring you.'

Tears leaked from my eyes and I remained slumped on the bed, rocking myself backwards and forwards as I stared at the phone in my hand. Why would she run away? Where would she go? Would something terrible happen to her? What can I do to help? Had something happened that Mrs Hastings hadn't told me? I dismissed the latter as Mrs Hastings would never shirk away from giving bad news.

I had to do something. A cold shiver ran through me, yet my hands were hot and sweaty as I paced up and down the room. How can I help? Justin must be informed. Paris's willful behaviour was his fault as it had started after her trip to visit him in Germany. I didn't intend to fight this last battle alone and he must shoulder some responsibility. With trembling hands, I phoned through to the farmhouse.

Deryn's soft Welsh accent crackled down the phone line, 'Hello, Jessica, how's London?'

'Paris has run away from school.' The words tumbled out.

'What can I do to help? You must be distraught.'

'Please find Justin and bring him to the house phone, he needs to know we are losing control of Paris and that he's not got through to her yet.' I waited, holding the phone tightly in my sweaty hand.

'Hello Jessica,' the shaky voice reverberated down the phone line, he had obviously guessed something had happened.

'Paris has run away from school and they don't know where she is...' A large crash occurred, and the distant voice of Deryn shouting, 'Quick! Come and help!'

'Justin, Justin...' I bellowed down the phone.

Deryn's voice reached me loud and clear, 'Justin has

collapsed and is unconscious, I will ring for an ambulance and inform the police.'

102

The two days of turmoil caused by Paris absconding from school had left its toll on me. Walking alone through the fields and countryside near the farm became the only activity which afforded release. The bleak wind-swept moorlands matched my mood but the colours and textures in the landscape were a sight of beauty. Unable to eat or sleep, my mind whirled from one disastrous scenario to the next.

Sitting in the rocking chair next to the Aga, exhausted both mentally and physically after a long trek, I rocked rhythmically backwards and forwards. Apart from the long walks, I'd sat for hours in this chair with thoughts in turmoil asking the same questions over and over again. Had any harm come to Paris? Would Justin die? What would happen next?

Although Justin had been transferred from intensive care, he remained seriously ill. The ringing of my mobile jerked me away from the terror-ridden thoughts, and I flicked the phone open with shaking hands, 'Mrs Southwick. This is Sergeant Ibbotson, I'm happy to say we have found your daughter and she is safe and well.'

'Oh, what a relief.' My shrill voice trembled as tears

trickled down my face. 'Paris will be given a quick hospital check, and then we'll bring her home.'

Rushing to find Deryn, I gave her the good news and then found Liam sat in the barn on one of the hay bales staring at the floor.

'Paris is on her way home,' I blurted out, 'they are checking her over, but she is unhurt.' Slumping onto a nearby box. 'It has been the longest two days of my life.'

'I cannot imagine the anguish with your daughter missing for two days, but it's over.' His calm voice washed over me. 'Perhaps whatever has happened to her over those days will have a positive impact.'

I rounded on him as my annoyance flared, 'That's harsh and an unnerving viewpoint as I haven't even seen her yet.' I expected Liam to apologise, but he didn't and continued to stare at the floor.

'I was hoping to have a chat with you.'

'Oh Liam, surely you can understand I'm tied up with Paris.'

Again, there was no apology and his expression dulled, 'It can wait a few days.'

'Liam!' I slapped my thigh with the palm of my hand. 'You have been miserable for the last week and keep saying we would discuss it later. For goodness' sake tell me what the problem is.'

In a slow, calm voice, 'Mrs Southwick, I am giving in my notice that I am leaving your employment.'

'What!' His words flew at me like a slap across the face. Mrs Southwick! Why had he called me that?

'You're what? You can't leave.' I huffed with impatience as I swiped a hand across my tear-stained face, 'I can't manage without you.'

A pained expression flitted across his face and he gave a heavy sigh, his clenched hands rested on his knees.

'Liam,' I leapt to my feet and paced backwards and

forwards across the barn. 'Please stay, I don't want you to leave. Why do you want to go?'

'I shouldn't have mentioned my decision. It is inconsiderate of me. Don't worry I won't walk out on you until you have found a replacement.' He pushed back his chair and strode out of the barn without a backward glance.

'Liam, Liam, come back! Tell me what all this is about.' Disappearing around the corner of the barn, the familiar sound of the quad bike filled the air as he roared off down the track. Oh my God, what's the matter with him? I don't want him to leave. I couldn't do anything about it today, but I resolved to have a long chat with him as soon as possible and sort out the problem.

103

A police car bounced along the track towards the farm. My mind raced as I waited for it to make its slow journey to the house. The car reached the yard and a pale and shaky Paris stepped out and half collapsed into my arms and sobbed on my shoulder.

While she hugged me, Sergeant Ibbotson stood discreetly in the background watching the reunion. Eventually, I took Paris inside the house, ushered her through to the front room and sat her in one of the armchairs.

'Are you okay, darling?' Paris shook and shivered, and her pale face and red-rimmed eyes filled me with dread. 'A man attacked me, he tried to put his hand up my skirt.' I tensed and turned to the Sergeant who stood in the doorway.

'I can explain,' he mouthed.

'Stay there Paris, I need to talk to the Sergeant.'

Standing in the middle of the kitchen Sergeant Ibbotson explained, 'Louise, the friend who absconded from school with Paris, led the pair to find her former boyfriend in Bradford. Louise's parents had banned any contact because the supposed boyfriend is fifteen years older than their daughter.'

'Louise and Paris became lost in Bradford and finished up in the red-light district. A man approached Paris and she screamed. A prostitute saved your daughter. Realising that Paris and Louise should not be there, she rushed up and kicked the man and then flagged down a passing police car. It might have been traumatic, but witnesses stated that Paris hadn't been touched. She has been to the hospital and the doctor only gave her something to calm her down.'

'Thank you, Sergeant.'

'Do you want me to leave a WPC here?' I shook my head.

When I returned to the front room, Paris had curled up in the armchair. With dirty, untidy hair and a face streaked by tears she looked young and vulnerable. Just to make doubly sure and ease my concerns, 'It's distressing but did the man touch or hurt you?'

Paris sobbed a little and in a stuttering tone, 'No, he used disgusting words and gestures as he approached me. I screamed and another woman, who was nearby, kicked him.' I nodded to the Sergeant, who gave me a wave of goodbye.

I calmed Paris as much as possible. Within ten minutes her tears had ceased and some colour had returned to her face. Liam appeared in the doorway.

'Hello. Why have you come back?'

'Deryn is at the hospital with your husband. David has gone to Braxton, so there is no one to drive you and Paris to the hospital, so I returned with a car.'

'Is dad in hospital?' Liam nodded at Paris. He went to speak but changed his mind and pressed his lips together.

'Yes, I patted her arm for reassurance, he became ill after you left.' Liam continued to stare intently at Paris.

'How is he?'

'Very poorly.' I caught hold of her hand and gave it a squeeze. I sensed Liam wanted to tell Paris what had happened. 'Can we go and see him,' Paris interrupted. 'Please, I want to, I do feel strong enough.'

104

As we walked into the hospital, I attempted to cheer her up and announced, 'Clyde is coming over to the hospital later.' A puzzled expression crossed her face and she frowned, 'If Clyde is at home, why didn't he come to meet me?'

I took a deep breath and ignored the question. As we approached the room assigned to Justin, Paris pointed along the corridor at Deryn, 'And why is she here!' Her voice held a hint of malice.

But I had no influence over what would happen today. No matter how much I had pleaded, it had fallen on deaf ears. Clyde would be here soon. Deryn had been magnificent, as after the phone call, she'd had to cope with the man she thought might die as he lay slumped on the floor in the hall.

'Oh my god, Dad,' cried Paris as she noted the monitoring equipment around and above the bed. Tubes and wires were connected to her father who lay back on the pillow, eyes closed and his face pale. Paris sobbed although rather over dramatically, but I kept my thoughts to myself.

Deryn stood with her hands on her hips on the far

side of the room, 'Paris, stop that wailing! Sit in that chair and talk to your father. He needs your support and your loud howling is not going to help. Stop crying!' Already pale, Paris turned white, and her hands clenched into fists at her side. Deryn grabbed her hand and although Paris squirmed, she guided her to the seat by the bed, then left the cubicle to talk to Liam, who had waited outside in the corridor.

I sensed the atmosphere and knew why Liam had been so insistent on bringing Paris to the hospital. I gulped as I heard Clyde's voice. Nervously I moistened my dry lips. He had arrived outside the cubicle and I stared at him through the small window as he smiled and chatted with Liam and Deryn. As he entered his face showed a grim determination.

I muttered, 'Not now,' but I knew my words would have no effect. Clyde acknowledged me with a nod, he stood still and in a quiet voice uttered one word. 'Paris.'

'I'll be back in a minute, Dad, Clyde's here.' Paris smiled as she approached her brother, but he didn't react. With a quizzical expression she clutched hold of her brother's hand. 'Come on. Let's go for a cup of coffee. Mum will sit with Dad.'

Clyde grabbed Paris by the arm, 'No. Dad needs you. You will stay here until he recovers.'

'Clyde, you're hurting.' He twisted her around to face her father and the monitoring equipment and held her firmly by the shoulders, 'Your thoughtless and self-centred actions caused this. He had a major breakdown and collapsed unconscious when mum told him you'd run away.' I stood in silence as the scene unfolded, unable to intervene. 'Look, you did this to dad! He almost died.' Paris sobbed. 'Tears are not good enough. Your selfish attitude is to blame. I've had enough of you. Dad needs you now, but I never want to speak to you again. Now get

on with it,' and he shoved her roughly towards the bed
and stormed out.

105

Clyde and I parked the bikes in Bateman's car park. 'Two months have passed since you last spoke to Paris, can you forgive her?'

'Is she coming home soon?'

'Yes, next week.'

'I will make peace with her but will never let her forget the anxiety she caused.'

'The shock of your reprimand at the hospital has had a marked effect on her. Since then she has been a changed and reformed character.'

I stopped in front of the two new bungalows constructed from local limestone. The setting was perfect; just on the edge of the village on a small rise of ground, which gave them panoramic views of the surrounding countryside. Today was the official handing over of the keys to the proud new owners, although they'd already moved in the previous week.

A large group of villagers had assembled, and as I handed the keys to George and Maureen, the local press took photographs. George and Aggie insisted we had a cup of tea before leaving. Aggie smiled as we sat in the warm spring sunshine in the garden, 'You are looking radiant Jessica, it must be a weight off your shoulders now that your husband has gone.'

'Yes, it is, they offered a deal if he pleaded guilty. The case had been badly handled in Germany and the authorities wanted a swift conclusion. Justin accepted the lesser charges and received a suspended sentence, but he's not coming back to Mossmoor. The last six weeks have been bliss.'

George relaxed back in the garden chair, ''Tis a pity that Welsh lass, Deryn, isn't here as she worked hard to make it happen, I've never met a woman like her before.'

'At one time I thought she might stay, but she suddenly decided to leave not long after Justin returned to Germany. Miles also decided to return to London, so the house is empty now.'

'Here's Liam,' George pointed to the lane. 'Is he still leaving?'

'Well I don't want him to go and have not attempted to find anyone else, with the hope that he will change his mind, but he is adamant.'

'A fine man, one of the best,' Aggie watched Liam approach, 'and now he needs a wife so that he can settle down.'

'Aye,' George nodded in agreement, 'He's a good farmer with plenty of ambition, you're right Aggie, he needs a good woman.' As Liam passed their new bungalow, George shouted and waved from our seats in the garden and invited him for a cup of tea. Liam joined us but as usual there was no smile and he said little.

106

I'd travelled with Liam to the Agricultural Merchants and he had packed some animal feed in the back of the vehicle.

He didn't put the keys in the ignition instead he rested his hands on the steering wheel and gazed through the windscreen, 'I've told you before how much I like you. I've been willing to be patient, as you've had so much on your plate. But my feelings for you haven't changed.'

'Life is quieter, and before you speak, I will be delighted to have a date with you.'

In a slow and deliberate voice, 'I've been thinking about how I feel.' I gave him a gentle smile of encouragement. 'I have decided to leave your farm, it's best if I go as soon as possible, without any more delays.'

'Liam you talked about me, and then changed to talking about the job, I don't understand.'

'I hoped, at one time, it might go even further than evenings out together as my feelings have increased since we first met. That's only a pipe dream, as you live and work in a different world.'

'That isn't true.' He took a deep breath, so I waited as I didn't want to interrupt him.

'Last month, at a day's notice you whizzed off to China. It's normal for you but I've never been to London.' I didn't want him to talk like this, but he found personal conversations difficult and I had no intention of arguing.

'You are a rich woman, and I'm only skilled in sheep farming and don't even have my own farm,' he continued to grip the steering wheel, 'and I don't think I ever will.'

'Neither of the things you say make any difference as far as I'm concerned, it's what you think of me as a person, that's what counts.'

'Jessica, you are a special and beautiful woman, who would make any man proud, but I am adamant you are out of my league.'

'Oh, don't say that Liam, I don't want to hear you speak that way.'

'I thought I could carry on working for you, but it gets to me seeing you every day, I can't cope anymore. Anyway, I expect now everything is settled, you will return to London, like the others.'

'I'm not going anywhere, I'm staying in Mossmoor as it is my home now. Please reconsider.'

He shook his head and started the car, the jut of his jaw told me he would not continue the conversation. After a few miles, he asked, 'How's Paris?'

'A completely transformed character.'

'That's good.'

I remembered Liam's actions the night she had come back with the police. 'You wanted to make sure she visited the hospital that night, didn't you?'

'Yes, she had to realise the consequences of her action. She hadn't been hurt as I'd checked with the policewoman who brought her back.'

'Thank you, Liam, I didn't think so at the time, but you were right.'

I desperately wanted to talk about him and me, but

he'd made his decision. Any romance between us had finished before it had started.

With an effort I pushed his words to the back of my mind and changed the topic of conversation, 'You might be able to help me with Paris, I need an idea.' I almost heard him give a sigh of relief that I wouldn't return to his decision about leaving. 'A mother will be soft with her only daughter.'

The comment brought a brief smile to his lips, 'You are allowed to be.'

'I've assured her that if she keeps up her current attitude, then she shall have a reward in the summer. Ideally, something we might do together.'

Liam drove on a few miles then slapped the steering wheel with the flat of his hand, 'I've an idea, but I don't know whether it's feasible.'

'Go on.'

'Whenever she dresses up, she favours one particular designer, it's written on the labels.'

'Yes, it's Pierre Lyons, she has always liked his work and her wardrobe is full of his designs.'

'I assume he is a real person.'

'Yes, of course.'

'Why not take Paris to meet him?'

'That's a brilliant idea.'

'Do you know him?'

'No, but Camilla who came to Mossmoor will know him and provide an introduction.'

The exuberant mood of the morning had gone. Liam had effectively dumped me. It had never developed as a relationship, but I kept trying to think of something that would change his mind. Life on the farm without him didn't seem possible.

His occasional and rare smile brightened my day. How can I prevent him leaving? I wouldn't see him for a few days as I would be in London. Perhaps an idea might occur to me.

Angela would miss him as she'd taken to following him around the farm like a pet dog. Remembering Angela and her love of chocolate cake bought a small grin of amusement to my lips.

107

'Jessica, how lovely to see you.' Miles gave me the most wonderful hug. 'We haven't met for over a month, let's have a drink and catch up.'

'I'd love to Miles, but I must find a hotel as I will not be able to travel home as there is a problem with the trains.'

'Don't be daft, stay with me.'

I shivered as I didn't want to get into a pressurised or compromising position, 'No thanks, Miles.'

'Come on, I live around the corner, so we can walk. I've plenty of drink in and I'm due home for dinner at seven o'clock, so I'll ring and say there is an extra.' I relaxed in one way but then worried about imposing on his new girlfriend.

As we crossed the road, 'I know a piece of news that will interest you, Robert and Cate have split up.'

'They weren't together for long, was it Cate's fault?'

Miles gave me a sideward glance, 'Why would it be her fault?'

'Never mind, why did they break?'

'It surprised me, but Robert's wife asked him back.'

'I thought they were divorced.'

'Yes, but then she contacted him and suggested they try again.'

'So, he dropped Cate and returned to her?'

'Yes, the decision came as a surprise.'

The divorce from Justin neared completion. Miles had been convinced I would have Justin back. He had been back to his former ebullient and confident self by the time he returned to Germany. When the trial finished, I had wondered whether he would ask.

Would I have him back? No, but after a lonely year in the big old farmhouse would I change my mind?

Miles opened the front door of the flat, 'Prepare for a surprise! We're here.' Leading the way into the kitchen, I followed but stopped and my mouth gaped open. 'Jackie!'

'Hello, Mrs Southwick.'

Is Jackie too young for him? What will Liam say? Has he taken advantage of a country girl in London?

Miles chuckled, 'Bit of a surprise? I'm off to shower and change so you two can catch up.'

At least he had been diplomatic. Within minutes we sat in the lounge, each with a glass of wine. Jackie had taken me by surprise because I nearly had to look twice. Her hair had been neatly styled, which coupled with delicate make-up, gave a softness that I'd never seen before. The tomboy appearance had vanished.

For the first time since I'd known her, she wore a dress which accentuated her good figure. 'Don't look so nervous, Mrs...'

'For goodness' sake,' I laughed, 'it's Jessica.'

Jackie smiled, 'I can tell what you're thinking but I've a separate room. I stayed with a couple and then they decided to split up. Miles saved the day and I moved in here.'

'Are you sure it's okay?' My heart thumped with anxiety. 'Are you all right?'

'London is fantastic, I'm brilliant and my course is superb. I've learned so much in a few weeks.'

'I was concerned, as I had introduced Miles.'

I put my wine glass back on the table and studied her face searching for answers, 'I've told mum and dad.'

'What did they say?'

'They have met Miles and liked him, but I did say he is not my boyfriend.' She giggled.

My eyes opened wider, 'What does that mean?'

'Well, we go out a lot in the evening together.' I'd never seen Jackie so radiant and full of life. London and her engineering course suited her, although I understood Liam's concern about his kid sister being in the city. 'I've been to the ballet.'

'Ballet?' My eyebrows shot up once again, 'Did you enjoy the performance?'

'It was great.' I found it difficult to understand that Jackie enjoyed the ballet, but she had changed from the tomboy who worked on the farm. A softer more feminine young woman sat beside me. Jackie beamed. A sound of movement in the hall, Jackie called out, 'Miles can you see to the oven, I'm chatting with Jessica.'

'Will do!'

Jackie tucked a lock of hair behind her ear, 'He is only six years older than me and I don't notice.'

I'm six years older than Miles and I also hadn't noticed.

Jackie whispered to me, 'I hope it becomes more than two people sharing a flat,' and with that Miles arrived to top up the wine.

108

Following several texts from people in London during my day working at FCI headquarters, I had made arrangements that I hoped would work. By early evening I sat in the bar area of the hotel, choosing a comfortable armchair in the spacious lounge, with a good view of the entrance and a large G&T in front of me.

David, following an earlier text, walked into the bar and kissed me gently on the cheek.

'You are looking smart, David.'

'Thank you, I thought I should, as I'm taking a special lady out to dinner.'

'Do you know David I think you are right.'

A confused expression crossed his face, but the smile soon returned.

'As you will know far more restaurants in London than me, can you suggest a good place to dine.'

David with his back to the hotel entrance didn't see who had just arrived. She spotted me and walked in our direction.

'Jessica...' but Cate's voice trailed away. 'David, what are you doing here?'

'Cate...?' They gaped at me.

'I intended contacting Cate as I had come to London, David texted me, so I thought....' My voice trailed away. They were lost for words.

Would my match-making work? 'I've designs to finish this evening. David mentioned he was taking a special lady out to dinner, So...' and I winked at Cate.

'Oh, Jessica,' Cate gave a shy giggle and hugged me.

'Thank you,' David smiled, 'As always Jessica, you think and care about other people.'

'Leave, enjoy! And don't forget the last time I saw you together.' David remembered and blushed. Cate smirked.

109

Nervousness ran through me every time I had to meet with Camilla. Summoned as soon as I walked into the building, I waited outside her office and wondered about the reason.

Since her visit to Mossmoor we'd not spoken. 'Come in, it shouldn't take long.' Her open-handed invitation to take a seat did nothing to calm my nerves. Renowned throughout the business for lack of small talk, I waited.

Sitting in the chair behind her desk, she came straight to the point, 'Every article Caroline Darken has written gives you heavy criticism. Ron is worried she might try to derail the success of the Mossmoor Collection. What's the situation with her?'

I bit my lip and drew my hands together in my lap, under Camilla's intense stare, 'Caroline used to work for me as a junior designer.'

'What happened?'

'Many years ago, I designed a collection of fashion accessories and used some of her ideas, but she doesn't believe I gave her credit.'

'Should you have done?' Camilla had ways of finding the truth.

'Yes, in retrospect, I should have given her due acknowledgements.'

'Okay, an honest answer. Not good, but you haven't used anyone else on your current designs.'

'No, they are my own work.'

'All in the past now, but I must make sure she doesn't affect the Mossmoor Collection as it's a huge success.'

A flick of her hand indicated the meeting had finished but I needed to ask, 'What will you do?'

Camilla frowned, 'Caroline is a good journalist, so I shall get a headhunting firm to entice her to work for us in our public relations department. My guess is she will succumb to the lure of international travel.'

As I returned to my desk my phone rang, 'Mrs Southwick, this is Gerald Arthurton, your solicitor, your divorce is fully complete.'

'Thank you, Mr Arthurton, that is the best news I've had in a long while.' Instead of settling down to work for the day I tidied my desk and packed my briefcase. I put on my waxed jacket, took the lift and crossed the entrance foyer.

My god, as I closed on her, I became certain. 'Deryn, what on earth's the matter?' I hadn't seen her for ages. Each time I'd been to the London office, I'd expected to meet her, but she had never been there, so I assumed that Camilla had sent her off to solve problems in far off places.

'Ah, hello, Jessica,' She did not step forward to hug and kiss me as usual. Had I upset her? We'd been good friends in Mossmoor.

'Are you okay?' She didn't appear her usual vibrant self and looked worried. 'You look ill, what's happened?'

Deryn stared at her hands clenched in her lap. She squeezed them so hard the whites of her knuckles showed. Then tears rolled down her face. 'I am sorry.'

'About what? You're making no sense and you look weak and fragile. Are you ill?'

She became agitated and kept turning her face from me, 'I can't stay here talking to you, I can't.

'Are you ill?'

'I've just been sick.'

'This early in the..... You're pregnant.'

'Yes, I am...' she dissolved into a flood of tears. I reached out to comfort her, but she backed away.

'What's the matter? Why won't you let me help you?'

'I can't... I can't... I've let you down. It's terrible.' She gulped back some of the tears and then tried to speak again.

'We became good friends...' but that brought more tears from Deryn.

'Come on,' catching one of her hands and not letting go, 'Tell me as I'm not leaving until I know what the problem is.'

Staring at the floor she mumbled, 'I'm pregnant and the father is Justin.'

I froze and had a momentary flashback to the first time I'd told Justin I was pregnant. I recovered and focused on Deryn. 'It's a surprise, a big surprise, but in many ways, it is nothing to do with me. Justin and I are divorced. I am Jessica James, again.' Deryn appeared confused. 'The divorce came through this morning. Are you with Justin?'

Deryn nodded, 'He's living in my London flat.'

I tried to get my mind around what I had been told, 'I have no ill feeling towards you, Deryn. Now give me a hug.' I grasped my friend and whispered, 'Enjoy your baby.' Deryn gave me a faint and pale smile as I stood up, and with head held high, I left the building.

110

As I walked away tears filled my eyes. Why was I crying?

My mind drifted back to when I'd met Justin, a young couple so much in love. I no longer loved him. Perhaps in the future we might become friends again.

Over a cup of coffee and a large muffin at the station, I attempted to calm my racing thoughts. Images of Deryn and Justin together kept appearing. No this wouldn't do. Then another thought hit me. What about Paris? She idolised her father and didn't like Deryn. No point worrying about that now.

I am a free and single woman. The divorce announcement changed everything. A broad smile covered my face. I yearned to return home to the old farmhouse and the rolling moorlands. Yes! The new me. With an exciting future ahead.

Deryn's news urged me on. The train home took ages. The next task focused on Liam, as I could not allow him to leave the farm. And I became clear as to how to solve the future. When I reached Macclesfield, I set off in search of a hardware shop and eventually left with a wrapped parcel. A taxi took me across the moors and dropped me on the lane at the bottom of the track.

I stopped at the sign, Cloughside Farm – The Home of the Southwick Family. I picked up a stone and after a few hits, the sign broke away and fell in the ditch. The Southwick family no longer existed. That part of my life had passed. I was Jesse James.

Then I walked along the track. The mud coated my fashionable red high heels, but I didn't mind. I let my eyes wander towards the familiar distant moorlands. I smiled, I had hated them so much when I first came here to live, but now their beauty struck me. The contours and the rolling skyline filled me with pleasure, I wasn't a townie anymore. The door to the main store stood ajar so I marched straight towards it. Liam just inside the store stacked feedstuffs on the shelves.

I stood motionless in the doorway, but he hadn't seen me. Sunlight from the small window, streamed across him, as though he was in a spotlight.

'Liam.'

'Jessica, you surprised me, I thought you were in London.'

'I've come back as I wanted to say something.'

'You've come from London to say something, not to me I assume.'

I nodded, 'Liam, do you remember the conversation when we drove to the merchants to get the chicken feed.'

'Yes, of course, I remember.' A sullen expression swept across his face. 'I don't want to repeat that conversation, I've made my decision and now if you'll excuse me, I have work to do.'

He hadn't looked at my face while delivering this speech but had focused his attention on the shelves nearby. He continued to sort boxes. I'd been dismissed! He was stubborn at times. A wave of panic swept over me. The package rested in my hand, it had appeared the perfect solution, but would it work? I tried to sound calm although my stomach churned, and I trembled.

'I remember exactly what you said, and I've come back from London to tell you that I am not prepared to accept it, you will have to think again.'

Liam went to speak, but before he uttered a word, I handed him the parcel, on which was clearly written, Liam Drinkwater.

'Don't say a word until you have opened it.'

He slumped down on a nearby sack of potatoes and stared at me, but he had no smile. He handed the parcel back to me.

'I don't want a leaving present, I've enjoyed working here, and I've good memories to take with me. That's all I want. Have you found a new employee? I'd like to leave soon.'

Without hesitation I gave the parcel back to him. 'Open it.' My voice sounded authoritative and cool, which was the opposite of the tension that coursed through my body.

He gazed at the parcel which I'd dumped back into his lap. A frown appeared as he moved it around in his hands. The suspense tightened the muscles in my stomach, and I gulped. My plan wouldn't work unless he opened it. My heart skittered.

Every movement from him filled me with anxiety and I hardly dared to breathe. He pulled at the tape around the thick paper of the parcel, and ripped it apart, and then his mouth opened but no words emerged. He sat unmoving. The silence between us lengthened and my heart hammered. Would my idea to keep Liam on the farm work? I didn't want him to leave. Cloughside Farm wouldn't be the same if he wasn't here.

Finally, he lifted my present out of the paper and held it out in front of him. I'd given him a new sign for the farm entrance, Cloughside Farm – The Home of Liam and Jessica Drinkwater. I held my breath and my heart thumped. What does he think?

He clutched it in his hands and stared for what seemed like an eternity. Then he gazed at me. How would he react? He slowly stood with his eyes fixed on my face. Then he smiled, stepped forward, pulled me to my feet and wrapped his arms around me. Laughter bubbled through him. Relaxing his hold, he turned his head towards me and kissed me lingeringly on the mouth.

Warmth and desire flooded through me and my breath quickened. Then he scooped me up and carried me across the farmyard. As we neared the house he stopped, put his head on one side and declared the day was a chilly one for Spring. Time to light the fire in the front room he announced with a glint in his eye. Longing whispered through me and love for this gorgeous man overwhelmed me. It hadn't been love at first sight and it had taken me too long to realise the depth of my love for him. The future for me as a country girl was full of promise. I couldn't wait.

Enjoy this book? Please leave an honest view.

You can make a big difference to my writing and stories. Reviews are the most powerful tools in my arsenal for drawing attention to my books. Honest reviews of my books help bring them to the attention of other readers.

If you've enjoyed this book, I would be very grateful if you could spend a few minutes leaving a review (it can be as short as you like) on the book's Amazon page.

Receive T M Goble's Monthly Newsletter containing:

Information about future publications (there many books to come across different genres)

Deriving plots and characters

Choosing Locations

Researching books (both fiction and non-fiction)

Recipes (cookery books)

No spam from me guaranteed.

Web address: www.tmgoble.com

Printed in Great Britain
by Amazon